THE HILDEGARD SEEDS

VATICAN SECRET ARCHIVE THRILLERS
BOOK TEN

GARY MCAVOY

LITERATI
EDITIONS

The Hildegard Seeds

Vatican Secret Archive Thrillers series - Book 10

Copyright © 2025 by Gary McAvoy

Hardcover ISBN: 978-1-954123-63-2
Paperback ISBN: 978-1-954123-64-9
eBook ISBN: 978-1-954123-65-6

Library of Congress Control Number: 2025902003

Published by:
Literati Editions
PO Box 5987
Bremerton WA 98312
Email: info@LiteratiEditions.com
Visit the author's website: GaryMcAvoy.com
R0425

BOOKS BY GARY MCAVOY
FICTION

FICTION

The Hildegard Seeds

Covenant of the Iron Cross

The Apostle Conspiracy

The Celestial Guardian

The Confessions of Pope Joan

The Galileo Gambit

The Jerusalem Scrolls

The Avignon Affair

The Petrus Prophecy

The Opus Dictum

The Vivaldi Cipher

The Magdalene Veil

The Magdalene Reliquary

The Magdalene Deception

NONFICTION

And Every Word Is True

PROLOGUE

DISIBODENBERG, GERMANY – 1106 CE

Born in 1098 into the noble Saint-Clair family in Bingen, Germany, Hildegard von Bingen's destiny was shaped by both privilege and tradition. As the tenth child of Mechtild of Merxheim-Nahet and Hildebert of Bermersheim, she was offered to the Church at the age of eight—a common practice among noble families seeking to fulfill their spiritual obligations and secure divine favor. Presented as a tithe to the Benedictine monastery at Disibodenberg, young Hildegard entered a world of strict devotion and rigorous education, bound to a life of service to God but destined to reshape the spiritual and intellectual landscape of her time.

Throughout her life as a Benedictine nun, Hildegard von Bingen held numerous esteemed roles, besides becoming a Benedictine abbess, across an array of disciplines such as religion, music, medicine, and natural sciences. Her literary legacy encompasses a diverse range of works from theological writings and scientific dissertations to extensive correspondence. She engaged in written dialogues with the era's luminaries, including popes and emperors. In her explorations of medicine and natural history, Hildegard's work mirrored the period's conceptions of these domains, weaving together empirical observations with profound theological reflections. Moreover, she was a prolific musical composer, having created an extensive catalog of hymns and sequences. Her music, noted for its originality and expressive quality, stands out as a remarkable testament to her creative genius during her time.

From her youth, Hildegard was plagued by severe headaches, which might have been more than mere physical ailments. Indeed, she regarded such painful experiences as mystical visions, a perspective she maintained throughout her life, becoming known as a Christian mystic. These visions, which she meticulously described in her seminal work, *Scivias* ("Know the Ways"), suggest a profound spiritual connection, framing her migraines not just as physical afflictions but as gateways to divine revelation.

In her early fifties, while serving as the founder and abbess of the Benedictine abbey in Rupertsberg, Germany, Hildegard developed a curious language referred to as *Lingua Ignota*, or Unknown Language. This unique vocabulary featured a lexicon of approximately one thousand words, most of which were original creations, though some drew inspiration or were adapted from Latin and German. The precise intention behind the creation of *Lingua Ignota* remains an enigma. It is speculated that it might have served mystical or religious functions, perhaps as a covert means of communication among the nuns of her convent, or as a linguistic embodiment of her visions and divine encounters. Regardless, this language stands as a monument to her inventive prowess and her eagerness to delve into and articulate the spiritual and mystical beyond customary forms of communication.

Despite her many skills and interests, however, Hildegard was foremost a pioneer in natural herbal remedies for addressing a range of afflictions: leprosy, plague, smallpox, measles and scarlet fever, dysentery, St. Anthony's Fire, tuberculosis, malaria, malnutrition, and periodontal diseases, many of which were common and pervasive due to the living conditions, hygiene practices, and inaccurate medical knowledge in twelfth-century Europe.

HILDEGARD'S FAME for her medicinal knowledge spread far and wide, attracting people from distant lands to seek her guidance and remedies. Pilgrims and travelers would make the arduous journey to the convent at Rupertsberg, where she resided, in hopes of receiving a glimpse of her wisdom. Many sought relief from ailments that had plagued them for years, while others came seeking preventative measures against the rampant diseases of the time.

Hildegard's apothecary was a sight to behold. Its shelves were lined with jars containing herbs, roots, and ingredients collected from the surrounding forests and gardens. She carefully crafted tinctures, salves, and potions, each tailored to the specific needs of the individual seeking her aid.

But it wasn't just the physical ailments that drew people to her doorstep; her gentle demeanor, wise counsel, and unwavering faith also offered solace to the weary souls who crossed her path. Hildegard listened intently to their stories, offering comfort and encouragement along with her herbal remedies.

As word of her healing abilities continued to spread, so too did tales of her mystical visions and divine revelations. Some whispered that she possessed powers beyond human comprehension, that she communed with angels and received visions of the future. Others believed her to be a chosen vessel of God, sent to bring light and hope to a world shrouded in darkness.

Hildegard, however, saw herself not as a miracle worker or a prophetess but simply as a servant of God, using the gifts He had bestowed upon her to help those in need. She remained steadfast to her calling, and her days were spent in prayer and contemplation, seeking guidance and strength from above to aid her in her mission.

THE CRISP AUTUMN air carried the scent of fallen leaves as a simple farmer named Friedrich and his daughter, Liesl, stood before the gates of the Rupertsberg convent. The journey had taken days, and Friedrich's boots bore the dust of long-traveled paths. Liesl, pale and frail, clutched her father's arm for support, her breath shallow.

"Stay close, Liesl," Friedrich murmured, his voice thick with worry. "We're almost there. Hildegard will know what to do."

The gate creaked open, revealing a serene nun who regarded them with calm curiosity. Friedrich stepped forward, bowing his head.

"Forgive my intrusion," he began, his voice trembling. "I am Friedrich, a farmer from Mainz, and this is my daughter. We have come to seek Hildegard's help."

The nun studied them, her gaze lingering on Liesl's gaunt frame. "Follow me," she said simply, leading them through the stone corridors to a room filled with the scent of herbs and beeswax candles. There, seated at a simple desk, was Hildegard von Bingen.

"Mother Hildegard," the nun announced softly, "this man and his daughter have come from Mainz seeking your aid."

Hildegard rose, her presence commanding yet gentle. She approached Friedrich, her gaze filled with understanding.

"You have traveled far," she said, her voice soothing. "What troubles you?"

Friedrich dropped to his knees, clasping his rough hands together. "Please, Mother Hildegard," he begged, his voice breaking. "My daughter Liesl—she suffers terribly. No healer, no remedy… nothing has helped. I fear I will lose her."

Liesl stood silently, her eyes hollow but hopeful. Hildegard knelt beside Friedrich, placing a hand on his shoulder.

"Rise, my son," she said gently. "Your burden is great, but you are not alone. Bring Liesl to my apothecary, and we will seek God's guidance together."

With a grateful nod, Friedrich helped Liesl follow Hildegard to the apothecary, a room filled with various containers of dried herbs, as well as pestles, implements, and wooden boxes of roots and flowers. Hildegard motioned for Liesl to sit on a small stool, then knelt to examine her.

"Tell me, Liesl," she said kindly, "where does it hurt?"

"My stomach," Liesl whispered, her voice weak. "It's like a fire that never goes out."

Hildegard placed a gentle hand on Liesl's abdomen, her experienced fingers feeling for the signs. After a moment, she looked up at Friedrich. "Her symptoms suggest an imbalance of black bile," she said. "It is as though her body fights a shadow from within."

"Can you help her?" Friedrich asked, his voice barely audible.

"I will do all that I can," Hildegard assured him. She rose and began gathering ingredients from her shelves, speaking as she worked. "This," she said, holding up a dried gall of a rare herb, "is from the *Ricinus aureum*. It holds the power to cleanse the humors and restore balance. Combined with other herbs, it can help Liesl's body heal from the cancer that burdens her."

She ground the gall with other herbs, her movements precise. "This mixture will become a tea," she explained. "It will ease the pain and draw out the sickness. But the tea alone is not enough. She must avoid heavy foods and eat only what is light and nourishing—barley bread, cooked apples, and broth will strengthen her."

Hildegard finished the preparation, pouring the ground herbs into a small pouch. "Friedrich," she said, handing it to him, "follow my instructions carefully. Brew this tea twice a day, and ensure Liesl rests. Faith and patience will be as vital as this remedy."

Friedrich's eyes brimmed with tears as he took the pouch. "Thank you, Mother Hildegard. May God bless you for your kindness."

Weeks passed, then months, as Friedrich followed Hildegard's guidance with unwavering dedication. One spring morning, he returned to the convent, his steps lighter than they had been in years. Beside him walked Liesl, her cheeks rosy, her eyes bright.

Hildegard greeted them at the gates, her smile serene. "Friedrich," she said, "your joy speaks before you do."

"Mother Hildegard," Friedrich said, his voice thick with emotion, "you saved her. Look at her—she's strong again. I can never thank you enough."

Liesl stepped forward and curtsied. "Thank you, Mother," she said softly. "I feel like myself again."

Hildegard rested her hand gently on Liesl's head.

"Give thanks to God, child. I am merely His servant. Go, live your life in health and gratitude."

As Friedrich and Liesl departed, Hildegard watched them with quiet satisfaction. Another life restored, another purpose fulfilled. Though her fame spread far and wide, she remained steadfast in her humility, committed to serving those who came to her in need. There were those who offered her money for her help or for her formulas, but her calling was to freely serve those in need, not take from the needy nor to satisfy human greed.

That night, in her prayers before bed, she had yet another vision, this one troubling. Hands, like claws, reached out to her table of herbs, clutching not for help but from callous avarice while a multitude of the sick stood behind, seeking help, finding none. She rose from her knees, unsteady from the vision and looked at a journal that she had been keeping as well as some of her medicinals. She closed her eyes, her fingers floating over the vials at her table. Then she looked heavenward and nodded before picking up the journal and a couple of vials. She settled them in a velvet satchel bag, tied it tight, and left her room, firm in the knowledge of what she must do.

Preserve the healing potential God had gifted her.

Protect the future of healing.

Follow His call.

ONE

PRESENT DAY

The sun rose over Geneva with a muted brilliance, as the city grieved the loss of a man whose influence had shaped lives and legacies for decades. Baron Armand de Saint-Clair, patriarch of the Saint-Clair family and steward of Banque Suisse de Saint-Clair, had passed peacefully in his sleep at the age of ninety-four. His death, though not unexpected, cast a long shadow over a legacy that had endured for centuries. To Hana Sinclair, his beloved granddaughter, the loss was more than personal—it was the end of an era, a final chapter in a story that had defined her life.

Banque Suisse de Saint-Clair, founded by the family in the early eighteenth century, was more than a financial institution. For over three hundred years it had been a cornerstone of Swiss banking, renowned for its stability, discretion, and impeccable reputation.

Armand, who had overseen the bank's operations for over half a century, had been its modern-day face, a man respected in boardrooms and capitals alike. Now, with his passing, the responsibility of preserving that legacy fell entirely to Hana, his sole heir.

The estate, an opulent manor nestled on the city's outskirts on the shore of Lake Geneva, buzzed with activity as preparations for Armand's funeral and the inevitable transfer of his holdings to Hana were underway. Hana sat in the study, surrounded by legal documents, her laptop open as she responded to a flurry of emails from attorneys, board members, and diplomats offering condolences. She had always known this day would come—her grandfather had prepared her meticulously for it—but no amount of preparation could dull the ache of losing him.

"Mademoiselle Hana," came the soft voice of Frederic, the baron's longtime aide, from the doorway. "The florists are here to finalize the arrangements for the memorial service." It would take many days to prepare properly for a funeral of the size that Armand's death would entail. Numerous decisions needed to be made.

"Thank you, Frederic," Hana replied, setting down a stack of papers. Her voice was calm, though inside, she felt like she was holding herself together by sheer will. "Is that something you could attend to?"

Frederic nodded and disappeared down the hall. Hana glanced around the study, the room that had always been her grandfather's sanctuary. It was filled with artifacts from centuries of family history: fine oil portraits of Saint-Clair ancestors, antique furniture, and shelves lined with aged leather-bound volumes. Above the mantelpiece hung a portrait of Armand in his prime, his piercing blue eyes and confident smile captured with remarkable realism. Hana felt her chest tighten. She had seen the man behind that portrait age with grace and humor, but the essence of his vitality had never faded. Until now.

While organizing Armand's personal papers in the study that afternoon, Hana noticed a sealed envelope tucked inside a small leather portfolio. Her name was written on the envelope in Armand's elegant handwriting. Inside it was a letter and an ornate brass key.

With a trembling hand, she opened the letter and read it in a whisper.

"'My dearest Hana,'" it began, "'If you are reading this, I am no longer with you. Do not let my passing weigh you down too heavily; I have lived a life filled with joy and purpose, much of it because of you. But as I leave this world, I entrust you with a legacy far more important than the bank or the estate. Enclosed is a key. It opens a safe hidden in the study wall, behind the third shelf of the bookcase. Inside, you will find something that has been in our family's care for centuries. What you learn there may challenge your understanding of who we are and where we come from, but I trust you to use this knowledge wisely.'"

Hana stared at the letter, her pulse racing. Rising from her seat, she walked to the bookcase and carefully removed the books from the third shelf. Behind them, as Armand had described, was a concealed panel. She pressed it, and with a faint click, it swung open to reveal a small steel safe.

Using the key, Hana unlocked the safe and pulled out its contents: an ancient leather-bound manuscript, two glass vials filled with a fine golden powder, and a faded photograph of an abbey she didn't recognize. The manuscript was inscribed with a title in a strange language she couldn't decipher, but one name stood out, written at the top of the first page: Hildegard von Bingen.

Hana's hands trembled as she turned the brittle pages, scanning unfamiliar symbols and dense text. She had no idea why her grandfather had kept something like this hidden, but she knew she couldn't unravel its meaning alone. She needed someone who could decode the manuscript, someone with both the historical and theological expertise to guide her. Her thoughts immediately turned to her fiancé, Father Michael Dominic, at the Vatican. The late Pope's edict that permitted priests to marry had allowed them to make marriage plans—if they so chose. Michael had confessed his love, as she to him, but no marriage arrangements had yet been discussed. Now any such plans would be delayed anyway, as she had to wend her way through her family's private and business affairs due to her grandfather's death.

As the significance of her inheritance bore down on her—both the financial empire and this mysterious new responsibility—Hana realized her grandfather's true legacy was far more than she had imagined. But as she began to dig into the manuscript's origins, she could not know the danger it would bring or the powerful forces potentially mobilizing to claim it for themselves.

THE NEXT MORNING, Hana sat at the desk in Armand's study, the manuscript spread out before her. The fragile pages seemed to hum with significance, their elegant script etched in a language she couldn't understand. Next to it, the small vials of golden powder caught the morning light, their contents glinting like tiny pieces of captured sunlight. She turned her phone over in her hands, debating, then tapped Michael's number. Her heart calmed slightly when his warm voice answered.

"Good morning," he said, his tone steady and reassuring.

"Good morning," Hana replied softly, a smile in her voice. "I hope I'm not interrupting anything important."

"You're never an interruption," Michael said, his voice softening. "How are you holding up?"

Hana exhaled, her eyes drifting to the portrait of Armand above the fireplace. "I'm managing. There's so much to do—arrangements for the funeral, the bank, the estate… but I've found something, Michael. Something I think you need to see."

Michael's tone shifted, curious. "Oh? What is it?"

Hana hesitated, glancing at the manuscript. "A letter from my grandfather led me to a hidden safe in his study. Inside, I found a manuscript—it's old and handwritten—along with two vials of what looks like a powdered substance. The first page bears the name

'Hildegard von Bingen,' apparently an ancestor of mine. Does that mean anything to you?"

There was a pause, and when Michael spoke again, his tone was laced with both surprise and intrigue. "Hildegard von Bingen? Yes, absolutely. She was a twelfth-century Benedictine abbess—a mystic, theologian, and scholar. She wrote extensively about medicine, music, and natural philosophy. If her name is on the manuscript, Hana, it could be something extraordinary."

Hana leaned forward, her fingers grazing the edge of the fragile pages. "The script—it doesn't look like anything I've seen before. It's intricate, almost like a cipher."

"That sounds like her *Lingua Ignota*," Michael said, his voice quickening. "It's the language Hildegard invented. She claimed it was divinely inspired, a way to express spiritual truths that couldn't be captured in ordinary language. Very few examples of it have survived."

Hana stared at the script, her journalist instincts now fully engaged. "So you think this could be authentic? Something she wrote?"

"It's possible," Michael said. "If it is, this manuscript could be invaluable. Hildegard's writings were centuries ahead of her time, especially in medicine and natural remedies. Did your grandfather give any indication of where he got this?"

"Not exactly," Hana said, leaning back in the chair. "In his letter, he said it's been in our family's care for centuries. He didn't explain how, just that it was part of our ancestry and that it contains some knowledge that he says could be challenging. Maybe he just means the language, but I don't even know where to begin. I already feel fatigued with everything else to be done and now this…"

Michael's voice softened, reassuring. "You've already begun. And I have no doubts you can handle your family's affairs. But you shouldn't handle all this alone. I'll come to Geneva and give you a hand."

Hana sat up straighter. "You would do that?"

"Of course," Michael said without hesitation. "This isn't just a historical discovery—it's deeply personal for you. Besides, if it's *Lingua Ignota* and tied to Hildegard, it may require theological context to understand fully. I was planning on coming soon to help you with Armand's funeral plans anyway; I'll just leave a little earlier now."

Hana let out a small breath of relief. "Thank you, Michael. I don't know what I'd do without you."

The priest's voice warmed. "You won't have to find out. We'll figure this out together."

For a moment, Hana allowed herself to relax, the impact of the manuscript and its mysteries momentarily lessened by Michael's presence, even across the miles. "Let me know when you're on your way. I'll be waiting."

"I will," Michael said. "And Hana… be careful. If this is what we think it is, it's not just rare—it's quite valuable. Keep it safe."

Hana nodded, even though he couldn't see her. "I'll keep that in mind."

When the call ended, she placed her phone on the desk and stared at the manuscript once more. Its looping script and cryptic annotations seemed to challenge her, daring her to uncover its secrets. Michael's words echoed in her mind: "*divinely inspired… centuries ahead of her time.*"

But what had compelled her grandfather to keep such a thing hidden? And why reveal it to her now, after his death? As she sat in the stillness of the study, she couldn't shake the feeling that Armand had known this discovery would lead her somewhere far more dangerous than he had let on.

STILL SITTING AT THE DESK, Hana absently turned one of the vials of golden powder in her hand, its shimmering contents catching the morning light, each tiny fleck reflecting the swirling questions in her mind. Michael's reassurances had soothed her nerves for now, but there was still so much she didn't understand. The name Hildegard von Bingen carried weight, especially with Michael's explanation of her significance, but the powder—what was its purpose? Could it be linked to medicinal remedies, which likely meant herbals in those days since Michael had mentioned her expertise in medicine?

Her thoughts turned to someone else who might be able to help. It had been a few years since she had last spoken with her old university friend, a botanist now working at the famed Conservatoire et Jardin botaniques de Genève—the city's most renowned botanical gardens and the largest in Switzerland—but the memory of their lively conversations over wine and books brought a smile to Hana's lips. If anyone could offer insight into these mysterious vials, it was Élise Gauthier, a woman whose passion for historical botany was rivaled only by her sharp wit.

Setting the vial carefully back on the desk, Hana picked up her phone and scrolled through her contacts. She hesitated only a moment before tapping Élise's name. The call connected after a few rings, and a familiar, cheerful voice answered.

"Hana! *Mon Dieu*, it's been forever! How are you?" Élise exclaimed, her warmth cutting through Hana's apprehension.

Hana smiled, leaning back in her chair. "It has been too long. I'm… managing, I suppose. My grandfather passed away recently, so things have been a bit overwhelming."

"Oh, Hana, I am so sorry to hear this. Armand was a legend—what a loss for all of us. You must be drowning in arrangements and responsibilities."

"I am," Hana admitted, her voice softening. "But Élise, I've also come across something… unusual. Something I think you might be interested in."

"Now you've got my attention," Élise said, her tone light but curious. "What sort of unusual? Don't tell me you've uncovered another family scandal. Those were always the best stories."

Hana laughed despite herself. "Not this time. It's something far older—and stranger. I found a manuscript in my grandfather's study. It's attributed to someone in our family named Hildegard von Bingen."

There was a pause on the line. When Élise spoke again, her voice was tinged with disbelief. "Hildegard von Bingen? The abbess? The medicinal healer? Are you serious?"

"Dead serious," Hana said. "So, you've heard of her?"

"But of course."

"Well, the manuscript is written in a strange language—Father Michael Dominic of the Vatican thinks it might be her secret language called *Lingua Ignota*—and it was hidden alongside two small vials of golden powder. Michael is flying in tomorrow from Rome to help me figure it out, but I also thought of you. If this powder has anything to do with plants or remedies, you might be the best person to shed some light on it."

Élise's excitement was palpable. "Hana, this is incredible! Of course, I'll come. If this powder is botanical, it could be linked to one of Hildegard's medicinal recipes. Do you know how rare it is to find something like this intact?"

"I had a feeling you'd say that," Hana said, a grin tugging at her lips. "I'll send you the address. Can you come by tomorrow afternoon? Michael will be here by then, and we can go through everything together."

"*Absolument*," Élise said without hesitation. "I'll bring some tools and a portable analysis kit—nothing invasive, but enough to get a preliminary sense of what might be in those vials. Hana, I'm telling you now, if this powder is related to her legendary cures, we might be looking at something revolutionary."

"Let's not get ahead of ourselves," Hana said, though Élise's enthusiasm was contagious. "I'll see you tomorrow, then."

"Tomorrow," Élise confirmed. "And Hana... thank you for thinking of me. I can't wait to see this with my own eyes."

They ended the call, and Hana leaned forward, resting her elbows on the desk. The study felt quieter now, but the air seemed charged with the potential of what lay ahead. She glanced at the manuscript again, its cryptic script both beautiful and inscrutable. Between Michael's theological expertise and Élise's botanical knowledge, she felt they were on the verge of unraveling a mystery centuries in the making. A mystery that her ancestors had for centuries felt worth hiding and that her grandfather had charged her with revealing. For all the other tasks ahead of her, this seemed the most inspiring and pleasant.

CHAPTER

TWO

The afternoon sunlight poured through the tall windows of Armand's study, casting warm patterns across the polished wood floors. Hana stood near the desk, her nerves and excitement barely contained as she waited for her two guests to arrive. The manuscript lay open on the desk, accompanied by the vials of golden powder, which gleamed in the light like tiny treasures. After she had handled what she could for this morning about the bank and the funeral, she had carefully prepared the space, ensuring that both Michael and Élise would have everything they needed to dive into this mystery.

The sound of the doorbell echoed through the house, and moments later, Frederic ushered in Michael, travel-worn but smiling warmly. Hana moved to greet him, the tension in her chest easing at the sight of his familiar face. He kissed her, then pulled her into a deep hug, and she allowed herself a moment of comfort before stepping back.

"You made it," she said, her voice soft but steady.

"I wouldn't miss this for anything," Michael replied. His eyes moved to the desk, where the manuscript and vials awaited. "Is that it?"

Hana nodded, but before she could voice her thoughts, the doorbell chimed once more. In a matter of moments, Élise Gauthier swept into the room, her presence almost tangible with vibrant energy. Clad in a perfectly tailored jacket, her ensemble was completed by a sleek black bag slung over her shoulder, embodying the very essence of the self-assured scientist Hana recalled so vividly.

"Hana!" Élise exclaimed with bright enthusiasm before her sharp green eyes shifted to meet Michael's gaze. "And this must be the renowned Father Dominic. Hana's spoken quite a bit about you."

Michael extended his hand, accompanied by a warm smile that reached his eyes. "It's just Michael, please. And you must be Élise. Hana mentioned you have a wealth of expertise in historical botany—your insights will be invaluable."

As Élise clasped his hand, her expression grew even more radiant. "Any friend of Hana's is a friend of mine," she declared warmly. Then, with a sweeping gesture toward the desk, she added, "And this—this is truly remarkable. I've been pondering it ever since Hana called me yesterday. I can hardly wait to examine it up close."

Hana gestured for them to join her at the desk. "All

right, let's get started. Michael, why don't you explain what we're dealing with here? Élise, you can start with the powder after that."

Michael stepped closer and spied the photograph she had found in the safe first. "Ah, yes, this is the Rupertsberg Abbey, the one Hildegard von Bingen founded." Then he glanced toward the manuscript, his expression shifting to one of reverence the more he examined the journal. "This," he began, his voice steady, "appears to be a manuscript attributed to Hildegard von Bingen, a twelfth-century Benedictine abbess who was not only a theologian but also a visionary, composer, and botanist. She believed her knowledge was divinely inspired and used it to write about subjects as varied as music, natural medicine, and the cosmos. The language you see here is likely *Lingua Ignota*, or 'Unknown Language,' a unique script Hildegard created to express spiritual truths she felt ordinary language couldn't capture."

Élise leaned in, her fingers trailing just above the fragile pages. "It's exquisite," she murmured. "The precision, the fluidity of the script—it's extraordinary. And you're saying she invented this language herself?"

Michael nodded. "She claimed it was revealed to her in visions. Very few examples of *Lingua Ignota* survive, so this manuscript is potentially a major discovery. But there's more. Hildegard was also a healer, and her writings on plants and their uses were centuries ahead of their time. Those vials"—he gestured toward the small bottles of golden powder—"may contain a formula tied to her medicinal theories."

Élise's eyes lit up as she picked up one of the vials. "May I?"

"Of course," Hana said.

Élise retrieved a small, portable analysis kit from her bag, its sleek design indicating both precision and frequent use. She opened the kit with practiced ease, revealing an array of neatly arranged tools: a glass slide, a fine metal spatula, reagent vials, and a compact handheld microscope. Her movements were deliberate as she carefully removed the sealing wax from the wooden stopper of the vial, setting it down gently. She selected the spatula, using it to scoop a minute sample of the fine, golden powder from the vial. She placed it carefully onto the glass slide, ensuring there was no contamination from external particles.

Next, she reached for a dropper filled with a clear reagent solution, allowing a single droplet to fall onto the powder. The liquid spread across the slide, creating a faint fizz as it interacted with the substance. Élise leaned in, adjusting the microscope's focus knob with expert precision, her brow furrowing as she examined the reaction closely. The handheld device, though small, provided a powerful magnification, revealing the crystalline structure of the substance in striking detail.

Her mind raced as she noted the characteristics: irregular edges on the crystals, their slight refractive glint, and a faint discoloration at the edges that hinted at impurities. She jotted down observations in a small notebook, her pen moving rapidly. Then, as part of her systematic procedure, she reached for a second reagent, adding it to the slide to observe any further reactions.

The powder darkened slightly upon contact, a change that confirmed one of her suspicions. Élise straightened, her expression a mix of intrigue and concern as she leaned back, processing the implications of what she had just seen.

"Well?" Hana asked, her voice filled with anticipation.

"It's botanical, without a doubt," Élise said, her tone serious. "And… remarkable. There are traces of gall-derived tannins, which were often used in medieval medicine for their anti-inflammatory and astringent properties. But this isn't just ordinary gall powder. There are also faint residues of something metallic—gold, possibly, though I'd need a more sophisticated lab to confirm it."

Hana tilted her head, curiosity in her eyes. "You mentioned 'galls.' What are those?"

Élise smiled, pausing for a moment to gather her thoughts. "Galls are like little growths or bumps that form on plants, usually on leaves, stems, or branches. They're created when a plant reacts to something irritating it—often tiny insects, mites, or even fungi. Similar to how an oyster makes a pearl, in fact. For example, a wasp might lay its eggs on a leaf, and the plant responds by growing a protective structure around it. That structure becomes the gall, keeping the irritant—in this case, insect larvae—from invading the plant itself. It creates a unique shape or pattern for each type of insect or fungus, so galls can look like little spheres, spikes, or even tiny flowers. They're fascinating because they show how plants and other organisms interact in really intricate ways."

"So they're recognized today in medicine as useful?" Michael asked.

"Actually, ancient civilizations noticed their potential, and over the centuries, naturalists marveled at their unusual forms. But Hildegard, to our best understanding of her history, went a step further: she didn't just study these growths—she discovered how to use them as potent remedies, turning nature's oddities into life-saving medicine, when so little else was available in her day."

"And I heard you also mentioned gold?" Michael echoed, his interest piqued.

"Yes," Élise said, looking up. "In trace amounts, gold was sometimes used in alchemical preparations during the Middle Ages. It was believed to have purifying properties, both physically and spiritually. If Hildegard included it in this powder, it might have been part of a larger formula—possibly something meant to treat a serious ailment."

Hana frowned. "Could it be medicinally significant today?"

Élise hesitated, then nodded slowly. "It's possible. Modern medicine has rediscovered some of the benefits of medieval remedies, especially plant-based ones. And gold is used for some medical purposes today, for instance, to treat rheumatoid arthritis, in implants, and in nanomedicine.

"If this powder is what I think it is, it might have

properties we don't fully understand yet. But I'd need proper lab equipment to analyze it further."

Michael crossed his arms, his brow furrowed in thought. "If this powder is medicinal, it would align with Hildegard's teachings. She believed in the interplay between the spiritual and physical, that healing the body was tied to healing the soul. This could be an extension of that philosophy—something she felt was too important to lose, or to leave unguarded."

Hana glanced between the two of them. "So, what do we do next?"

Élise carefully resealed the vial and set it back on the desk. "First, I'll take a sample to my lab at the Conservatoire. I can run tests there and give us a clearer picture of what we're dealing with. But Hana…" She paused, her expression serious. "If this is as significant as it seems, you need to be cautious. The pharmaceutical industry is cutthroat and people have killed for far less than a discovery like this."

Michael nodded in agreement. "She's right. Not only is that a danger, but there are unscrupulous collectors of historical artifacts. The significance of Hildegard's manuscript and this powder could attract the wrong kind of attention."

Hana exhaled slowly, the weight of their words settling over her. She had thought of this "gift" from Armand as a pleasant diversion from the tasks ahead of her as his heir. Now she realized this could end up one more task… one with inherent dangers. "I trust both of you to help me figure this out. But if Armand thought this was worth hiding for centuries, there's no way I'm letting it fall into the wrong hands now."

Michael's gaze softened, and he placed a reassuring hand on her shoulder. "We'll uncover this together, Hana. Step by step."

Élise smiled faintly, her excitement tempered by caution. "Whatever this is, it's going to change things. Let's just make sure it's for the right reasons."

As the three of them stood around the manuscript, the sunlight faded, leaving the room cloaked in the quiet shadows of evening. And yet, the air seemed charged with something electric—an anticipation of the truths they were about to uncover, and the dangers they would undoubtedly face along the way.

CHAPTER
THREE

The quaint café in Geneva's Old Town was warm and inviting, its walls lined with shelves of old books that gave it a cozy, intellectual charm. Élise Gauthier sat across from Dr. Laurent Chevalier, her former mentor and a respected academic in medieval botany. The table between them was cluttered with papers, her cappuccino cooling as their conversation deepened. Laurent leaned forward, curiosity lighting his eyes.

"So, Élise," he began, his French accent lending an easy charm to his words, "you've been far too quiet about your latest work. That usually means it's something extraordinary."

Élise hesitated, her fingers brushing the edge of her notebook. The café was quiet, its early patrons engrossed in their own worlds. The warm familiarity of her mentor and the atmosphere lulled her into a sense of safety. Laurent had been a trusted friend and guide for years—surely it wouldn't hurt to share a little?

"Well," she began, leaning in slightly and lowering her voice, "I've been assisting an old friend… Hana Sinclair. You might have heard of her?"

Laurent nodded slowly. "The journalist? Yes, I've come across her name. What is it she has uncovered?"

Élise's enthusiasm bubbled to the surface, her voice quickening. "A journal, Laurent. A handwritten manuscript that we believe belonged to Hildegard von Bingen regarding her botanic medicinals."

His eyes widened in astonishment. "Hildegard? The medieval botanist and polymath? That's extraordinary!"

"It's not just the journal," Élise said, smiling. "Hana also recovered preserved botanical samples, perfectly intact. Can you imagine? Plant materials dating back to the twelfth century?"

Laurent leaned back, stunned. "Élise, that's incredible. If these samples hold any medicinal properties, this could change the way we understand medieval science."

Élise nodded, her voice quiet but fervent. "Exactly. There could be lost knowledge there, waiting to be rediscovered. It's why we've been so cautious. The implications are enormous."

Seated at a nearby table, a man dressed in a plain coat and scarf stirred his coffee absently, his attention half on his phone and half on the conversation drifting from Élise's table. He wasn't actively listening, but certain words—*Hildegard… botanical samples… medieval journal…*—snagged his attention.

He turned slightly, adjusting his seat to catch more of the conversation without drawing attention to himself. Élise's animated tone carried just enough for him to piece together fragments.

He leaned back in his chair, considering the information. Pulling out his phone, he opened a note-taking app and typed:

Journal. Hildegard von Bingen. Botanical samples. Names: Sinclair, Hana. Élise something.

The man didn't fully understand the significance, but he recognized its potential value. He was a man whose sharp eye and ear sought anything of value, and he had a nose that could sniff out anything that would benefit his pocket. Pausing for a moment, he added:

Look into Élise and Hana Sinclair—possible leads.

Satisfied, he glanced at his watch, pocketed his phone, took a final sip of his coffee, and stood, slipping out of the café without drawing attention.

Back at their table, Élise continued explaining the nuances of the discovery, oblivious to the unintended leak. Laurent smiled warmly. "Élise, you've always been drawn to groundbreaking work. This… this could be truly historic."

"I hope so," she replied with a soft laugh, closing her

notebook. "There's so much to do. I need to return to the lab—it feels like we've barely scratched the surface."

They exchanged goodbyes, and Élise left the café with her notes and a renewed sense of purpose. Outside, the narrow streets of Geneva felt as peaceful as ever, giving no indication of the storm brewing elsewhere.

But minutes later and miles away, the man's brief notes would soon reach someone who understood their full significance.

THE DARK GLASS doors of Zentara Biogenics's headquarters reflected the bustle of Geneva's financial district, a strikingly modern façade that gave no hint of the shadowy operations within. Christophe Vaux, Zentara's lead European research and development operative, entered the lobby with his usual calculated stride. His tailored suit and distinct features exuded control, but his mind was already spinning with the implications of what he had just overheard at a nearby café.

The elevator carried him swiftly to the top floor, where he entered a sleek, dimly lit office lined with bookshelves and cutting-edge technology. Vaux placed his briefcase on the desk and powered on the computer, pulling up two search windows: one for Hildegard von Bingen and another for Hana Sinclair. He adjusted his chair, leaned forward, and began to dig.

The first search was straightforward. Hildegard von Bingen, the mystic abbess of the twelfth century, was renowned for her groundbreaking work in music, natural science, and medicine. Her *Lingua Ignota* had long intrigued scholars and theologians, while her writings on healing and botanical remedies were still studied in niche academic circles. But it was an obscure reference in a digital copy of one of her surviving manuscripts that made Vaux sit up straighter.

The text described an "elixir of preservation," a formula Hildegard claimed to have received in a vision. It was said to blend the physical and spiritual, prolonging health and vitality, ostensibly providing a longer and healthier life. This was always a powerful claim and modern science had yet to achieve that goal. The vague description alone would have been enough to dismiss it as medieval mysticism, but paired with the whispers Vaux had heard about an ancient manuscript and mysterious vials in Hana Sinclair's possession, it felt like a thread worth pulling.

"Interesting," Vaux muttered to himself, leaning back in his chair.

He took a bit of time researching the first name only of an "Élise," assuming she worked at one of the prestigious labs near the café. With luck, he found a picture of the woman online: Élise Gauthier, a renowned biochemical scientist. Interesting, he thought.

He switched tabs to investigate Hana Sinclair. A few keystrokes brought up her profile: an investigative journalist of considerable reputation, her work spanning corruption exposés, historical mysteries, and daring pursuits of the truth. He scrolled through articles detailing her career, the announcement of her engagement to a Catholic priest in the Vatican, then froze at a photograph of her with Baron Armand de Saint-Clair, her late grandfather. The accompanying obituary confirmed what he already suspected—Hana was the sole heir to the Saint-Clair fortune and banking empire.

His curiosity deepened. The Saint-Clair name carried weight, not just in banking but in the preservation of European heritage. If Armand had hidden something connected to Hildegard von Bingen, it wasn't by accident. A family with centuries of influence would have had the means to safeguard anything valuable, including something as groundbreaking as an ancient medicinal formula.

He compiled his findings into a concise report and sent it to his superior: Alton Blackthorn, Zentara's enigmatic CEO. Moments later, his phone buzzed.

"Come to my office," Blackthorn's curt voice ordered.

A short while later, Vaux entered Blackthorn's office, a minimalist space with a commanding view of Lake Geneva and the Swiss Alps beyond. Blackthorn stood by the window, his hands clasped behind his back, his reflection well-defined against the glass. Without turning, he said, "You believe the Sinclair woman has something of value."

"I do," Vaux replied, his tone confident. "What we know so far matches pieces of Hildegard von Bingen's writings that have been lost to history. If the formula's benefits are proven to be true—a medicinal compound that could 'encourage health and vitality,' as the accomplished scientist I overheard stated, it could solidify Zentara's dominance in pharmaceuticals. Imagine the patents, the exclusivity. We're not talking about marginal gains; this could revolutionize medicine and extend our influence across every major market."

Blackthorn turned, his cold eyes locking on Vaux. "And the Sinclair woman? What's her role in this?"

"She's intelligent and resourceful, but presumably inexperienced when it comes to what we do," Vaux said smoothly. "She recently inherited the Saint-Clair legacy, so she may not even grasp the significance of what she's found and could be concentrating on more urgent matters now anyway. However, she has allies, notably her fiancé, Father Michael Dominic from the Vatican. He's a wildcard. A theologian of his reputation will recognize the value of Hildegard's work, and his connections to the Church could complicate things."

Blackthorn considered this for a moment, then walked to his desk. "Your recommendation?"

"We move quickly," Vaux said. "We're ahead of anyone else who might uncover something like this. With the right pressure, we can acquire the manuscript and the vials the woman mentioned. Once they're in our possession, we'll analyze the formula and, if it proves to hold the promise we hope it will, neutralize anyone who poses a threat to our control of it."

Blackthorn sat down, his hands steepled before him. "And if Sinclair refuses to cooperate?"

Vaux's lips curved into a faint smile. "Everyone has a price, Monsieur Blackthorn. If hers isn't money, it will be something else. But if persuasion fails, we have other methods."

Blackthorn nodded, satisfied. "Proceed then. Discreetly. And Christophe…" His voice hardened. "Failure is not an option. If this discovery is as valuable as you believe, then it must belong to Zentara—at any cost."

"Understood," Vaux said, inclining his head.

As he left the office, his mind was already racing. This was no ordinary assignment. The manuscript, the vials, and Hildegard von Bingen's legacy could represent a prize greater than anything he had pursued before. But Vaux knew one thing above all else: whatever Hana Sinclair thought she was safeguarding, she had no idea what forces she was about to face.

CHAPTER

FOUR

T he soft hues of dusk painted the sky over Lake
Geneva, the water shimmering like liquid
silver in the fading light. Inside the great room
of the Saint-Clair residence, the glow of a single lamp
cast a warm circle of light over the sofa where Michael
Dominic sat with Hildegard's journal resting on his lap.
Dressed casually in jeans and a black T-shirt, a rare sight
for a man so accustomed to clerical robes, he looked at
ease yet deeply focused. Hana lay against him, her head
resting on his chest, her legs curled up beneath her. One
of his arms rested around her shoulders, absently
stroking her arm as his other hand turned the fragile
pages of the manuscript.

The room was silent except for the occasional sound
of Michael murmuring words under his breath as he
attempted to decipher the ancient text. Hana, feeling the
rhythmic rise and fall of his chest beneath her, closed
her eyes briefly, savoring the rare quiet of the moment.

"'*Herba sacra*,'" Michael muttered, his brows furrowing. "'Sacred herb' in Latin."

"What more does it say?" Hana asked softly, opening her eyes and tilting her head to look up at him.

Michael squinted at the delicate script. "Something about a purification ritual involving *herba sacra*. It's vague... but it could refer to a botanical preparation of some sort. The context here is healing, perhaps something spiritual as well as physical."

Hana shifted slightly to see the page better. "And this is written in her *Lingua Ignota*?"

Michael nodded, tapping the margin where unfamiliar symbols intertwined with the Latin text. "Yes, but the structure is strange. Some sections seem almost like translations between *Lingua Ignota* and Latin, but others incorporate German. It's as if she was layering meanings—one for those who could read Latin, another for those who knew her invented language."

He flipped to another page and paused, his eyes narrowing as he traced the lines of text. "'*Corpus humorum sanitas*,'" he read aloud. "'Health of the body's humors.'"

"That sounds medieval," Hana remarked, a faint smile tugging at her lips.

"Very much so," Michael agreed. "In medieval times it was widely believed that we have four bodily fluids— blood, yellow bile, black bile, and phlegm. Hildegard's teachings aligned with that theory. She believed that balancing the body's humors was essential for health— common medical theory for the time. Still, she always added something uniquely her own, tying it back to her visions."

He turned the page and froze, his breath catching. His finger hovered over a particular line of text.

"What is it?" Hana asked, sitting up slightly.

Michael didn't answer at first, his eyes scanning the passage with growing intensity. "'*Malignus tumorum destructio*,'" he said, his voice laced with excitement. "'Destruction of malignant tumors.'"

Hana sat up fully, turning to face him. "Is she saying…?"

Michael nodded, his hand resting on the open page as he looked at her, his expression alight with realization. "This—this could be it! She's describing a botanical concoction, one designed to destroy malignant growths. It's not just metaphorical or spiritual; this is practical medicine. If this phrase means what I think it does, it could be a direct reference to a treatment for cancer."

Hana's eyes widened, her gaze darting to the vial resting on the nearby table. "You think that's what's in the vials? The formula she created?"

"It's possible," Michael said, his voice rising with excitement. "Hildegard's understanding of plants and their properties was centuries ahead of her time. If she discovered a combination capable of targeting tumors— malignant tumors, no less—it could explain why she encoded it so carefully, to be sure it wasn't lost in time."

Hana reached for the vial, holding it up to the light. The golden powder inside seemed to glow faintly, almost as if it carried its own energy. "If that's true,

Michael… if this really is a cure, it could change medical history."

Michael leaned forward, his elbows on his knees, his gaze fixed on the manuscript. "It would explain why your grandfather kept this safe. He must have known—or at least suspected—its significance. But there's more here. I need to translate the rest of this passage. There might be details about how the concoction was prepared or administered."

Hana watched him as he flipped back through the pages, his focus acute and unwavering. "This is bigger than just a historical discovery," she said softly. "If Hildegard really found a way to treat cancer… Michael, we have to be very careful."

Michael glanced up at her, his expression sober now despite the excitement in his voice. "I know. Something like this—if it's what I think it is—could save lives. But it could also be exploited. We have to protect it, Hana. Whatever it takes."

As Michael returned to the manuscript, his mind raced with possibilities. Hildegard's brilliance seemed to leap off the pages, her words carrying across centuries to reach them at this particular moment. But even as he worked, a quiet unease settled over him. If they had stumbled onto something this profound, and word got out about it, it wouldn't remain a secret for long—and a nagging sense of unease lingered, whispering that they weren't the only ones searching for it.

. . .

THE AIR in Élise Gauthier's lab at the Conservatoire et Jardin botaniques de Genève was thick with anticipation. The faint hum of analytical equipment underscored the meticulous work she had been conducting for hours, examining every particle of the golden powder from one of Hildegard's vials. Under the fluorescent lights, Élise's face was a mix of focus and excitement as she recorded her findings.

Adjusting the microscope, she leaned closer, her breath catching as the sample revealed its secrets. "Incredible," she murmured to herself, typing rapidly on her laptop. The chemical composition was fascinating—layers of botanical compounds, each more intricate than the last. But the final revelation came when she cross-referenced the molecular signatures with historical botanical databases. Her heart raced as the results came into focus.

She picked up her phone and quickly dialed Hana.

Hana was in the great room sitting beside Michael, who was still immersed in Hildegard's journal, deciphering the cryptic Latin and *Lingua Ignota*. The sound of her phone broke the silence, and she glanced at the screen.

"It's Élise," she said, answering on speaker. "Bonjour, Élise. What did you find?"

"Hana, you're not going to believe this," she began, her voice brimming with energy. "I've analyzed the powder more thoroughly, and while its potency has degraded over the centuries, I've identified its primary botanical source."

Michael leaned closer, intrigued. "Go on," he said, his voice steady but curious.

"It's from a plant known as *Ricinus aureum*, or 'golden castor,'" Élise explained. "It's a species thought to be extinct, but which was native only to certain areas in southwestern Germany—in the Black Forest, specifically. Historical records describe it as highly medicinal, used in medieval treatments for severe illnesses. Hildegard likely sourced it herself, which must have been the cornerstone of this formula."

Michael's eyes lit up. "*Ricinus aureum*. That aligns with Hildegard's teachings. She often wrote about using rare plants as divine gifts for healing. And you're certain the powder came from this plant?"

"Positive," Élise said. "The chemical signature is unmistakable. It has properties that could have been effective against cellular abnormalities—in modern terms, tumors. If the powder were fresh, it might have been remarkably potent. But after so many centuries, it's inert. Sadly, the botanical compounds have broken down almost completely."

Hana frowned, processing the information. "So even if we had the full recipe, the powder itself would no longer work."

"Exactly," Élise replied. "If *Ricinus aureum* still existed, it might be possible to recreate the formula. But as far as we know, the plant is extinct."

Michael straightened, his mind racing. "Extinct… or yet undiscovered. Hildegard was meticulous. The plant was rare even then. If she knew the importance of this plant, she might have hidden a source. She wouldn't rely on something this critical without safeguarding its future."

"That's possible," Élise admitted. "She was far ahead of her time, and she clearly understood the significance of this formula. But finding a plant that's been presumed extinct for centuries? That's a monumental task."

Hana glanced at Michael, seeing the wheels turning in his mind. "Do you think the journal might have clues about where she sourced it?"

"It's possible," Michael said. "She was precise in her records, even if she encoded much of her knowledge. If she intended for the plant to be rediscovered, she may have left breadcrumbs in her writings."

"There's one more thing," Élise added, her voice growing serious. "If the powder truly originated from *Ricinus aureum*, it might explain why your grandfather kept it hidden. This plant—and its formula—could be a miracle in the right hands. Big Pharma would likely kill for this kind of discovery, to be the only company to produce a cancer-curing drug."

Michael's expression darkened. "Then we need to act quickly. Élise, can you send me your findings, including any drawings or illustrations of the plant, if you have them? I'll cross-reference them with Hildegard's journal and see if we can locate a potential source for the plant."

"Of course," Élise said. "I'll email you everything I have. But be careful, both of you. This discovery is potentially so big that we should keep it quiet."

"Agreed, and thank you, Élise," Hana said. "We'll keep you updated."

The call ended, and Hana set the phone down, her gaze meeting Michael's.

"So now we're looking for a plant that's been extinct—or hidden—for centuries," she said, her voice laced with disbelief.

Michael closed the journal gently, his expression resolute. "If anyone could have preserved it, it was Hildegard. She believed in divine purpose, Hana. If she created this formula, she would've ensured the key to it wasn't lost forever."

"And if she didn't?"

Michael's lips pressed into a thin line. "Then we're holding a miracle we can't replicate."

Hana exhaled slowly, the burden of their task settling over her. "Then I think we should head to Germany to see what we can find. I have things under control enough here for now. There is much paperwork that needs to be dealt with by Grand-père's attorneys before I will be fully involved. And the funeral is such a huge affair that it will take a couple of weeks before any memorial. Fredric is helping with that. So"—she turned to Michael—"if you have the time, I'll order the jet for us. And we'd better hope Hildegard left us more than just breadcrumbs."

Michael reached for her hand, squeezing it gently. "I'm with you until this is resolved. We'll figure it out."

Outside, the evening settled over Geneva, but inside the study, the air was electric with purpose. The next step in their journey had revealed itself, and there was no turning back.

FIVE

Hana paced the kitchen as her tea was brewing, her phone pressed to her ear. She glanced at her packed bag by the door, her thoughts racing with anticipation. Élise picked up after a few rings.

"Hana," she said warmly, "you must have news. Are you making progress with the manuscript?"

"Hi, Élise," Hana replied, smiling. "Yes, actually, I wanted to call and update you. Michael and I are heading to Germany."

"Germany?" Élise's tone carried a spark of recognition. "I assume this has to do with *Ricinus aureum*?"

"Exactly," Hana said. "Thanks to your help identifying the plant, we've narrowed down its possible location. We think it's connected to the ruins of the Rupertsberg Abbey."

"I thought as much," Élise said. "That monastery

was central to Hildegard's work. If she grew something as significant as *Ricinus aureum* there, it makes perfect sense. That assumes, of course, that it's not extinct…"

"Michael agrees," Hana said. "And he's certain Hildegard left other clues in her journal for future generations. We're hoping to find more than just the plant—we might uncover something about the full formula. Talk soon." She ended the call and set her phone down on the table.

THE SUBDUED NIGHT-LIT corridors of the conservatory were silent, the faint hum of the building's ventilation system the only sound breaking the stillness. Deep in the research wing, the door to Élise Gauthier's laboratory stood ajar, the lock expertly bypassed. Inside, the sterile space was controlled chaos—glass-fronted cabinets filled with vials, jars, and meticulously labeled containers lined the walls, while Élise's desk, cluttered with notebooks and reference materials, sat beneath the glow of a green-shaded lamp.

Two figures, dressed in black and masked, moved with practiced efficiency, their gloved hands darting over surfaces and into drawers. Their purpose was singular: recover the notes and powdery botanical vial attributed to Hildegard von Bingen, a centuries-old recipe rumored to hold miraculous medicinal properties. Vaux had sent them with specific instructions: get anything connected but leave no trace of their theft. And leave something behind as well.

One operative, taller and broader in build, stood over a cabinet filled with glass vials, his flashlight beam illuminating their contents. Each label bore Élise's precise handwriting, listing plant species and chemical compositions. His partner, more wiry and agile, was crouched near the floor, prying open a storage bin beneath a counter.

"She's too meticulous not to have something," the taller man muttered, his voice low and edged with frustration. He swept the light across rows of containers, reading aloud. "*Salvia officinalis. Artemisia absinthium.* Nothing here matches the descriptions of what Vaux told us to look for."

The smaller operative, pulling aside a tray of soil samples, snorted softly. "Maybe she's smarter than we thought. Check for a hidden compartment. No way she'd leave something valuable out in the open."

Across the room, the wiry man shifted to Élise's desk, rifling through stacks of notebooks, handwritten notes, and folders. He paused over a set of pages detailing experiments in botanical preservation but found no mention of powdered formulas or Hildegard's name. He snapped pictures of anything that looked remotely relevant, the faint click of his phone camera barely audible in the stillness. He paused at the lab's computer but found it password-protected and moved on.

The tall man had turned his attention to the wall-mounted cabinets, pulling them open and scanning the shelves for any sign of concealment. His flashlight glinted off an empty display case. "She's cleared this out. I'd guess she assumed someone might come, so she's put whatever was in here somewhere else."

The wiry operative opened a drawer and pulled out a small metal lockbox, testing its weight. "Could be in here." He pulled out a lock-picking set and went to work. The tumblers clicked into place, and the box opened to reveal a neat arrangement of glass slides, each labeled with microscopic samples of plant tissue. Wrong plant names. He cursed under his breath and shoved it aside.

"Keep looking," the taller man snapped, his voice harsher now. "We're not leaving empty-handed."

The operatives worked in tandem, combing through every possible hiding place. They checked under countertops, removed vent covers, and even inspected the backs of cabinets for false panels. They overturned a potted plant, dug into its soil, and scanned the floor for signs of a loose tile or hidden safe. But after nearly an hour, their search yielded no sign of vials containing golden powder or related notes.

The wiry operative finally stood, rubbing his temples in frustration. "She's either locked it up tight or taken it with her. My money's on the latter. There's nothing here."

The taller man gestured toward a stack of folders. "We'll take what we can. Photos of her research, any notes, records of shipments—anything that gives us a lead."

The wiry man hesitated. "If she's moved it, she won't leave obvious clues."

"That's not for us to decide," the taller man said. "Let the analysts figure it out."

Before leaving, they meticulously wiped down every surface they had touched, leaving no trace of their presence. Except one. Carefully concealed, a bugging device would keep tabs on whatever work went on in this lab.

They slipped out as silently as they had entered, blending into the shadows of the conservatory grounds. The laboratory door clicked shut behind them, the faint sound swallowed by the night.

SIX

T he reconstructed Rupertsberg Abbey stood proudly on the rocky promontory overlooking the Rhine River, a serene testament to the resilience of faith and knowledge. The original structure, destroyed during the Thirty Years' War, had long since been reduced to ruins, but a modest Benedictine community had breathed new life into the site. Pale stone walls rose against the lush green hills, blending seamlessly with the landscape, while the gleaming glass panes of a vast greenhouse hinted at the abbey's deeper purpose—a living sanctuary for Hildegard von Bingen's botanical and spiritual legacy.

The grounds were quiet except for the rustle of wind through the abbey's herb gardens. Sister Amalia, the abbess of the Benedictine community, stood near the entrance, gazing toward the river with an expression that mingled pride and contemplation. A plaque set into the stone wall nearby bore the Latin inscription: *"Fides et Natura in Unitate"*—Faith and Nature in Unity.

Another sister approached, her hands clasped. "Shall I prepare the greenhouse for the evening, Sister Amalia?"

Amalia nodded but didn't turn from the view. "Yes, Sister Clara. And check the sanctum before you lock the doors. Some of the specimens will need more moisture tonight."

Clara inclined her head and departed toward the greenhouse, her habit swishing softly against the gravel. Amalia let her gaze linger on the river for a moment longer, as if searching the horizon for a sign.

As the sisters went about their evening tasks, the story of Rupertsberg whispered from every corner of the grounds. Built in 1150 by Hildegard von Bingen, the abbey stood as a beacon of spiritual and intellectual life. Its walls housed not only Hildegard's theological insights but also her revolutionary contributions to music, medicine, and botany.

That golden age ended in 1632 when Swedish troops swept through the region during the Thirty Years' War and razed it to the ground. For centuries, only ruins and scattered artifacts remained, visited by pilgrims who came to touch the echoes of Hildegard's vision.

It wasn't until the early twentieth century that the Benedictine Order, inspired by her teachings, decided to return to the site. They rebuilt the abbey on its original foundations, not as a traditional convent but as a center for her legacy. Here, they cultivated medicinal plants, preserved her writings, and taught her philosophy of harmony between faith and nature.

Today, the abbey had become a sanctuary not only for the sisters but also for scholars, botanists, and theologians seeking to connect with Hildegard's work.

The greenhouse was the crown jewel of the property —a towering structure of glass and steel that seemed to breathe life into Hildegard's vision. Inside, the air was permeated by the scent of herbs, flowers, and earth. Hundreds of plants grew in meticulously organized rows, their leaves glistening with dew. Many of the species were mentioned in Hildegard's books *Physica* and *Causae et Curae*, resurrected through painstaking research and cultivation.

At the heart of the greenhouse was a sanctum, a raised platform surrounded by locked glass walls. Here, the sisters kept their rarest specimens—plants that existed nowhere else in the world, either saved from extinction or rediscovered in old texts. Apart from the library and archives, these were the most guarded treasures of Rupertsberg, tied to Hildegard's vision of healing and divine harmony. Some plants were rumored to possess properties that could heal the gravest ailments—or cause untold harm in the wrong hands.

Sister Clara moved quietly among the plants, misting their leaves and checking the temperature controls. As she passed the sanctum, she paused, her gaze lingering on the delicate plants within, aware of the sanctity of her charge.

As dusk settled over the monastery, the bells of evening prayer rang out, echoing across the valley.

Sister Amalia stood at the greenhouse entrance, watching Clara finish her rounds. The abbess's voice broke the silence.

"Rupertsberg has always been a place of power," she said softly, more to herself than to Clara. "Hildegard knew it. The plants and seeds she nurtured here—they were not just medicine for the body but for the soul."

Clara turned, her expression serene. "Yes, Sister. I feel the peace of this sacred place." Then she frowned, recalling the abbess's words, suddenly concerned. "A place of power? Power of healing, do you mean?"

Amalia's mouth tightened into a firm line. "Power of any kind in this world… it can be a heady treasure for some. It is not ours to keep, Sister. But it is ours to protect—until the heir of the Saint-Clairs reaches out to us. They are the rightful beneficiaries of Hildegard's legacy."

As the final rays of light disappeared from the glass panes, the sisters secured the doors and returned inside the abbey for evening prayers. In the stillness that followed, the greenhouse seemed to pulse with quiet vitality, its secrets lying in wait for the hands—whether worthy or unworthy—that would one day unveil them.

CHRISTOPHE VAUX'S expression remained stoic, though his piercing gaze betrayed a flicker of satisfaction as he watched Blackthorn read the pages printed out from the phones of his henchmen. Originally, Vaux had hoped that his crew could find the formulary that might "encourage health and vitality," which, alone, was highly valuable to Zentara Biogenics. But Élise's notes had offered a greater treasure: a cure for cancer. The rewards would be staggering. And Zentara would want it.

"You brought back only notes?" Blackthorn looked up at Vaux, his tone precise, almost surgical.

Vaux squirmed, then caught himself, and sat straighter. "This is quite a bit, I'd say."

Blackthorn glowered at his man. "You'd say? Her analysis of the powder from the galls, her assumptions, yes, but where is the powder itself that she analyzed? I need that. I expected that."

Vaux nodded. Of course, he wanted it all. Vaux had been on-site in South America when Blackthorn's minions took over an Amazon area where certain rare plants had been found medicinally active. He had seen the charred earth and the ruined lives left in Blackthorn's path. Not that Vaux cared. But he knew that Blackthorn stopped at nothing to get what he wanted. Now Blackthorn wanted—no, expected—Vaux to get hold of the powder that Élise had been analyzing.

Moments later, after Blackthorn had left, Vaux stood, his shadow long against the glow of the surveillance screens of his office. Somewhere in the network of operatives he controlled, he had set his plans in motion. Now, his task wasn't just observing or gathering intel—he was preparing to strike.

∿

THE NIGHT WAS COLD, and Geneva's streets were quiet except for the occasional crunch of snow under hurried footsteps. Élise Gauthier left her lab, her bag slung over her shoulder and her thoughts preoccupied with the data she had gathered that day. The analysis of the *Ricinus aureum* powder was yielding promising results, and the complexity of Hildegard's encoded recipe was beginning to align with modern biochemical insights. She couldn't wait to share more of her findings with Michael and Hana.

But as she turned down a less-traveled side street, a subtle prickle of unease made her glance over her shoulder. The streetlights cast eerie shadows, and the faint hum of the city seemed unusually distant. She quickened her pace, her boots clicking against the pavement, her breath visible in the chill.

Then, she saw it—a dark van parked at the corner. Two figures emerged, moving with an unsettling purpose. Her instincts screamed danger.

Before she could react, they were on her. A gloved hand clamped over her mouth, silencing her cry, and the other grabbed her arm in a vice-like grip, pulling her forearms tight, grabbing her purse, then zip-tying her wrists behind her. The second man quickly pulled a black hood over her head, plunging her into darkness. Her heart pounded and adrenaline surged as she struggled against them, but their grip was unyielding.

"Don't fight," one of the men growled in a low, accented voice. "You'll only make it worse."

The world shifted as they lifted her off her feet, carrying her like a sack of grain. She felt herself being shoved into the back of the van, the smell of rubber and oil overwhelming her senses. The door slammed shut, and the vehicle lurched forward.

Inside the van, Élise's mind raced. Her heart hammered as she tried to make sense of what was happening. She thought of the *Ricinus aureum* powder, her research, and the cryptic significance of Hildegard's work. Could this be connected? Michael had warned her about third parties potentially having an interest in their activities, but she had dismissed the idea of being personally targeted. Now, she wasn't so sure.

The men spoke in low tones, their voices muffled but intense.

"Zentara wants everything she's got," one whispered.

"I doubt she'll talk," the other replied. "Not without persuasion."

The mention of Zentara sent a chill through Élise. The biogenetics conglomerate's shadowy influence had grown increasingly apparent in recent news, something concerning illegal acquisitions of ancient artifacts and bio-engineering projects with unsettling implications. But what did all that have to do with her?

The van stopped abruptly, throwing Élise forward. She rolled over, her cheek stinging where it had struck the rough surface of the floor. Moments later, she felt herself being yanked upright and pulled out of the van. The night air bit at her exposed skin as they dragged her into what felt like a large, cold space—maybe an abandoned warehouse, judging by the echo of their footsteps.

They forced her into a chair, and a few moments later, the hood was ripped off, and the sudden brightness of a single overhead bulb made her squint. The building's interior was dark except for that singular bulb, and bare of all but a wooden table and some equipment, along with the dumped contents of her purse. Two men loomed over her, their faces partially obscured by scarves and hats. One of them stepped forward and leaned in close.

"Élise Gauthier," he said, his tone calm but menacing. "We know who you are, and we know what you've been working on."

"I don't know what you're talking about," Élise said, her voice shaking despite her efforts to sound defiant.

The man chuckled. "Don't play games. Hildegard von Bingen's work—the powder, the formula, the analysis. We know you have it. Our employer wants it, and you're going to give it to us."

Élise's mind raced. The powder wasn't with her; it was safely put away in the lab's secure storage. But her research notes and preliminary findings were accessible from her phone, linked to the lab's network. If they got hold of those, Zentara might unravel everything.

"I don't have it," she said firmly, meeting the man's cold gaze. "The powder isn't with me."

The second man stepped closer, his patience clearly thinner. "Then where is it? Don't make us take this further."

Élise hesitated, her thoughts a whirlwind. She couldn't let them take everything she had worked on.

But if she refused, they might escalate the situation, and she wasn't certain she could outlast their threats.

"I need my phone," she said finally. "I can access the data from my lab remotely."

The men exchanged a glance before one of them roughly cut off the zip tie on her wrists while the other grabbed her phone from the contents of her purse and shoved it into her hand, keeping a close watch as she unlocked it. Élise's fingers trembled as she navigated to the lab's secure database. She hesitated briefly before downloading a set of heavily abridged research notes. The real breakthroughs were stored offline, inaccessible even to her from here.

"Here," she said, handing the phone back. "That's everything."

One of the men plugged her phone into a laptop sitting to one side on the table and began transferring the files. As the progress bar crept across the screen, the other leaned in close again. "I hope, for your sake, that you're not lying. Our boss doesn't take kindly to deceit."

"I gave you what I have," she said through clenched teeth. "Now let me go."

"Not until you tell us where the powder—"

Sudden barking and snarling sounded just outside the door. A man's voice said, "What is it, boy? Watcha find?"

Élise opened her mouth to yell just as duct tape covered her lips and the hood whipped back over her head. She heard the clamor of running feet and a door slam. Her breath came in short gasps as she tried to struggle free. A car engine rumbled nearby, and the barking seemed to follow that sound.

Élise pushed up with her feet, then tumbled down hard, the chair smacking the concrete floor. The barking returned, and moments later, the warehouse area's security guard ripped off the hood and the tape, looking at her in surprise.

She trembled. Slowly, she realized she was in an isolated and mostly deserted section of Geneva's industrial district. The guard was full of questions, and as grateful as she was for his rescue, she felt compelled to avoid answering too much. She had learned the hard way already: knowledge had a way of leaking out and bringing danger in.

SEVEN

Earlier that day, Michael had sat at Hana's coffee table, Hildegard's manuscript spread out before him on the polished oak surface. The faint aroma of coffee and freshly purchased Bündner Nusstorte, a popular caramelized nut-filled Swiss pastry, drifted his way as Hana carried in the treats, but he seemed oblivious, his eyes fixed on the delicate script of the *Lingua Ignota*. Hana leaned in, her arms resting on the table, as she studied his notes.

"This part," Michael said, pointing to a line he had carefully translated, "isn't merely about her botanical experiments. It's a directive. She left instructions for someone—likely a descendant or a keeper of her legacy."

Hana frowned, brushing a strand of hair from her face. "A directive? You think she meant someone in my family?"

"Possibly. Or perhaps she intended her work to

reach someone with the capacity to understand it when the time was right." He shifted slightly and tapped another section of text. "Here, she writes of a *Sanctum Vitae*—a sanctuary of life—hidden within the grounds of Rupertsberg Abbey."

"Rupertsberg… I'm anxious to see it. I read up on it after you said we needed to meet today to make our travel plans." Hana's brow furrowed as she dredged up memories from her studies. "That's where she founded her first abbey, isn't it?"

Michael nodded. "Exactly. The original abbey still exists as a convent today as it did centuries ago, although some sections have been renovated in more recent times. And this phrase—" He pointed to another passage, his voice lowering slightly as though the words carried a weight even centuries later. "'Seek the *arbor vitae* where the winds cross, where the sanguine and choleric meet beneath the roots of the earth. There the humors will mingle, and the cure may be found.'"

Hana sat back, staring at him. "*Arbor vitae*? Tree of life? That sounds… symbolic."

"It could be," Michael agreed. "But in this context, I think it's more specific. Hildegard often used metaphors to describe natural phenomena. This likely refers to a particular tree or stand of trees where the plant grows."

"Wait," Hana said, her thoughts snapping into place like a rapidly solving equation. "You think there's something—something physical—left at the abbey of Rupertsberg?"

Michael nodded. "A map, I believe it implies here. She wrote this for a time when her work would be understood and needed. And if her descriptions are correct, the abbey might still hold what we're looking for."

Hana's gaze dropped to the manuscript, then to the vial of golden powder resting in its small ornate case on the table. Her grandfather's unexpected bequest had been full of mysteries, but none as compelling as this. "How do we even find it? I assume this 'map' isn't sitting out in the open."

"It won't be," Michael said. "We'll have to search the foundations and any surviving structures carefully. And..." He paused, his expression contemplative. "We might need help."

"Help?" Hana raised an eyebrow. "Let me guess... Karl and Lukas?"

Michael allowed a slight smile. "They'd be invaluable. Their training, their discretion... This isn't the kind of mission we can undertake alone."

Hana laughed softly, shaking her head. "Mission? Michael, you make it sound like a covert operation."

"In a way, it is," he said seriously. "If we're correct about what Hildegard left behind, it's something that needs to be handled with care. Not everyone would see the value in preserving her work as she intended."

"Fair enough," Hana conceded.

"I'll contact Karl and Lukas before we leave; we can pick them up in Rome on the way. Their assistance will be essential once we reach Rupertsberg."

"Good," Hana said, already pulling out her phone. "I'll make arrangements with the pilot. We'll leave as soon as everything's ready."

Michael glanced down at the manuscript one last time, his fingers brushing over Hildegard's elegant script. Her words seemed to carry a resonance beyond their literal meaning, as though the centuries between them were collapsing into a shared purpose.

"May her wisdom guide us," he murmured under his breath.

Hana looked up from her phone. "What was that?"

"Nothing," Michael said, closing the journal carefully. "Just a thought. Let's hope Rupertsberg holds the answers we need."

KARL LEANED against the stone wall of the Swiss Guard barracks in Vatican City, the late afternoon sun casting long shadows over the courtyard. He glanced at his watch, waiting for Lukas to finish his shift so they could grab a quick espresso before the evening briefing. Just as he was about to check his messages, his phone buzzed in his pocket.

The name **Michael Dominic** appeared on the caller ID. Straightening his posture, he answered. "Hi, Father Michael. What can I do for you?"

"Hey, Karl," Michael's voice came through the line, calm but with an undercurrent of urgency. "Are you and Lukas free to talk for a moment?"

Karl glanced toward the gate where Lukas was finishing up his post. "We're both on duty, but it's quiet at the moment. Let me grab him."

"Good. I'll wait," Michael replied.

A minute later, Karl and Lukas stood in the shaded corner of the courtyard, Lukas rubbing the back of his neck and looking slightly puzzled. "What's this about, Father?" Lukas asked.

Michael's tone was direct. "I have a situation that I need your help with. It's related to the Apostolic Archives, but it will take us out of the Vatican—into Germany, actually."

Karl raised an eyebrow. "Germany? That's a bit far afield for Archives work. What's the project?"

Michael hesitated, knowing he needed to explain just enough to secure their assistance without overwhelming them with unnecessary details. "Hana has inherited a manuscript written by a twelfth-century Benedictine abbess named Hildegard von Bingen. It contains information of great historical and possibly medical significance. We've determined that part of what she left behind points to the Rupertsberg Abbey in the Rhineland, where Hildegard lived and worked. We need to retrieve something that may still be hidden there."

Lukas frowned. "Rupertsberg? You think there's something left after all this time?"

"I do," Michael said firmly. "The manuscript suggests Hildegard left instructions for future generations. I believe she hid something in the monastery's foundations—something critical to understanding her work."

Karl crossed his arms, his expression thoughtful. "What kind of help are you expecting from us? Security? Logistics?"

"Both," Michael admitted. "We'll need to search the

site carefully, and your training will be invaluable. You're experienced in handling unexpected challenges, and I trust you both implicitly."

Lukas exchanged a look with Karl. "Sounds intriguing, but this isn't exactly standard duty for us. How are we supposed to clear this with our commander?"

Michael had anticipated the question and had already prepared his answer. "I'll handle that. I'll frame it as an Apostolic Archives project—an extension of my role as prefect. Technically, it falls under Vatican business, so there shouldn't be an issue approving a short absence. It's only for a couple of days."

Karl's lips quirked in a faint smile. "You've thought this through."

"Of course," Michael replied. "I wouldn't involve you if it weren't important."

Lukas tilted his head. "What about Hana? Is she coming along?"

"She's the reason we're going," Michael said. "Hildegard's journal belongs to her family. She's already making arrangements for transportation."

"Transportation?" Karl asked, curious.

"Her grandfather's jet," Michael explained. "It's faster than commercial flights and allows us more discretion."

Lukas gave a low whistle. "Nice! So when do we leave?"

"As soon as I clear things with your commander," Michael said. "Be ready to pack light. We'll pick you up at Ciampino Airport in the morning. I'll send you the details once everything is confirmed."

Karl nodded, his expression resolute. "Understood. Let us know as soon as it's a go."

"Thank you both," Michael said, his tone warm with genuine appreciation. "I couldn't ask for better allies."

The call ended, and Karl tucked his phone back into his pocket. He glanced at Lukas, a hint of amusement in his eyes. "Private jets and ancient monasteries. You ever think this is what we'd be doing when we signed up as Swiss Guards?"

Lukas smiled smugly. "Not even a little. But with Father Dominic, I've learned to expect the unexpected."

"Let's get that espresso," Karl said, slapping him on the shoulder. "Sounds like we'll need the energy."

The two walked off toward the barracks café, their steps already carrying a sense of purpose. Somewhere in the back of their minds, they both knew this would be no ordinary assignment—it never was with Father Dominic. And they were ready.

CHAPTER
EIGHT

The low hum of the Dassault Falcon 900 filled the cabin as the jet climbed smoothly into the morning sky above Geneva. Hana leaned back in her seat, gazing out the window at the Alps receding into the distance. Across from her, Michael sat with his hands folded, staring at nothing in particular. His brow was furrowed, and the faint tension in his posture hadn't gone unnoticed.

"You're thinking again," Hana said with a small smile, turning her attention to him.

Michael blinked, startled out of his reverie. "I always am," he admitted, a faint smile tugging at the corner of his mouth.

"Want to share?" she asked gently.

He hesitated, his fingers tightening slightly around the armrest. "It's about us," he said finally, his voice quiet. "And what comes next."

"You mean our engagement?" Hana asked, her tone even, though her heart gave a little flutter.

Michael nodded. "It's… different now. I've been thinking a lot about what this will mean—for me, for us, for the life we'll share."

Hana reached out, resting her hand on his. "Michael, I know how much being a priest means to you. Talk to me. What's on your mind?"

He exhaled slowly, his gaze dropping to their joined hands. "It's not just about being a priest. It's about balancing what I've committed my life to with what I want to build with you. I've spent so long thinking of the priesthood as a vocation of singular devotion—an all-encompassing calling. Now… now I'm trying to imagine being both a good priest and a good husband. And now, with the added responsibilities of your family, you need my support. I need to be there for you."

Hana gave his hand a gentle squeeze. "And you are. Like now."

"Yes, but…" Michael said, meeting her eyes. "The Church allows marriage now, sure, but if I continue to serve as prefect of the Apostolic Archives, can I fully commit to that while also being a supportive enough husband, the kind you deserve?"

Hana's expression softened. "Michael, you don't have to choose between those two parts of yourself. They're both grounded in love and devotion. You wouldn't be the man I fell in love with if you weren't so dedicated to your faith and your work. And I know you'll bring that same dedication to our marriage."

"But what if I fail at one or the other?" Michael

asked, his voice heavy with doubt. "What if trying to balance both means I fail at both?"

Hana leaned forward, her voice firm but tender. "You won't. You're not doing this alone, Michael. Marriage is about partnership. We'll figure it out together. And let's not forget—your vocation isn't just about the Archives or the Church. It's about serving others and living a life of purpose. Marriage doesn't take that away; it adds to it."

Michael was silent for a moment, her words sinking in. "It's not just the practicalities," he said finally. "It's the perception. People will see me differently—as a priest who's married. There will be scrutiny, expectations, judgments. I wonder if I'm ready for that."

Hana gave him a small, reassuring smile. "You've faced scrutiny your whole career. You've been questioned, doubted, and challenged—and you've always risen above it. This won't be any different. You'll set an example, Michael. You'll show that love and faith aren't competing forces; they're complementary."

Michael leaned back in his seat, exhaling deeply. "I wish I could be as confident as you are."

"You will be," Hana said, resting her head on his shoulder. "You just need time to let it all sink in. But no matter what, I'm here. We'll face everything together."

Michael tilted his head, resting it lightly against hers. "You make it sound almost easy."

Hana chuckled softly. "It's not easy. Nothing worth having ever is. But I believe in you—in us."

The cabin grew quiet for a moment, the hum of the engines filling the space. Michael closed his eyes briefly, the tension in his shoulders easing as Hana's words reassured him.

"You're incredible, you know that?" he said finally, his voice warm.

Hana grinned. "I've heard that before."

Michael laughed softly, his first genuine laugh since boarding the plane. "Thank you, Hana. For understanding—for believing in this."

"Always," she said simply, her voice filled with quiet conviction.

As the jet cruised through the morning sky bound for Rome, their hands remained entwined. The decision wasn't without challenges, but the love between them—and their shared determination—was more than enough to guide the way.

THE JET HUMMED STEADILY as it cruised at altitude, the Italian coastline still an hour away. Michael sat across from Hana in the spacious cabin, a small table between them covered in open books and loose notes. He was engrossed in Hildegard's cryptic recipe while Hana absentmindedly stared out the window, her mind flitting between Armand's funeral arrangements and the mounting tension surrounding Élise's work.

Her phone buzzed, cutting through the quiet. She glanced at the screen and saw Élise's name as she swiped to answer.

"Élise. Hi," she said but was met with silence. "Élise? Everything okay?" she asked, her voice edged with concern.

"No," Élise said, her tone shaky and rushed. "I—something happened. I need to tell you."

Hana immediately put the call on speaker, gesturing for Michael to listen. "You're on speaker. Michael's here, too. What's going on?"

There was a brief pause, and when Élise spoke again, her voice was tight and urgent. "I was kidnapped. Zentara's men—they took me. Just hours ago."

Michael straightened in his seat, his face darkening. *"What?!* Are you alright? Where are you now?"

"I'm bruised up a bit but spent the last several hours at the hospital getting checked out. Thankfully, a security guard dog smelled trouble and… well, I'm okay but I'm still shaking." Élise paused. "I'm in Geneva now, safe, but Zentara's reach is long."

Hana frowned, her confusion evident. "Who? Zentara? I've never heard of them."

Michael nodded, leaning forward. "Neither have I. Who are we dealing with, Élise?"

Élise exhaled audibly, the frustration and fear mingling in the sound. "Zentara Biogenics. On the surface, they're a pharmaceutical company—cutting-edge, focused on biotech innovations. But beneath that, they're something much darker. They're known for skirting ethical boundaries, smuggling, and even black-market dealings. They'll stop at nothing to acquire what they want."

Hana gripped the edge of the table, her pulse quickening. "What did they want? The powder?"

"Yes, but they didn't get it," Élise assured her. "It's still secure in the lab. But… they wanted my research, my notes. Somehow, they knew I was working on Hildegard's formula, and they were desperate for details. I… I gave them an abridged version."

Michael's features tightened with concern. "Abridged?"

"I only gave them surface-level information," Élise explained. "Basic observations, preliminary analyses—enough for them to understand the significance of what I'm working on, but not enough to replicate it or get to the real breakthroughs."

Michael raised an eyebrow. "Breakthroughs? Why would they care about Hildegard's work from centuries ago?"

"They're not after Hildegard for any historical significance," Élise explained. "If her formula is what we think it is—something with revolutionary medical applications—they'll exploit it. Patent it, monetize it, and control it. They'd use it for profit, not for healing. And they'd bury anyone who gets in their way."

Michael pinched the bridge of his nose, processing Élise's words. "If they're this dangerous, you need to be extremely careful. They've already crossed the line by kidnapping you. What's to stop them from trying again —or worse?"

"I know I should have been more careful," Élise said, her voice trembling. "But that puts everything we've discovered in jeopardy—puts it directly in the public eye, and I think that could be even worse. For now, I've locked everything down at the lab. The powder is secure, and my files are encrypted. But this… this is bigger than I realized. They won't stop with me. If they figure out that you two are involved, they might come after you as well."

"They'd have no reason to," Hana said, though her voice lacked conviction. "They don't even know we're connected to the research."

"I wouldn't bet on that, Hana," Élise warned. "Zentara doesn't leave loose ends. If they think you're helping me, you'll be on their radar. And who else would such a Hildegard legacy involve but an heir to that very legacy: the Saint-Clair family. You."

Michael leaned back, his expression grim. "We can't let this stand. If they're targeting you and trying to hijack Hildegard's work, we need to find a way to stop them. They can't be allowed to control something this important."

Hana nodded. "Élise, are you sure you're safe for now? Do you have someone with you?"

"I'm home," Élise replied. "I've contacted a trusted colleague at the university—someone who knows about Zentara and can help keep an eye out. But I'm still shaken. This feels like the beginning of something much worse."

"It might be," Michael admitted. "But we'll do everything we can to make sure they don't get what they're after."

Hana's jaw tightened. "We need to figure out what Zentara knows and how they're planning to act next. We're in the air now, en route to Rupertsberg Abbey to find out more about what Hildegard discovered, but we'll get back to you as soon as we can. In the meantime, Élise, you need to stay vigilant. Don't go anywhere alone, and don't trust anyone you don't know."

"I'll be careful," Élise said. "But please, watch yourselves too. Zentara doesn't play by the rules. They're dangerous."

After the call ended, the cabin fell into a tense silence. Hana stared at the phone, her fingers drumming against the table. "Zentara," she murmured. "Some unscrupulous company willing to kidnap is… terrifying."

Michael nodded, his expression grim. "If they've gone this far already, they'll only escalate. We need to stay one step ahead of them."

"And protect Élise," Hana said, determination flashing in her eyes. "We're not letting them win."

The thrum of the jet carried them forward, but now the atmosphere felt heavier, the stakes impossibly higher. They exchanged a glance, both silently resolving to do whatever it took to keep Hildegard's work—and Élise—safe.

CHAPTER
NINE

The Falcon touched down smoothly on the runway at Ciampino Airport under a bright Roman sky. Hana peered out the window, spotting Karl and Lukas on the tarmac near the private Signature terminal.

"There they are," Hana said, leaning back in her seat. "Right on time, as usual."

Michael smiled faintly. "Punctuality is one of their superpowers."

"Punctuality and looking like they're guarding the Pope even when they're off-duty," Hana added with a grin.

The jet rolled to a stop, and moments later, the door hissed open. Karl was the first to climb aboard with his luggage, grinning broadly when he saw Hana.

"Hey, Cousin!" he called, throwing his arms wide. "It's been too long."

Hana laughed and stood to hug him. "What are you

talking about? You were visiting us in Geneva just last month!"

"Still too long," Karl insisted, squeezing her tightly before stepping aside to let Lukas on board.

Michael gestured for Karl and Lukas to sit as the jet began taxiing back to the runway. Once everyone was settled, he leaned forward, his expression a mix of excitement and gravity.

"First, I should say thanks for coming along. This is important to both of us," Michael began, glancing briefly at Hana. "It's about a project tied to Hana's family history. She inherited a journal from her grandfather—a manuscript written by Hildegard von Bingen, of all people. He'd had it secreted away but left her with the task of bringing it to light."

"Hildegard von Bingen?" Karl repeated, eyebrows raised. "As in, the visionary saint? That Hildegard?"

Michael smiled. He knew that Karl shared his own love of Church history. "The same. It's an extraordinary document, detailing her work with a plant called *Ricinus aureum*. It's a gall-producing plant she believed had profound healing properties."

"So, we're going to Germany *why*?" Lukas asked.

"She left clues in her manuscript that suggest the plant's location is tied to the ruins of her abbey at Rupertsberg. That's why we're going to Germany—to see if we can find more of her work and, possibly, the plant itself."

Karl leaned back, whistling softly. "That's incredible. Many plants have revolutionized medicine in the past, of course. So you think this plant might still be out there?"

"If it is," Hana said, "it could lead to major medical breakthroughs. But even if we only find her notes or some remnants of her work, it would be a huge historical discovery."

"And you called us because...?" Lukas teased, though his tone was light.

"Because I know how handy you two are," Michael said with a grin. "This isn't just an archaeological expedition. And there's always the chance of unexpected challenges. We've already had a kidnapping—"

"*What?*" Karl looked sharply at Hana.

"No, not me. But it is related to what we're doing. I'll tell you about it later. Having two Swiss Guards—especially ones who know us well—seemed like a smart choice."

"A kidnapping?! You bet we're in," Lukas said, concerned.

Karl nodded firmly. "Of course. Family first—and I wouldn't miss this for the world."

"Good," Michael said, relaxing slightly. "We'll land in Frankfurt, rent a car, and drive to the abbey. It should be straightforward but stay sharp."

The jet lifted off smoothly, the ground falling away beneath them. The four settled into a full briefing conversation, the excitement for their journey growing.

• • •

Two hours later, the Falcon touched down at Frankfurt Airport. The group disembarked and headed to the car rental counter in the main terminal, where Karl took charge of the arrangements.

A sleek black Range Rover SUV awaited them in the lot. Lukas slid into the passenger seat while Karl took the wheel, and Michael and Hana settled in the back.

The drive from Frankfurt to the small town of Bingen am Rhein was stunning, with vineyards blanketing the rolling hills and the Rhine River occasionally glimpsed through the trees. Hana couldn't resist rolling down her window to take in the fresh autumn air.

"Almost there," Karl announced, glancing at the GPS. "Five minutes."

Michael leaned forward from the backseat. "Rupertsberg should be on a hill overlooking the river. Some of the abbey was destroyed centuries ago, but much of the original still remains, now with some renovations."

"And we're looking for what exactly?" Lukas asked.

"Anything that could point us to Hildegard's *Sanctum Vitae*—her sanctuary of life," Michael explained. "If she left instructions or maps, they're likely hidden there."

"And if we don't find anything?" Lukas pressed.

"Then we regroup and keep searching," Michael said simply. "Hildegard's work is too important to give up on. And we aren't the only ones who think that's true." On the plane, Hana had already filled the guards in on what happened to Élise.

They fell into a companionable silence as Karl guided the Range Rover into a small gravel parking lot. The abbey and its ruins came into view—a collection of crumbled stone walls, weathered by centuries but still hinting at the grandeur they once held.

Hana stepped out of the car, pulling her scarf tighter against the cool breeze. "Well," she said, looking up at the ruins, "let's see what secrets Hildegard left behind."

Karl clapped her on the shoulder. "Let's do it."

Together, the four of them set off toward the abbey, their shared excitement and determination driving them forward.

HANA'S GAZE swept over the ancient beauty of the abbey, with its weathered stones standing like sentinels of a bygone era. But what truly caught her attention was the large greenhouse nestled on the grounds, its glass panels gleaming in the sun. Inside, two figures in black habits moved among rows of plants, their hands busy tending to the greenery.

"Well, that's unexpected," Hana said, nodding toward the greenhouse. "Look at the size of that greenhouse."

"No kidding," Michael said, stepping beside her. "Let's find out who that is inside."

The group approached the greenhouse, their footsteps crunching on the gravel. One of the nuns, a middle-aged woman with streaks of silver in her hair, looked up as they neared. She set down her watering can and wiped her hands on her apron, stepping toward the entrance.

"Good afternoon," she said in German, her voice warm and welcoming. "Welcome to Rupertsberg Abbey. I'm Sister Amalia. How can I help you?"

Michael stepped forward, his tone respectful but friendly. "Good afternoon, Sister. I'm Father Michael Dominic, and these are my friends: Hana Sinclair, Karl Dengler, and Lukas Bischoff. We've come here because of a connection to Hildegard von Bingen."

Sister Amalia tilted her head, her curiosity piqued. "Hildegard's legacy is why we maintain this abbey and greenhouse. But may I ask, what brings you here in particular? This is not a site many people visit."

Michael gestured toward Hana. "Hana recently inherited a journal from her grandfather, Baron Armand de Saint-Clair. The manuscript contains references to Hildegard's work—specifically to a plant called *Ricinus aureum*. We believe Hildegard left clues here at Rupertsberg about her research."

At the mention of Armand de Saint-Clair, Sister Amalia froze. Her expression shifted to astonishment as she turned to the younger nun beside her.

"Sister Clara," Sister Amalia said, her voice filled with disbelief. "Did you hear that?"

Sister Clara nodded, her wide eyes fixed on Hana. "She said Armand de Saint-Clair!"

Hana glanced between the two nuns. "Yes, he was my grandfather. He passed away recently."

Sister Amalia clasped her hands together, a mixture

of awe and relief on her face. "You're his granddaughter?"

"Yes," Hana said slowly. "Is that significant?"

Sister Amalia exchanged a look with Sister Clara before turning back to Hana. "It is more than significant. We've been waiting for someone from the Saint-Clair family to come for years. Hildegard's writings spoke of a time when her most sacred knowledge would pass to a rightful heir—someone connected to her work through lineage, intellect, and faith. Your grandfather's name was known to us, and we are so sorry for your loss. But we were told to watch for his descendant."

Hana blinked, stunned. "You've been waiting for me?"

Sister Clara stepped forward, her voice gentle. "We didn't know who it would be, only that someone would come. Hildegard entrusted part of her legacy to our community, but she foresaw that a time would come when it needed to be shared beyond these walls. It appears that time has come."

Michael's brow furrowed with curiosity. "What exactly did Hildegard entrust to you?"

Sister Amalia gestured for them to follow her. "Come inside. It's easier to explain if you see it for yourselves."

The group entered the greenhouse, the warm, humid air a stark contrast to the cool autumn breeze outside. Rows of herbs, flowers, and other plants stretched before them, their vibrant colors and earthy scents filling the space. Hana's eyes widened as she took in the collection.

"This is incredible," she murmured. "You've preserved her work."

Sister Clara nodded. "The greenhouse is dedicated to Hildegard's plants—those she used for healing, food, and even pigments for her illuminated manuscripts. Each plant has its purpose, and the Benedictines have cared for them for generations."

Hana scanned the rows, looking for the plant described in her grandfather's manuscript. "Is *Ricinus aureum* here?"

Sister Amalia shook her head. "No. The plant you seek could grow only in the Black Forest, far from here. Hildegard wrote that its galls held extraordinary properties, but they were rare even in her time and could only be harvested at the right time of year. This season—autumn—made them most potent, she wrote."

Michael folded his arms, processing this information. "So the *Ricinus aureum* isn't part of the greenhouse collection?"

"It never has been," Sister Amalia confirmed, her voice carrying a reverence that matched the gravity of the sacred trust she had spent her life safeguarding. "Hildegard herself believed the plant should grow wild, untouched by human hands, in its natural environment. She believed its power—both physical and spiritual— came from its unbroken connection to the earth, where it thrived untainted by cultivation or interference."

Hana's shoulders sagged. She'd had such hope. "So it wasn't preserved here by Hildegard at all. And now it's extinct."

The two nuns looked at each other, a grin growing

on Sister Amalia before she looked back at Hana. "Why, dear, I never said that."

"But I thought that—"

The two nuns laughed lightly, covering their mouths, before Amalia said, "*Ricinus aureum* is believed to be extinct because we, the sisters, intentionally fostered that belief. This was Hildegard's vision: that the plant remain hidden, shielded from the corruption and exploitation of the world."

Sister Amalia's gaze shifted to the dense forest visible through the abbey's window. "The fallacy of its extinction was a deliberate act of preservation. As knowledge of Hildegard's writings spread, her other botanical discoveries were harvested, studied, and commercialized even in her own day. She feared that *Ricinus aureum*, with its unparalleled properties, would meet the same fate—or worse, that its potential would be weaponized. By allowing the world to forget it ever existed, we have ensured its survival."

She hesitated, her fingers brushing against a rosary hanging from her belt. "But more than that, Hildegard believed this plant to be a divine gift, a symbol of balance and healing meant for a time when humanity truly needed it. Until then, she entrusted its care to us, warning that if it were found too soon, its misuse could bring harm instead of salvation. That why we maintain the illusion of its extinction—it is an act of obedience to her wisdom and a protection of the sacred trust she placed in us."

Hana turned to Michael, her expression resolute. "Then we'll have to go to the Black Forest."

"First," Sister Amalia said, interrupting gently, "there's something else. Beneath the ruins of our other monastery is a small chamber—the *Sanctum Vitae*. Hildegard left it for the one who would continue her work. That chamber holds the knowledge you'll need to understand her writings fully."

Michael exchanged a glance with Hana, his eyes bright with anticipation. "Then we'll start there." Sister Amalia's gaze rested on Hana with an intensity that seemed to pierce the layers of any uncertainty surrounding them. "For that, we must go to Eibingen Abbey, where our community lives," she said, her voice steady but shaded with urgency. "What you seek—what belongs to you—is there, safeguarded for generations. The ferry will take us across the Rhine; we mustn't delay." Her words hung in the air like a promise and a warning as the distant toll of the abbey bells of Eibingen called them toward the next step in their journey.

CHAPTER
TEN

The low hum of the ferry's engine blended with the rhythmic lapping of water against the hull as it cut smoothly across the Rhine. The group stood near the railing, the chill autumn breeze carrying the faint scent of the river. The scenery was breathtaking, with vineyards climbing the hills on either side of the water and the golden hues of fall glowing under a soft, overcast sky.

Hana had called Élise before they set out just to confirm that she was still fine. Now she tried to relax, tightened her scarf around her neck, and glanced at Michael, who stood beside her, his hands gripping the railing as he gazed at the far shore. Behind them, Karl and Lukas were engaged in quiet conversation, their voices low but relaxed. Sisters Clara and Amalia sat in quiet reflection inside the ferry.

"I didn't realize we'd be taking a ferry," Hana said,

leaning closer to Michael. "This feels... almost too picturesque for what we're doing."

Michael smiled faintly. "There's something fitting about crossing the Rhine on this journey. Hildegard herself would have traveled these waters countless times. It feels like we're walking in her footsteps."

"Or floating in her wake," Hana teased, her smile softening as she turned her gaze back to the river. "It's strange to think that she left all of this—her work, her legacy—intended for someone like me. I mean, I'm just a journalist."

Michael looked at her, his expression thoughtful. "You're not 'just' anything, Hana. Hildegard's writings speak to people who are curious, bold, and willing to follow the truth wherever it leads. That's you to a T."

Hana laughed quietly. "Flattery will get you everywhere, Father Dominic."

"Not flattery," Michael said, his tone sincere. "Just the truth."

Karl joined them at the railing, pulling his jacket tighter against the breeze. "I'll admit," he said, nodding toward the distant shoreline, "this is turning out to be more interesting than I expected. I didn't think we'd be tracking down ancient maps and hidden chambers when I agreed to come along."

"It is a bit surreal," Hana admitted. "But you're enjoying it, aren't you?"

"Of course," Karl said with a grin. "Anything that gets me out of the routines of the Vatican for a few days is a win. Besides, this is family business now. How could I miss it?"

Lukas walked up, his hands in his pockets. "I've never seen this part of Germany before. It's beautiful. Hard to imagine we're here for anything other than sightseeing."

"Well," Michael said, "I wouldn't call what we're doing sightseeing. But I'll admit, the setting doesn't hurt."

As the ferry neared the opposite bank, the outline of Eibingen Abbey came into view atop the hill. Its modest, pale stone chapel seemed to glow against the backdrop of dense forest and rolling vineyards.

Hana's breath caught as she took in the sight. "That's it, isn't it?" she asked, glancing at Michael.

He nodded. "That's the chapel where Sister Amalia said the reliquary is kept."

"It's smaller than I imagined," Hana said.

"Small but significant," Michael replied. "Hildegard spent her later years at the Eibingen Abbey which she founded in 1165. Some of her most personal writings and work were preserved there."

The ferry bumped gently against the dock, and the group disembarked, their steps purposeful as they made their way to the waiting car. Sister Clara took the wheel, guiding them up a winding road through the vineyards and toward the monastery. The air was crisp and quiet as they arrived at the chapel, its simple façade exuding an air of timeless reverence.

"Welcome to Eibingen," Sister Amalia said, her voice warm. "This is where Hildegard's final legacy resides."

Hana looked up at the chapel, her heart beating

faster. "The reliquary," she said. "You really think it holds a map?"

Sister Amalia smiled gently, looking into Hana's eyes. "Not just a map. A guide. Hildegard left it specifically for the one she knew would continue her work."

Michael stepped forward, his tone curious but respectful. "How has it been kept all these years? Surely others have been curious about its contents."

"They have," Sister Clara said. "But Hildegard's instructions were clear: it was not to be opened or disturbed until the rightful descendant arrived. The sisters of Eibingen have honored that directive for centuries, just as my sisters at Rupertsberg carry on her work in the greenhouse. And we have"—she hesitated, then smiled—"others who look out for us and our work as well."

"This is… incredible," Michael said, glancing at Hana. "This is exactly what we've been searching for."

Sister Amalia led them down the age-worn steps of an ancient stone stairway and gestured toward the doors of a small chamber: the *Sanctum Vitae*. "Come. It's time to see what Hildegard left for you."

Hana hesitated for a moment, her nerves catching up with her excitement.

Michael placed a reassuring hand on her shoulder. "Ready?" he asked softly.

She took a deep breath and nodded. "Let's do this."

With that, the group followed the sisters into the chamber, the shadows of history and discovery pressing down on them as they approached the reliquary.

. . .

THE SANCTUM VITAE of Eibingen was a serene and humble space, its stone walls illuminated by the soft light filtering through high stained-glass windows depicting Hildegard's visions. The faint scent of beeswax candles mingled with the cool, earthy air. Hana, Michael, Karl, and Lukas followed Sister Amalia and Sister Clara down the central aisle, their footsteps echoing softly.

At an altar, a small but ornate reliquary rested on a raised stone platform. Its intricate gold-and-silver filigree seemed to glow in the dim light, and at its center was a polished crystal window that shimmered faintly. Hana's breath caught as she took in the craftsmanship.

"That's it," Sister Amalia said, her voice reverent. "This reliquary has been here for nearly nine hundred years, entrusted to us by Hildegard herself."

Michael stepped closer, his eyes scanning the reliquary. "It's extraordinary," he said. "And you're certain it contains a map?"

Sister Amalia nodded. "Hildegard's instructions were explicit. This reliquary holds a parchment—a guide she wrote for her successor. Oral legend tells us she described it as a map, but none of us have ever seen its contents. Only the rightful heir was to open it."

Hana hesitated, her heart pounding. "You really think that's me?"

"Yes," Sister Clara said, her voice calm but certain. "Hildegard's writings speak of the Saint-Clair lineage and its connection to her work. Your grandfather's name, Armand, was mentioned specifically as history unfolded over the years. We believe that Hildegard knew that when the time was right, someone from your family would come."

Hana turned to Michael, her hands trembling slightly. "This feels… overwhelming. What if they're wrong? What if this isn't meant for me?"

The abbess held up her hand to stop Hana's objection. "It was not just hearing the name 'Saint-Clair' that convinced us you are the one we've awaited for centuries. It was your name."

The team all looked at Hana, who looked as surprised and puzzled as they were.

Sister Clara spoke up with a bit of a chuckle. "Hana."

Amalia took Hana's hand. "Hildegard wrote of her successor as being one who would 'come with grace and be favored by God to continue His good work.' Grace. Favor. Those are the meanings behind—"

"Hana!" Michael beamed. "The Hebrew meaning behind the name Hana. Of course." He gave her a reassuring smile. "Hana, you wouldn't be here if it weren't meant for you. Everything we've uncovered points to this moment. Trust in that."

Karl stepped forward, his tone light but supportive. "And if you need a push, just think of Élise. We need to get through all this, to make things right. We're all behind you. You've got this, Cousin."

Hana let out a nervous laugh, then turned back to Sister Amalia. "What do I do?"

Sister Amalia gestured toward the reliquary. "Simply

open it. The clasp is unlocked. Hildegard left it that way so it could be accessed at the right time."

With a deep breath, Hana stepped up to the platform. She reached out, her fingers brushing against the cool metal of the reliquary. After a moment of hesitation, she gently lifted the clasp and opened the lid.

Inside was a rolled parchment, tied with a faded ribbon. Hana carefully lifted it, her hands trembling as she untied the ribbon and unfurled the delicate sheet.

The group leaned in, their eyes scanning the parchment. It was a map, beautifully illustrated, with hand-drawn details of a dense forest. Beneath the map, in Hildegard's elegant script, was a set of instructions written in Latin.

Michael read aloud, his voice steady. "'Seek the *arbor vitae* where the shadows meet. Beneath its protectors, the galls of gold grow—nature's secret gift to heal the afflicted.'"

Hana traced her finger along the map. "This is the Black Forest," she said, her voice filled with wonder. "It's exactly as Sister Amalia said—the *Ricinus aureum* grows there."

"And their galls," Michael added, "are the essential key to completing her formula."

Karl and Lukas exchanged a glance, their expressions a mix of anticipation and determination.

Sister Amalia smiled, her voice soft. "This is why Hildegard entrusted us with the reliquary. She foresaw that her work would need to continue beyond the monastery's walls. You are the one to carry it forward, my dear Hana."

Looking up from the map, Hana's expression was resolute. "Then we're going to the Black Forest."

∼

EARLIER, at Rupertsberg Abbey, a drone had hovered quietly over the grounds, its near-invisible presence blending seamlessly with the twilight sky. Below, within the greenhouse, the camera feed captured the unmistakable figures of Father Michael Dominic, Hana Sinclair, and the Swiss Guards as they spoke with an older nun.

Inside their parked surveillance van a mile from the abbey, Christophe Vaux and Vincent Garonne watched the feed intently. The live audio from the drone's parabolic microphone filled the small space, crisp and clear.

"...*untouched by human hands,*" Sister Amalia was saying. "*Hildegard believed the Ricinus aureum's power comes from its purity, its connection to the earth as God intended.*"

Vaux leaned forward, his intense blue eyes narrowing. "There it is," he murmured. "The confirmation we've been waiting for. The plant exists; it's *not* extinct!"

Vincent, his agile fingers tapping away at the tablet to stabilize the feed, smirked. "And these fools are walking right into it for us. Let's see what else the good sister has to say."

The drone's microphone zeroed in as Hana's voice cut through the audio. "*If it's so powerful, why keep it* hidden? Wouldn't sharing it have helped countless people throughout the years?"

The nun's tone turned somber. "*Because knowledge and power without understanding lead to destruction. Hildegard foresaw its misuse—by the greedy, the reckless, or those seeking dominion. This plant's power could heal, yes, but in the wrong hands, it could also devastate. That is why we have kept its existence a secret for centuries.*"

Vaux exchanged a knowing glance with Vincent. "Greedy, reckless dominion? Sounds like us."

"Maybe we should send her a thank-you note," Vincent quipped, before adjusting the drone's position slightly.

As Sister Amalia continued, the drone's audio feed wavered for a moment. Vincent frowned, making minor adjustments. "Rotor's off-balance again. It's making noise. Too faint for most to notice, but we should watch it."

Vaux kept his eyes fixed on the screen.

The live feed continued from some distance outside a tall window, showing Sister Amalia leading everyone down a stone stairway. The drone's powerful parabolic microphone picked up most of her words as she spoke again.

"*Hildegard's notes also ref… a location in the Black Forest,*" she said. "*She believed Ricinus aureum thrived there as well, hidden deep in its untouched wilderness. If you wish to follow her work, that is where your next steps will take…*"

Hana's voice followed quickly. "*The Black Forest? That's our next destination, then.*"

"*Yes,*" Amalia replied. "*But tread carefully. The forest*

holds secrets that have swallowed many who...." The drone finally lost the signal as they descended the steps.

Vaux sat back, his expression thoughtful.

"The Black Forest," he mused, more to himself than to Vincent. "They're heading straight for it. Get the team ready. By the time they get there, we'll already be in position."

Vincent leered, his tension easing as he packed away the equipment. "They have no idea what's waiting for them."

"Let's keep it that way," Vaux said, his voice cold and measured. "The *Ricinus aureum* belongs to us now."

CHAPTER
ELEVEN

T he Range Rover hummed steadily along the winding roads of southern Germany, its tires gliding over asphalt framed by fields of gold and green. Lukas drove with quiet focus, his keen eyes scanning the road ahead, while Karl sat beside him, occasionally checking their route on his phone. In the back seat, Hana and Michael shared the map Hildegard had left behind—a relic from another time, its faded parchment and intricate markings both mysterious and compelling. The sisters had remained at the Eibingen Abbey, glad for the opportunity to share the good news of the arrival of Hildegard's heir with the other sisters in that convent.

The landscape unfurled like a living tapestry. Golden fields of wheat stretched out beneath a cloudless blue sky, their edges dotted with red poppies and the occasional stone farmhouse. Vineyards climbed gently sloping hills, their neat rows a testament to centuries of careful cultivation. As they passed through small villages, the team caught glimpses of timber-framed houses with flower boxes bursting with late-blooming geraniums, their colors vivid against the whitewashed walls. Church spires rose gracefully above the rooftops, their bells tolling faintly in the distance.

Occasionally, the road curved alongside the Rhine, its waters glittering in the afternoon sun. Small fishing boats bobbed gently, their wakes spreading in delicate ripples. Hana leaned closer to the window, captivated by the serenity of it all.

"This part of the world has a way of making you forget time," she murmured, almost to herself.

Karl glanced at her in the rearview mirror. "Enjoy it while you can. The Black Forest is beautiful, but it's a different kind of wild."

They pulled into a quaint Gasthaus at the edge of a quiet village surrounded by fruit orchards. The scent of fresh bread and roasting meat greeted them as they parked beneath a large walnut tree. Opting for the terrace, the team sat at a wooden table shaded by a leafy canopy. The sounds of rustling leaves and faint laughter from other diners provided a peaceful backdrop.

Lukas unfolded a napkin and looked over the menu. "We're making good time," he said, glancing at Karl. "Still two hours to the forest, though."

Hana was only half-listening, her attention drawn to the view of the village square. An elderly man tended to a flower stall, and children chased each other around a fountain. It was a snapshot of serenity, one that felt far removed from their task ahead.

The waitress arrived with steaming plates of bratwurst, sauerkraut, and fresh-baked pretzels, along with frothy mugs of beer for Karl and Lukas and sparkling water for Hana and Michael. As they ate, conversation turned to the map.

"You've studied it enough," Karl said, leaning back in his chair. "Do you think this really leads to the location?"

Hana hesitated, her fingers brushing the edges of the old parchment resting beside her. "If Hildegard went to such lengths to preserve it, it has to mean something. But I won't believe it until I see it. I mean, how much can change in nine hundred years?"

By late afternoon, the landscape had transformed. The open fields and vineyards had given way to dense forests, the towering trunks of pines and firs casting dark shadows across the road. The light dimmed as the SUV climbed higher into the hills, the air cooler and tinged with the earthy scent of pine needles.

When they finally stopped, it was at the edge of a secluded clearing near the Triberg Waterfalls area, as revealed on Hildegard's map. The forest loomed before them, dark and impenetrable, its canopy of oak trees so thick that little sunlight reached the ground. Lukas cut the engine, and for a moment, there was only silence— deep and unnerving, broken only by the occasional trill of a bird.

Hana got out and sat on a large rock, unfolded the map, and spread it across her lap. The parchment's edges were frayed, and its ink had faded in places, but the markings were still clear: a series of routes crisscrossing the Black Forest, ending in a symbol near the bottom of the page.

"This is it," she said, her voice quiet but steady. "The location Hildegard marked. If the *Ricinus aureum* is anywhere, it's around here."

Michael leaned closer, studying the map. "How far?"

"Not far, close to the waterfalls," she replied, glancing at Karl. "But we'll have to go on foot from here."

Karl stepped forward, his gaze fixed on the dense woods ahead. "Then let's waste no time."

Hana rolled up the map and slipped it carefully into her bag. She took one last look at the clearing, the trees pressing in like sentinels, before stepping ahead into the shadows.

The dense foliage swallowed them as they moved deeper into the Black Forest, the towering evergreens forming a living cathedral overhead. The air grew cooler, damp with the scent of moss and earth. Hana walked at the front with Lukas, her bag slung over one shoulder and her eyes scanning the faint trail ahead. Karl brought up the rear, his gaze flicking between the shadows, both beside and behind them, ever watchful.

They walked for what felt like hours, their boots crunching on the soft, pine-needle-strewn ground. The only sounds were the occasional rustle of leaves and the distant calls of forest birds.

Michael broke the relative silence. "Are we close?" he asked, his voice low but clear.

Hana paused, pulling the map from her bag once more. She unfolded it carefully, the parchment crackling faintly in the stillness. Tracing their path with her finger, she glanced around, aligning the landmarks on the map with the terrain around them.

"We're close," she said. "If we keep heading this way, we should reach the waterfalls soon. The symbol Hildegard marked is somewhere beyond them."

Karl stepped up beside her. "Good. We should move faster. This place isn't as quiet as it seems."

Hana frowned. "What do you mean?"

Karl gestured subtly toward the trees. "The forest has its own rhythm, its own sounds. But now and then, I hear something out of sync—branches snapping, movement too deliberate. If we're not alone, we'll know soon enough."

The sound of rushing water reached them, faint at the beginning but growing louder as they continued. The trail opened up, and they emerged onto a rocky outcrop looking up at the Triberg Waterfalls. The sight was breathtaking.

Cascading from a towering height of over 160 meters above them, the falls tumbled over rugged rock formations in a series of powerful steps as they have for centuries. Each cascade sent a fine mist into the air, creating shimmering rainbows in the sunlight that filtered through the forest canopy. The Gutach River surged below, its waters rushing over smooth stones and feeding the lush vegetation that clung to the riverbanks.

The area was alive with movement. Ferns swayed gently in the breeze, and moss-covered rocks glistened with moisture. The air smelled fresh, clean, and alive with the earthy aroma of wet stone and greenery.

Hana stepped forward, captivated by the scene. "It's so beautiful," she whispered.

Michael nodded. "It feels untouched. As if time hasn't reached this place. And to think that Hildegard herself may have walked this very path."

Karl remained behind them, scanning the area with the practiced eye of a protector. His hand rested lightly on the hilt of his sheathed knife. "We should keep moving. If there's a path beyond the falls, we'll need to find it."

Hana knelt by the edge of the stream, dipping her fingers into the cool water, then swiping them dry on her jacket before taking out the map for another look. Her brow furrowed. "The route Hildegard marked doesn't show a specific trail here, but it suggests we follow the river upstream."

Michael crouched beside her, studying the map over her shoulder. "That would make sense. If she wanted to hide something, it would be beyond a natural barrier like this."

Karl turned back toward the forest, his expression darkening. "Then let's go. The longer we stay here, the more vulnerable we are."

Hana rose to her feet, tucking the map safely back into her bag. As they moved toward the narrow path skirting the falls, a lingering dread coiled in her chest, whispering that the forest was watching them, its ancient trees silent witnesses to their search.

The trail grew narrower and more treacherous as

they followed the river upstream, weaving through dense undergrowth and over slippery rocks. The sound of the falls gradually faded, replaced by the steady murmur of the river. Occasionally, Hana would pause to consult the map, her fingers brushing over the faded ink as if seeking guidance.

Suddenly, Karl raised a hand, motioning for silence. The group froze, listening intently.

A faint rustle echoed through the forest, followed by the unmistakable snap of a branch. It was distant but deliberate, not the random sound of falling debris.

"Stay close," Karl murmured, his voice barely above a whisper. "And stay alert."

Hana exchanged a worried glance with Michael but nodded, gripping the strap of her bag tightly.

They pressed on, the rustling behind them growing fainter but never entirely disappearing. The forest seemed to thicken the farther upstream they went, the undergrowth tangling their path and the towering evergreens blotting out most of the sunlight. The air grew damp, heavy with the scent of moss and earth.

The river's flow became calmer here, its waters meandering through a narrow gorge carved by time. Smooth stones jutted out, forming natural stepping-stones that glistened in the dim light. Hana paused near the water's edge, consulting the map again.

"The symbol Hildegard marked is just beyond this point," she said, her voice barely carrying over the sound of the water. "We're very close now."

Michael crouched beside her, studying the faded ink. "Does it say anything about landmarks?"

Hana traced a finger along the parchment. "Not explicitly, but the symbol is near what looks like a clearing, surrounded by water on three sides. If we keep following the river, we should find it."

Karl's voice broke through their conversation. "We're not alone."

Both Hana and Michael turned to him. He was standing a few paces behind them, his stance rigid, one hand resting on the hilt of his knife. His gaze was fixed on the tree line, his eyes scanning for movement.

"What do you see?" Michael asked, his voice low.

"Nothing yet," Karl replied. "But I can feel it. Someone—or something—is watching us. They're staying just out of sight. For now."

They moved carefully now, their senses heightened. The trail became steeper, forcing them to climb over roots and rocks. The sound of the river grew louder again, signaling another cascade ahead. The forest seemed alive, its ancient trees towering like sentinels, their branches knitting together to create an almost impenetrable canopy.

Michael paused to catch his breath, leaning against a moss-covered boulder. "Hana, are you sure this is the right direction?"

She nodded, panting slightly as she adjusted her bag. "It has to be. The map—"

A sudden movement in the periphery of her vision made her freeze. She turned quickly, scanning the dense foliage, but saw nothing. Just the forest, silent and still.

"What is it?" Michael asked.

Hana hesitated. "I thought I saw something—someone—in the trees."

Karl stepped between them and the tree line, his knife now unsheathed. "Stay together. If they're here, they won't risk showing themselves unless we give them an opening."

Michael exchanged a look with Hana, his expression grim. "We keep moving. If they want us to stop, they'll have to make the first move."

The river curved abruptly, and the group emerged into a small clearing. It was as Hana had described from the map—water surrounded the area on three sides, with only a narrow path leading farther into the forest. The ground was softer here, covered in a thick carpet of ferns and wildflowers. The air felt different, charged with a subtle energy that was almost tangible.

"This is it," Hana said quietly, stepping forward. She knelt near the center of the clearing, her fingers brushing the earth. "This matches Hildegard's description perfectly."

Michael joined her, his eyes scanning the surroundings. "If the *Ricinus aureum* is here, where do we start looking?"

Hana opened her bag, pulling out a small notebook where she had copied key passages from Hildegard's journal. "It's supposed to grow in shadowed places, near water but away from direct sunlight. The leaves look like this," she pointed to a photo of an illustration that Hildegard had penned, "and be about a meter tall. We should check along the edges of the clearing, near the rocks."

Karl remained at the clearing's edge, his eyes never leaving the forest. The rustling they had heard earlier was gone, replaced by an unnerving stillness.

"They're out there," he said quietly, not looking back at the others. "Whoever's been following us—they're waiting for something."

Michael straightened, his expression determined. "Let them wait. We didn't come this far to turn back now."

Hana held a small journal in one hand, her other hand resting lightly on a bag slung over her shoulder. The team gathered around her before splitting up. "According to Hildegard's notes," she said, her voice low, "the galls of *Ricinus aureum* should be unmistakable —small, golden, and shaped almost like clusters of teardrops. They're supposed to grow on the undersides of the leaves, just near the veins."

Michael nodded, scanning the shady areas under the branches of the nearest oak. "And they'll only be on mature plants. The younger ones won't have yet developed the symbiotic relationship with the insects."

The team split into pairs, moving to opposite ends of the shadowed clearing. Michael and Hana walked along the bank of the river, where the dappled light filtered weakly through the dense canopy above. Karl and Lukas took the opposite side, weaving through the undergrowth with practiced efficiency.

They moved cautiously, eyes scanning every branch and leaf. Hana paused beneath a particularly old oak, its trunk gnarled and thick with moss. She crouched down, carefully parting the ferns at its base to inspect any plants hidden among the ferns.

"There," she whispered, pointing to a plant. She gently lifted a leaf, and beneath it, a cluster of broad, deep-green leaves, tiny golden galls clung to the underside of a small plant with foliage similar to but distinct from the oak, matching the description of *Ricinus aureum*. They were luminous, their tiny pebbled surfaces reflecting the faint light like drops of molten gold. Each gall was about the size of a large bead, with a slightly translucent sheen that seemed almost unnatural.

Michael knelt beside her, pulling a small knife and tweezers from his satchel. "Hildegard wrote that the galls are fragile. We'll need to be careful taking samples."

Hana held the branch steady as Michael used the

knife to gently sever the stem of a single leaf, being mindful not to crush the sensitive galls. He placed it carefully into a sample vial filled with a small amount of high proof ethanol, then slipped that into a padded specimen box lined with soft material.

"Do we need more than one?" Hana asked, her gaze darting around the plant's other branches.

Michael nodded. "If we're going to study them—and if they're as important as Hildegard believed—we'll need multiple samples. But we shouldn't take too many. They're likely part of a delicate ecological balance."

On the opposite side of the clearing, Karl and Lukas worked methodically, moving from under one tree to another. Karl scanned the plants while Lukas inspected the undersides of the foliage. The babble of the nearby river filled the silence, punctuated by the occasional rustle of leaves as they brushed past.

Lukas paused beneath a particularly ancient oak, its massive limbs reaching outward like a protective canopy. "I think I've found some," he called softly, motioning for Karl to join him.

Karl stepped closer, recognizing the golden castors. He peered beneath the leaves where Lukas pointed. The golden galls were there, clustered in tight groups near the veins of the leaves. Some were smaller, likely newly formed, while others were fully developed and glistening in the muted light.

"Those match the description," Karl said. He pulled a Swiss Army knife from his belt. "Hold the branch steady."

Lukas steadied the branch as Karl carefully pried

one of the larger galls free. It came loose easily, rolling into his palm like a precious gemstone. He placed it into the sample vial containing ethanol to preserve its integrity.

"Let's take a few more," Karl suggested. "If this is what we're looking for, we don't want to miss an opportunity."

The two pairs met back in the center of the clearing, their findings spread out on a flat rock. Each sample was carefully stored in a protective container, the golden galls gleaming against the soft padding.

"These are incredible," Hana said, leaning closer to examine them. "No wonder Hildegard kept their location hidden. They look… otherworldly."

Michael nodded. "The fact that they've survived for so long in secrecy is a testament to how rare and protected they are. But now the question is—what exactly are they capable of?"

Karl glanced over his shoulder, his expression guarded. "We'll need to figure that out quickly. If we've found these, so could whoever's been following us."

Lukas nodded in agreement, his voice low. "We need to move. Staying here too long makes us sitting targets."

Michael carefully packed the remaining galls, securing the box in his bag. "Let's head back to the car."

The team had just finished packing their samples and started heading back when the sound of crunching footsteps echoed through the clearing. Hana turned sharply, her heart racing, but Michael raised a calming hand. Emerging from the shadows of the forest were four men, each dressed in weathered hiking gear, their faces flushed as if from exertion. The leader, a tall man with a friendly smile and a trimmed beard, raised a hand in greeting.

"Afternoon," he called out in German, his voice carrying easily across the clearing. "Didn't expect to run into anyone out here. Beautiful spot, isn't it?"

Karl stepped forward, his posture relaxed but subtly guarded. "It is," he replied with a friendly nod. "Didn't think we'd see other hikers this far off the main trail."

The bearded man chuckled. "We like to go off the beaten path. Name's Daniel, by the way," he said, extending a hand. "These are my friends—Tom, Erik, and Jonas. We're amateur biologists, you could say. Studying the flora of the Black Forest. What about you? Finding anything interesting?"

Karl clasped Daniel's hand briefly, his expression neutral. "Karl. And these are Michael, Hana, and Lukas." He gestured toward Lukas, who remained a few steps behind. "We're just doing a bit of exploring ourselves. Nothing too exciting."

Hana forced a polite smile, slipping her hands into her pockets to keep herself from fidgeting. "The forest is full of surprises, isn't it?"

Daniel grinned. "It is. Especially these oaks. Did you know some of them are host to fascinating gall formations? Tiny homes for all kinds of insects. We've been cataloging some of the rarer types." He gestured vaguely at the surrounding trees. "Find anything unusual?"

Michael stepped in smoothly, his tone conversational. "We've noticed a few galls here and there. Fascinating structures, really. But we're not biologists, so we wouldn't know what is unusual."

Erik, a stocky man with a backpack that looked suspiciously high-tech, crouched to inspect a nearby branch of an oak tree. "Even the common ones are interesting. Nature has a way of surprising you."

Lukas finally spoke, his voice measured. "You're pretty far from the usual hiking trails for amateur biologists."

Jonas, the youngest-looking of the group, laughed easily. "That's part of the fun. The best discoveries aren't on the map. What brings you all this way?"

Karl's smile didn't waver. "Same thing, I suppose. Enjoying the peace and quiet. We came across this spot and decided to take a break."

Daniel's eyes flicked briefly to the bags the team carried before returning to Karl. "Well, you've picked a good place. The oaks here are some of the oldest in the forest. Great for finding unique specimens."

Hana felt a prickle of unease but kept her expression neutral. "It's definitely peaceful. Do you come out here often?"

"First time in this part of the forest," Daniel replied smoothly. "But we've been to a lot of similar spots. You find anything worth keeping, though, you've got to be careful. Some of these galls are fragile. Easy to crush them if you're not careful."

Karl's eyes narrowed slightly, though his smile remained. "Good advice. We'll keep that in mind."

Daniel glanced at his companions. "Well, we won't

keep you. Just thought we'd say hi. Always nice to meet fellow nature enthusiasts."

Michael nodded. "Likewise. Safe travels."

"You too," Daniel said, turning to leave with a casual wave. His group followed him back into the trees, their voices fading into the distance.

The team stood in silence for a moment, watching the hikers disappear. Lukas broke the quiet first. "Friendly bunch."

"Too friendly," Karl muttered, his voice low. "They were watching us more than the trees."

Hana shivered slightly, glancing at Michael. "You think they were just hikers?"

Michael shook his head. "No. But I'd venture a strong guess they're from Zentara."

"I agree," Karl said, his tone grim. "They were fishing for information, noticeably about galls. And they've probably figured out more than we'd like."

Hana bit her lip. "What do we do now?"

Karl scanned the tree line one last time. "We stay on guard and keep moving. Whatever they wanted, we're not giving them another chance to get it."

THE FOUR MEN regrouped a safe distance from where they had encountered Michael and the team, the dense forest muffling their voices as they spoke in low, hurried tones. Daniel leaned against a moss-covered tree trunk, his expression dark with frustration.

"They're definitely onto something," he muttered, adjusting the straps on his hiking pack. "Did you see how careful they were with those bags? Whatever they found, they didn't want us anywhere near it."

Erik crossed his arms, his thin face taut with irritation. "We should've pressed harder. Asked more questions, maybe even suggested helping them. They wouldn't have turned us away so easily."

"Not without risking suspicion," Jonas interjected, squatting to tie his bootlaces. "They were already wary. That one man—Karl?—he was watching every move we made. If we'd pushed, we'd have blown our cover."

Daniel exhaled, running a hand through his beard. "Fine, but we're still empty-handed. If those were the specific galls required for the formula, and they've already taken samples, we're behind."

Tom, the quietest of the group, finally spoke, his voice calm but edged with annoyance. "Behind, but not out. We know they were looking around those oaks, and our recording of Sinclair's conversation pointed us here. They can't have gotten everything. There's got to be more."

Daniel nodded. "Maybe. But we know our instructions." He reached into his pocket for a cigarette and lit it, pulling in a lungful of smoke before exhaling. He gave them a nod, and they headed toward the oak trees where they had watched the team work earlier.

CHAPTER

TWELVE

The Range Rover hummed softly as it wound through the dense, shadowy roads of the Black Forest. The air outside was crisp, and the towering pines blurred into a curtain of dark green. Inside, the team sat in a heavy silence, each lost in their own thoughts after the tense encounter at the forest's edge. Karl drove with quiet focus, Lukas in the passenger seat scanning the road for signs of trouble.

In the back, Michael sat with Hildegard's journal balanced on his lap, the faint glow of a reading light casting a soft halo over the delicate pages. Hana was next to him, her head leaning back against the seat, her eyes half-closed in weariness. Every so often, she glanced sideways at him, sensing his growing tension as he worked through the manuscript.

Michael's pen moved steadily across his notebook as he translated another passage, his brow furrowing with each line. The Latin phrase had stopped him first: *Vir*

Dei inter amorem et sacramentum—"A man of God between love and sacrament." He swallowed hard and traced his fingers lightly over the text, his heart racing as the imagery unfolded.

"I saw a tree, its roots tangled deep in the soil, pulling nourishment from the Earth. Its branches reached upward to touch the heavens, bearing flowers that shone like the sun. At the base of the tree stood a man, his garments torn, his face shadowed by doubt. To one side lay the sacred tools of the Church—the chalice, the cross. To the other stood a woman, her hand extended, her face filled with light. The man reached for both but could not grasp either fully. A voice, gentle and stern, called out to him: 'Your path is to nurture the fruit of this tree, but you cannot do so while torn asunder. Choose to bring forth its gift. Waver and the tree will wither.' Then the light faded, and I saw him kneel before the tree, his hands placed over its roots, and the flowers swelled into fruit."

Michael exhaled abruptly, the meaning of the vision hitting him like a blow. He shut his eyes briefly, pressing his fingertips against his temples.

"Michael?" Hana's voice was soft but concerned. She turned toward him, catching the faint sheen of sweat on his forehead. "What is it? You're pale."

He glanced at her, his expression conflicted, and gestured to the journal. "This passage... it's—" He stopped, his words failing him momentarily.

Hana sat up straighter, her hand gently brushing his arm. "Talk to me," she urged.

Michael opened his notebook, pointing to the translation he had scrawled. His voice was quiet, almost hesitant. "It's a vision. Hildegard wrote about a man standing at the base of a tree, torn between his faith and his love. One path leads to the Church, the other to a woman. The vision says he cannot 'nurture the fruit of this tree' unless he resolves the conflict in his heart. And if he doesn't… what he's meant to protect will wither."

Hana's eyes glistened as she processed his words. She glanced at the journal, then back at him. "You think it's… about you?"

Michael let out a breath that was almost a laugh, but there was no humor in it. "I don't know. Maybe it's my own guilt projecting onto the text, or maybe it's more than that. But it's too close, Hana. Too close to what I've been wrestling with since—" He hesitated, his eyes locking with hers.

"Since us," she finished softly, her voice steady despite the flicker of fear in her eyes.

He nodded, the impact of it clear in his expression. "I've been trying to keep both paths open, to hold onto my priesthood while being with you. But this… it's as if Hildegard is warning me that I can't do both. Not without consequences."

The car hit a small bump, jostling them slightly. Hana leaned closer, her hand slipping into his. "Michael, you've been carrying this alone for too long. Whatever choice you have to make, you don't have to face it on your own. We'll figure it out together."

He stared at her, the warmth of her hand grounding him. "I don't want to lose you, Hana," he said quietly, his voice trembling. "But I don't know how to reconcile this with everything I've committed my life to."

"You don't have to answer that now," she said gently. "But whatever you choose, I'm here. For as long as you'll have me."

Michael glanced down at their joined hands, her steady grip grounding him as his thoughts swirled. "Hana, I've always believed my faith was my anchor, the one thing I could rely on to guide me. But now, with you… it feels like I'm being pulled in two directions. Both paths feel right, and yet they contradict each other."

Hana tilted her head, studying him. "Does it have to be a contradiction? Can't your faith and… us coexist? I never intended to pull you away from what matters to you. Just… to be with you at the same time."

Michael shook his head, his expression pained. "That's the thing. It's not you pulling me, Hana. It's me. I've changed—because of you, because of us. And I don't know how to reconcile that with the vows I took."

Hana tightened her grip on his hand, her voice firm but gentle. "Michael, you're allowed to change. Faith isn't about staying the same; it's about growing, adapting, and finding meaning. Maybe what you're feeling isn't a conflict but a new way forward."

He looked at her, his eyes searching hers. "And what if that means leaving the priesthood? Turning away from everything I thought I was meant to be?"

"You haven't turned away from anything. You've

dedicated your life to helping people, to protecting what's sacred. That doesn't disappear if you choose a different path."

Michael let out a long breath, leaning back against the seat. "You make it sound so simple."

"It's not simple," Hana admitted. "It's messy, and it's painful. But Michael, whatever you decide, it has to be what feels true to you. Not what you believe others expect of you, not the Church… or me. Not even what you think you're supposed to do. What do you want?"

The question hung in the air between them, raw and unspoken. Michael closed his eyes for a moment, his thoughts a tangle of memories, faith, and love. Finally, he opened them, looking directly at Hana.

"I want you," he said softly. "But I'm afraid of what that means."

Hana's lips curved into a small, bittersweet smile. "Then let's figure it out."

Michael nodded, a flicker of relief crossing his face. For now, it was enough—their shared determination to navigate the uncertainty ahead. He squeezed her hand gently, the significance of Hildegard's vision still weighty but no longer unbearable.

THE SUV HUMMED STEADILY as it cruised north on the autobahn, the dark forest giving way to rolling hills. Inside, the atmosphere was quiet but uneasy, the team replaying their strange encounter with Daniel and his group in the Black Forest. Karl drove with practiced precision, his gaze flicking between the road ahead and the mirrors. Lukas sat in the passenger seat, his trained eyes scanning the surrounding traffic for anything out of place.

In the back, Michael was bent over Hildegard's journal, tracing the ornate script with his fingers as he worked on another translation. Hana sat beside him, her head leaning against the seat as she alternated between watching him and staring out the window.

Karl slowed the SUV, his gaze on the rearview mirror. Lukas noticed the action first and turned to look behind them.

Michael suddenly became alert and asked, "Is it those men? Are they following us?"

Karl answered, "No, it's worse than that."

All the car's occupants turned to see what had aroused Karl.

Far back on the horizon, a plume of smoke rose. It was directly behind them, in the forest where the last remaining live *Ricinus aureum* lived under the protective arms of the now burning oak trees.

"Is that… ?" Hana asked, her voice tight.

No one answered. They all knew it was Zentara.

Michael glanced at the journal in his lap, his grip tightening. Whatever secrets Hildegard's legacy held, they were clearly worth chasing—and fighting for.

THIRTEEN

The faint glow of Frankfurt Airport's lights bathed the private hangar in an eerie stillness as Michael followed Hana toward the waiting plane. The sleek aircraft hummed softly, its engines prepared for takeoff, and Karl and Lukas moved ahead, scanning the area with practiced eyes. The air was brisk, and Michael adjusted the strap of his satchel, feeling the weight of Hildegard's journal against his side.

The pilot stood at the base of the stairs, motioning for them to hurry. "We need to leave within the next ten minutes," he said, glancing at his watch. "Air traffic control has us on a tight window."

"We won't take long," Karl replied tersely, his gaze sweeping the perimeter of the tarmac. "We've just had too many surprises lately."

As Michael approached the stairs, a voice cut through the night behind him, calm yet commanding. "Father Dominic?"

Michael froze, his heart quickening as he turned. A tall man stood a few meters away, emerging from the shadows near the hangar. He was dressed in a dark trench coat, his hands visible and open at his sides in a gesture of non-aggression. His distinct features were partially illuminated by the airport lights, revealing an intense gaze framed by salt-and-pepper hair.

Karl immediately stepped forward, his hand moving to his sidearm. "Stay where you are," he barked.

The man raised his hands slightly, his expression unperturbed. "I'm not here to harm you. But I must speak with Father Dominic before he leaves. It's urgent."

Michael glanced at Karl, then at Hana, who had stopped halfway up the stairs, her brow furrowed in suspicion. "Who are you?" he asked, his voice steady but cautious.

The man took a step closer, his movements deliberate but non-threatening. "My name is Brother Gabriel. I represent the Order of the Green Flame, a group dedicated to safeguarding the legacy of Hildegard von Bingen. We work in partnership with Sister Amalia and her Benedictine order at Rupertsberg Abbey."

Michael's grip on the satchel tightened. "And why are you here now?"

"To ensure you understand the essence of what you carry," Gabriel replied, his gaze flicking briefly to the satchel. "The journal in your possession is not merely an artifact. It is a key—a map, if you will, to Hildegard's most profound secrets. But such knowledge comes with great responsibility and some danger."

Hana descended the stairs, her eyes narrowing. "Danger as in your 'green flame' order burning a forest? Stopping progress? Destroying—"

"No!" The man raised a hand. "Our mission is to protect. Not destroy, not burn. Our green flame represents the light of healing through nature. And… we failed." He shook his head as if the burden of failure fell on his shoulders alone. "We know what happens in this greedy secular world, and we know the fire was set purposely."

"Were all…?" Hana hesitated to ask.

Gabriel's eyes glistened with unshed tears. "All the living golden castors were destroyed. An accelerant was used to ensure that. The forest, damp as it was, didn't burn much further. But the real damage is something the authorities who put it out will never know. Centuries of secret protection over that singular patch was for naught."

"You seem to know a lot about what is going on, and about us, Brother Gabriel. How is that?"

Gabriel's lips curved faintly, but the smile was without warmth. "For many generations, Hildegard's legacy has been watched over by those who understand its significance. We have been observing your progress since you left the monastery. We didn't intervene sooner because we wanted to see if your intentions aligned with hers."

"And?" Michael asked.

Gabriel took another step forward, his voice

dropping slightly. "We know you mean well, Father Dominic. But you lack the context, the training, to fully grasp what you've uncovered. That journal holds more than recipes and records—it is a guide to something far greater. Something that can heal, but also injure."

Karl's wary voice cut in. "You're saying you've been following us? Watching us without making yourselves known? That doesn't inspire much trust. Why should we believe you aren't the very ones who set that fire?"

Gabriel met Karl's glare with calm resolve. "Our priority is not trust, but protection. If the wrong people gain access to what Hildegard left behind, the consequences could be injurious to the masses."

Hana took a step in his direction, her curiosity harboring unease. "If you're here to protect Hildegard's legacy, why not take the journal yourselves? Why approach me now?"

Gabriel's expression softened, though his intensity remained. "Because my brotherhood's task is one of protection, not implementation. It has been clear for centuries that only those chosen by Hildegard could properly make use of her sacred legacy. And we have stood guard throughout that time, as was ordained in Hildegard's visions. If we'd had any idea about the possibility of that fire, we would have acted. Stopped it. But we are acting now and know that you and your associates have been chosen for reasons beyond our understanding. And we know what you carry. We honor that. But know this: others are aware of the journal now. Powerful, dangerous others. One of them is now known as Zentara. And they will not hesitate to use Hildegard's work for their own ends."

Michael cocked his head. "One of them? Now? What do you mean?"

"The Order of the Green Flame has existed for nine centuries. And during that time, we've needed to act against numerous adversaries. One of them has persisted through most of that time, changing names, tactics, and goals as time went on. But always with greed behind its filthy acts. Today, that same entity is known as Zentara."

Hana crossed her arms, her skepticism clear. "So you're the 'others' that Sister Amalia said look out for Hildegard's work. But you're here to... what? Offer us protection? Guidance? Or are you just here to scare us into handing the journal and the galls over to you?"

Gabriel's gaze locked onto hers. "Protection, Ms. Sinclair. My order has resources, networks, and knowledge that you lack. We can assist you in reaching your destination safely while minimizing the risks to all involved. But if you refuse our help, you must know that you are walking into a storm far larger than you realize."

The faint hum of an approaching vehicle in the distance caught Karl's attention, and his posture stiffened. "We're out of time," he said, his hand gripping his weapon. "Michael, we need to move."

Gabriel nodded slowly and handed Michael a card with his phone number on it before stepping back into the shadows. "I've said what I needed to say. You must decide whether to trust us or not. But know this, Father

Dominic: the choices you make in the coming days will determine whether Hildegard's legacy heals the world —or works to harm it. Contact me if you ever need help making that choice."

Before anyone could respond, Gabriel turned and disappeared into the night, his dark coat blending into the shadows.

Michael exchanged a tense glance with Hana as Karl and Lukas hurried them onto the plane. The door closed behind them, and the engines roared to full power as the aircraft began to taxi. But even as they ascended into the night sky, Gabriel's warning echoed in Michael's mind, leaving a chill that no altitude could dispel.

FOURTEEN

The jet landed smoothly at Ciampino Airport in Rome, where Karl and Lukas would disembark to return to their duties in the Vatican. Michael and Hana stood near the open door of the aircraft as the two men prepared to leave.

"Be careful, both of you," Karl said, gripping Michael's arm in a firm handshake.

Michael nodded. "We'll be fine. But we'll keep you updated if we need anything. This isn't over yet."

Lukas, always less formal, gave Hana a brief, reassuring smile. "Don't let him overthink everything before you call for our help," he said, jerking a thumb toward Michael.

"I'll do my best," Hana replied with a knowing smile.

The two Swiss Guards stepped off the jet, their movements precise and practiced even in casual moments. As the door closed and the engines whirred back to life, the jet taxied down the runway. Moments later, it lifted into the air, the Eternal City shrinking below them. Hana gazed out the window at the domes of Rome, her thoughts shifting to the tasks ahead.

THE JET DESCENDED through a blanket of low-hanging clouds, Geneva's familiar outline emerging in the fading winter light. Snow dusted the rooftops and trees, giving the city an air of quiet elegance. Inside the cabin, the hum of the engines was a steady backdrop to the weighty silence between Michael and Hana.

Hana stared out the window, her face illuminated by the soft glow of the evening sun. She had spent many minutes earlier in their flight making calls to arrange for their pick-up as well as following up on numerous calls regarding her grandfather's affairs. Now, her expression was calm, almost detached, but Michael recognized it as the calm of someone holding a storm at bay. She clutched her carry-on bag tightly, as if the contents were the only anchor keeping her tethered to the present.

The pilot's voice crackled over the intercom, announcing their approach. Michael glanced at Hana, trying to gauge her mood. "Almost there," he said softly.

She turned toward him, her eyes betraying a flicker of gratitude for his presence. "It feels like another lifetime since we last here," she replied, her voice quiet.

"Geneva will always be your home, no matter how far we travel," Michael said, though he knew her thoughts were elsewhere—on her late grandfather, and the impending funeral. The responsibilities ahead weighed heavily on her, but she carried them with the same resilience he had always admired in her.

The jet landed with a gentle thud, the tires skimming the runway before settling into a smooth roll. Outside, the city awaited them, bustling yet serene, its orderly streets contrasting sharply with the whirlwind of events they had recently endured. As the aircraft taxied to the private terminal, Michael leaned closer to Hana. "Are you sure you don't want me to handle some of the arrangements? You've already been through so much."

Hana shook her head, her gaze steady. "No, I need to do this. Armand deserves that much. And besides," she added, her tone softening, "you have your own work to focus on. Hildegard's recipe isn't going to decode itself. There is still the possibility that, with these fresh galls and understanding her methods, great good can come from what we can learn, even if all the living plants were destroyed."

Michael offered her a small smile. "True. I hope so. But I'm always here if you need me."

The plane came to a stop, and moments later, the door opened to reveal a set of stairs leading down to the tarmac. The icy air rushed in, crisp and invigorating. Hana adjusted her coat as they stepped out, their breath visible in the chill. The lights of Geneva shimmered in the distance, a beacon of calm amid their storm.

A sleek black sedan awaited them on the tarmac, its driver stepping out to greet them with a polite nod.

"Monsieur Dominic, Mademoiselle Sinclair," he said in a thick Swiss accent, opening the door for them.

"*Merci*," Hana said, sliding into the back seat. Michael followed, the door clicking shut behind him. The driver returned to his seat, and the car pulled smoothly onto the highway, the low hum of the tires filling the cabin.

Hana stared out the window as the city unfolded around them. The elegant architecture, the pristine streets, the familiar landmarks—it all felt distant, as though she were observing it through a pane of frosted glass. Her thoughts drifted to Armand. His passing had left a void she couldn't yet articulate, a sense of loss that went beyond words.

Michael watched her out of the corner of his eye, sensing her turmoil. "You don't have to say anything," he said gently, breaking the silence. "But I'm here if you want to talk."

Hana hesitated, her fingers tracing the edge of her bag. Finally, she spoke. "It's strange," she began. "I've spent so much time preparing for Armand's funeral, but it still doesn't feel real that he's really gone. He was always the constant in my life, the one person who... truly understood me."

Michael nodded, giving her the space to continue.

"He would've loved knowing what we're doing," she said. "The mystery, the history, the challenge of it all. He always encouraged me to pursue the truth, no matter how difficult it was."

"And you've honored that," Michael said. "Your

work, your dedication—it's a testament to everything he believed in."

Hana looked at him, her eyes shimmering with unshed tears. "I just hope I'm doing enough," she whispered.

"You are," Michael said firmly. "Armand would be proud of you."

The car slowed as it approached the Saint-Clair estate. The driver pulled to a stop and stepped out to open the door for them. Hana exited first, the cold air biting at her cheeks, but she barely noticed.

Michael followed, taking in the familiar surroundings. The house was elegant and understated, its façade illuminated by warm light spilling from the windows. It had always been a sanctuary for Hana, a place where she could retreat from the chaos of her work. He hoped it would offer her some comfort now.

"I'll make some tea," Hana said, shrugging off her coat and heading toward the kitchen. Michael set his bag down and followed her, watching as she moved through the familiar motions. He knew her well enough to recognize that keeping busy was her way of coping.

As the kettle boiled, Hana leaned against the counter, her hands wrapped around the edge. "We have so much to do," she said, her voice tinted with exhaustion. "The funeral, the galls, Élise's analysis, Hildegard's recipe… it feels like it's all happening at once."

"We'll take it one step at a time," Michael said. "I spoke to Élise while you were making your other calls. She's doing fine and is excited about what we found. She's already preparing to analyze the galls tomorrow for us, and I'm making progress on the recipe. And the funeral… I'll be there for that too. Remember, you have people to help you with every task."

Hana nodded, her gratitude unspoken but evident in her eyes. "Thank you," she said softly.

The kettle whistled, breaking the moment. Hana poured the steaming water into two mugs, handing one to Michael before leading him into the living room. They sat in companionable silence, the force of the day slowly giving way to the quiet comfort of the moment.

"I keep thinking about what comes next. You're right —I can use others to help me," Hana said eventually. "If Élise can extract the compounds from the galls, and if we can decode Hildegard's recipe… we'll need someone who can take it further. Someone who understands medical science and the potential applications."

Michael sipped his tea thoughtfully. "I agree. Élise might have a contact in oncology. Someone who can bridge the gap between the ancient and the modern."

Hana nodded, her mind already turning over possibilities. "I'll ask her tomorrow. And I'll ask Frederic to help continue with the funeral arrangements. After that…" She exhaled, her resolve hardening. "We keep moving forward."

Hana met Michael's gaze, drawing strength from his steady presence. For the first time since Armand's passing, she felt a glimmer of hope—a reminder that even in the face of loss and uncertainty, they had people on their side and a purpose. And they wouldn't stop until they saw it through.

There was one thing he didn't share with Hana,

something she didn't need to worry about. How did Zentara's people know to be at the Black Forest? Those supposed hikers knew they had collected something from that patch of the forest. Did they know it was galls taken from the golden castor plants? If they had already known that the plants or galls existed and where they were, they would have taken them and/or burned them long ago. So... they knew Michael's team's plans. But how?

CHAPTER

FIFTEEN

The sterile hum of machinery filled the room as Hana and Michael stepped into Élise Gauthier's state-of-the-art laboratory. The space was a meticulous symphony of glass and steel, with shelves lined with neatly labeled reagents, microscopes gleaming under bright white light, and monitors displaying streams of data. The faint scent of ethanol and the sterile chill of climate control added to the clinical precision of the environment.

Élise herself was already at a workstation, her short, dark hair tucked behind her ears and a lab coat draped over her slim frame. She turned at the sound of their arrival, her ready, inquisitive eyes lighting up as they entered.

"Ah, you're here," she said in her crisp French accent. Her tone was brisk but not unfriendly, the voice of someone perpetually busy but always engaged. "You have the galls?"

Hana nodded, stepping forward and unzipping her carry-on bag. Inside, cushioned in protective foam, were several small vials containing the golden-brown galls of *Ricinus aureum*. She handed them over with care, as if she were passing off a priceless artifact.

Élise took one vial and held it up to the light, her gaze narrowing as she examined its contents. "Exquisite," she murmured, almost to herself. "The structure of these is extraordinary. The vascularization alone suggests complex biological activity. If the historical accounts are accurate, these may indeed contain unique bioactive compounds." She looked up at Hana and saw her friend's sad look.

"Hana, dear, what's wrong?"

"The fire. We were told it destroyed all the plants. So these"—she motioned to the galls—"are the last we will ever have of them."

Élise reached out and touched Hana's arm. "There is much we can learn, even from just one gall. Not all things in nature can indeed be replicated in a lab, but much can be as well. Trust me. We'll figure this out." She gave her friend's arm a little squeeze.

Michael stepped closer, his curiosity piqued. "How soon can you analyze them?"

Élise gave a small smile, her confidence apparent. "First, I need to prepare them. Let me walk you through the process."

She motioned for them to follow her deeper into the lab, past workbenches laden with precision tools and equipment. At one station, she placed the vial under a high-powered microscope. The image of the gall's intricate surface structure appeared on a large monitor, revealing a labyrinth of vascular channels and tiny spines.

"This is where we start," Élise said, pointing to the screen. "The outer layer must be carefully preserved to prevent the degradation of any active compounds within. To do that, we'll use a vacuum freeze-dryer. It removes all moisture without damaging the molecular integrity."

She opened one of the vials and placed the galls from it into a small freeze-drying chamber, its sleek design resembling a compact glass oven. As she activated the machine, a low hum filled the air, and the temperature on the display began to plummet. "This will take about an hour," she explained, "but it's essential to ensure we preserve the bioactive components. In the meantime, let's safeguard these others in here." She opened a climate-controlled cabinet used to preserve fresh specimens.

Hana watched her friend's actions intently, the scientific precision of the process providing a sense of reassurance. "What happens after the drying?"

"Once they're fully desiccated," Élise continued, "we'll mill them into a fine powder. But not just any milling. We'll use a cryogenic grinder. The galls will be cooled with liquid nitrogen to keep them stable as they're pulverized. This prevents heat from damaging sensitive compounds."

Michael raised an eyebrow. "And the powder? What will you do with it?"

Élise's smile widened slightly, her passion for her

work shining through. "The powder is where the magic —or, rather, the science—begins. I'll use liquid chromatography-mass spectrometry to isolate and identify the chemical compounds. This will allow us to determine if the historical claims about *Ricinus aureum* have any basis in pharmacological reality."

She glanced at Hana. "You mentioned earlier there's a recipe involved?"

"Yes," Hana replied. "Hildegard documented a preparation method in her *Lingua Ignota* in the manuscript you inherited from Armand. Michael's working on decoding it, but it's… complicated."

"Ah, Hildegard," Élise said, nodding appreciatively. "She was centuries ahead of her time. If her recipe aligns with making use of the compounds we find here, it could be a huge breakthrough."

A little over an hour later, the freeze-drying process was complete. Élise carefully removed the now crisp, lightweight galls from the chamber and placed them into a sealed container. From there, she moved to another station, where the cryogenic grinder awaited. The device resembled a cross between a laboratory centrifuge and an industrial blender, with a metallic bowl encased in insulation.

Using tongs, Élise placed the galls into the grinder's chamber. She pressed a button, and a jet of liquid nitrogen hissed into the container, enveloping the galls in a plume of frosty vapor. The room filled with the faint smell of cold metal as the machine roared to life.

"It's a precise process," Élise said over the noise. "We grind in short bursts to prevent any overheating. Even a few degrees of temperature rise can destroy sensitive compounds."

Moments later, the grinder stopped, and Élise opened the chamber. Inside, a fine golden dust sparkled under the lab's bright lights. She transferred the powder into sterile glass vials, each one labeled meticulously.

"This," she said, holding up one vial, "is what we'll analyze next."

She moved to another station, where a sleek machine with a tangle of tubes and sensors awaited. "This is the liquid chromatography-mass spectrometer," she explained, her tone almost reverent. "It will separate the compounds in the powder and identify them based on their molecular weight and structure."

As Élise began the analysis, Michael and Hana observed in silence, the hum of the machine filling the room. Data streamed across the monitor, a cascade of peaks and valleys representing the chemical compounds extracted from the powder.

An hour passed as Élise worked, her focus unbroken. Finally, she turned to Michael and Hana, holding a printout of the results. Her expression was a mixture of excitement and caution.

"These results are… intriguing," she said. "We've identified several compounds with known anti-inflammatory and anti-tumor properties. But there's one in particular—a previously unclassified alkaloid—that stands out. Its structure suggests it could have powerful medicinal applications, but we'll need further study to confirm."

Hana leaned forward, her heart racing. "Do you think it could work? Against cancer, I mean?"

Élise hesitated. "It's too soon to say for certain. What we've found is promising, but this is just the beginning. If we want to take this further, we'll need a specialist—an oncologist with experience in experimental therapies. Someone who can help us understand the potential applications and guide us through the next steps."

Michael nodded, his mind already racing with possibilities. "Do you have someone in mind?"

Élise considered this for a moment. "Yes. Dr. Margot Eberhardt. She's based in Lausanne and has worked extensively with natural compounds in oncology. If anyone can help us bridge the gap between ancient knowledge and modern medicine, it's her."

Hana exchanged a glance with Michael, her determination renewed. "Then let's contact her. This is too important to wait."

Élise nodded, her confidence unwavering. "Agreed. And in the meantime, I'll continue refining the analysis. If Hildegard's recipe in that manuscript Armand had holds the key to unlocking this compound's potential, we might be on the verge of something extraordinary."

SIXTEEN

The ethereal strains of Hildegard von Bingen's *"O viridissima virga"* filled the room, its haunting melody weaving a sacred atmosphere around the work in progress. Hana's home was transformed by the music, the modern furnishings fading into the background as the past seemed to press closer. The hymn's soaring notes, both calming and inspiring, felt like a bridge to the very mind they were trying to unravel.

Michael sat at the large oak table in the study, his collection of books and manuscripts spread out like an intricate puzzle waiting to be solved. A dim reading lamp cast a golden pool of light on the parchment in front of him—a carefully preserved copy of Hildegard's *Lingua Ignota*. The cryptic recipe written in her invented language was an enigma, each line tantalizing in its complexity.

The music swelled, the singer's voice—composed eight centuries earlier and recorded only a few decades ago by a Benedictine order—seeming to echo Michael's thoughts. He adjusted his reading glasses and leaned closer, muttering translations under his breath as he traced a line of the parchment with his finger. His notebook lay open beside him, already filled with dense, cramped handwriting.

Hana entered the room quietly, carrying two mugs of steaming coffee. She placed one next to Michael, who nodded in gratitude, his focus unwavering. Sliding into a chair across from him, she took a sip of her drink and listened to the music for a moment, letting its calm sweep over her.

"Any progress?" she asked, breaking the silence.

"Some," Michael replied, not looking up. He gestured at the parchment with his pen. "But it's slow going. Hildegard wasn't just writing a recipe—she was encoding an entire worldview. Every word is deliberate, layered with meaning. Take this line, for example." He tapped a section of the parchment. "'*Mixtum aureum fructum cum aqua vitae et calefaciens usque ad unum...*' 'Mix the golden fruit with the water of life and heat it up to one.'"

"'Golden fruit,'" Hana repeated, glancing at the script. "That must be the *Ricinus aureum*'s gall."

"Exactly," Michael confirmed. "But '*aqua vitae*'—the 'water of life'—is more ambiguous. It could be literal, referring to spring water or holy water, or symbolic, representing some kind of transformative element. And then there's 'heat gently until it becomes one.' It's clear she's describing a process, but it's maddeningly vague. How much heat? How long? And becomes 'one' what?"

Hana leaned forward, intrigued. "Do you think it's intentionally vague? Like she expected her readers, if they were the right people, to understand it instinctively? While the wrong people wouldn't understand?"

Michael exhaled, sitting back in his chair. "That's what makes this so frustrating. She was writing for a specific audience—people who shared her knowledge, her context. They would have understood her references intuitively. But for us, eight centuries later, those connections have been lost."

The music shifted to a slower, more meditative section, the melody wrapping around the room like a gentle embrace. Hana's gaze drifted to the books piled around Michael: medieval Latin dictionaries, studies on Hildegard's theology, and annotated volumes of her hymns.

"What about the music?" she asked suddenly. "You said she used music as a kind of code?"

Michael's eyes lit up. "Yes, that's another layer to this puzzle. Hildegard thought in harmonies, in patterns. The numbers she used in her language weren't just numbers—they were part of a symbolic system tied to her music and theology. For example..." He flipped to a page in his notebook, where he had jotted down chant notations. "These tonal sequences in her Gregorian chants match numerical patterns in the recipe. I think they might correspond to proportions, but I haven't cracked the code yet."

"So, the measurements in her recipe are hidden in her music?" Hana asked, her curiosity deepening.

"Possibly," Michael said, leaning forward. "Hildegard, while not a scientist by modern definition, was a pioneering scientific mind in her own right. She saw the world as an interconnected tapestry of sound, nature, and spirituality. Her recipes weren't just functional—they were philosophical. The process mattered as much as the result."

Hana sipped her coffee, her mind spinning. "It's amazing to think she could create something so advanced with the knowledge of her time. If we figure this out, Michael, it could be revolutionary."

Michael nodded. "It is extraordinary. If we can decode her instructions and align them with Élise's analysis of the *Ricinus aureum*, we might unlock something that bridges the ancient and the modern. But it's going to take time—and precision."

Hana turned back to him, her eyes filled with determination. "Then let's get to it."

The hymn reached its final, soaring notes, filling the room with a sense of reverence and quiet hope. As the music faded into silence, Michael returned to his translation, his pen scratching across the page. Beside him, Hana picked up one of the reference books, ready to help. Together, they worked under the glow of the lamp, Hildegard's legacy guiding them forward.

After a few minutes, Hana leaned back in her chair

and rubbed her eyes. The faint strains of fatigue were evident in her voice as she said, "Michael, I think we've earned a break. Let's go out for dinner. I've been meaning to take you to a little bistro in town—quiet, cozy, and not far from here."

Michael paused mid-translation, glancing at her over his reading glasses. "Dinner? Now? You're willing to leave Hildegard's secrets for a plate of coq au vin?"

She smiled knowingly, shutting the book in her hands with a soft thud. "Even Hildegard would agree we need to eat. And besides, a change of scenery might help us think more clearly. Who knows? Over a good meal, we might stumble upon a revelation."

Michael couldn't help but smile. "You're impossible to argue with when you've made up your mind, aren't you?"

"Always," she replied with a grin, already rising to fetch her coat. "Come on, it'll do us good. We'll pick up where we left off when we're back."

Reluctantly, Michael set his pen down, picked up the journal, and stood, stretching his arms. "All right, but if the food isn't as good as you're promising, I'm holding you personally responsible."

"You won't be disappointed," she assured him, her tone light and teasing as she led the way toward the door. "They layer slices of sweet onion and aromatic herbs between succulent chicken breast, then pour not just some white wine, but the best of Calvados apple brandy from Normandy over it all, cook it until…" and soon Michael was as anxious for dinner as Hana.

As they walked along the darkened path to her car,

neither noticed the shadowed figures slipping through the grounds, silent as the wind through the trees. The operatives had waited for this moment, for the estate to fall silent, its occupants far from reach. As Hana and Michael drove toward town, laughter filling the car, the intruders made their move.

SEVENTEEN

The team of four approached the house like wraiths, their black attire blending into the darkness. They had studied the layout meticulously, noting the estate's modern security measures and potential blind spots. Christophe Vaux had sent them with clear instructions: recover anything related to Hildegard's journal or the *Ricinus aureum*—the mysterious golden castor plant. All four of them knew what their fate would be this time after the Black Forest incident. True, they had gathered some of the precious galls that Zentara wanted, but then Daniel set them to destroy the plants. So much for understanding their instructions of "Don't leave any trace of what you've done." If the team failed again, there would be no room for excuses.

Daniel stroked his beard a moment, then signaled the team forward. Using advanced equipment, they deactivated the estate's perimeter alarms and scaled the stone wall surrounding the property. The main house loomed before them, its expansive windows darkened, save for a faint light spilling from the far wing where the estate's live-in caretaker resided.

They bypassed the front door, opting instead for a rear window that had been left ajar in the kitchen, no doubt for ventilation. One by one, they slipped inside, their footsteps noiseless against the marble floors.

The team split up, moving methodically through the house. The leader and one operative made their way to Hana's office. It was a spacious, elegantly appointed room, with mahogany shelves lined with rare books. The operatives worked quickly, rifling through drawers and scanning the shelves for anything resembling Hildegard's journal.

They found nothing, the space devoid of the item they sought. The leader's lips thinned into a line of frustration. He motioned for his partner to keep searching while he moved toward a tall cabinet at the back of the room.

Inside, he found a collection of folders and notebooks, many filled with Hana's detailed notes on her investigative work. One caught his attention—a slim notebook tucked between files. As he flipped through it, he recognized references to the *Ricinus aureum* and sketches of the strange galls they had secured in the Black Forest. Though the journal itself wasn't here, this notebook offered something tantalizing: coordinates scrawled on a page, accompanied by notes about an upcoming expedition to a remote site in Italy where Hana suspected similar botanical phenomena might exist. He tucked it into his jacket.

Meanwhile, another operative slipped into Hana's bedroom, his flashlight beam cutting through the darkness. The room was immaculate, with soft gray walls and understated yet luxurious furnishings. On a small table by the window lay a stack of letters and a slim laptop.

The operative ignored the letters, opting to scan the laptop. Unable to access its contents without potentially triggering security protocols, he tucked it quickly under his arm for later decryption. A soft sound from the hallway made him freeze, but after a tense moment, silence resumed, and he slipped out undetected.

In the kitchen, the fourth operative was securing their exit route when he spotted something intriguing: an ornate box on the counter. The lid was slightly ajar, revealing several small vials of liquid inside. Each was labeled in Hana's meticulous handwriting. Though the words were unfamiliar, one bore the word *Ricinus aureum*. He carefully pocketed the vial, certain that Christophe would be pleased with his find.

The team regrouped in the estate's library for a final search. One of the operatives ran a hand under the desk's edge, looking for a possible secret latch but, instead, inadvertently triggering a hidden sensor. A soft beep echoed through the room, and within seconds, the estate's alarm system roared to life. Lights flooded the once-shadowy corridors, and the distant sound of yelping dogs and shouts of guards erupted from the security wing.

The leader barked a sharp order, and the team swiftly moved toward their exit route. They scrambled back through the kitchen window into the night, slipping into the dense woods before security personnel could fully mobilize.

When Hana and Michael returned from dinner, they were alerted by the estate's security team and quickly reviewed the damage. The intruders, of course, were long gone. Hana's office displayed clear signs of a search: drawers were left open, and files were scattered across the floor. Worse, she discovered that her laptop had been stolen from her bedroom. Michael's instincts kicked in as they regrouped in her office and he assessed the scene with a penetrating gaze.

"It had to be Zentara's people. Obviously, they were looking for Hildegard's journal," he said gravely, picking up one of Hana's notebooks that had been tossed onto the floor. "And anything connected to the galls."

Hana frowned, crossing her arms. "They didn't find it. Nothing in my laptop will likely help them. The journal is with you, and Élise has the rest of the fresh galls. But…" She trailed off, her expression darkening as she looked inside the ornate box on the kitchen counter.

"What is it?" Michael asked.

"They took my vial of *Ricinus aureum* powder left from Hildegard, along with my field notes," Hana replied, moving to her desk. "Among which I'd written down coordinates for a potential site in Italy—a lead on where we might find more traces of the plants."

Michael exhaled. "Then Zentara has a new target."

Hana clenched her fists, her eyes narrowing. "And so do we."

EIGHTEEN

Hana was on her phone setting up the jet for a trip to Italy when the distinct chime of Michael's phone caught their attention. He glanced at the screen, the name Brother Gabriel glowing on the display. A twinge of curiosity mixed with caution flickered across his face.

"Brother Gabriel," Michael greeted as he answered, his tone measured.

"Father Dominic," came the familiar voice, soft but laced with urgency. "I've come across something... something you need to see. It concerns Hildegard's manuscript and the Order of the Green Flame's mission."

Michael sat upright, his curiosity piqued. "What do you mean?" He motioned to Hana, who interrupted her call, saying she would call back.

"There is much you don't yet understand about Hildegard's teachings," Gabriel said. "The manuscript you hold is just a fragment of a greater truth. Our Order has guarded her legacy for centuries, and it is time you saw what lies beneath Rupertsberg Abbey."

Hana leaned closer, her instincts catching the shift in Michael's demeanor. He nodded at her to stay silent for the moment.

"Why now?" Michael asked.

"Because Zentara is closer than ever to uncovering what we've safeguarded. There was an infiltration attempt on our archive two months ago. They failed, but not without leaving traces of their presence. It is only now that we've been able to ascertain the files that were compromised. We believe they're after the same knowledge you seek."

"So," Michael hesitated, "you're looking to protect us in some way?"

The sigh on the other end of the phone line was audible, as if the speaker had to reveal something distinctly uncomfortable. "Actually, I am requesting your help."

The line fell silent for a beat before Gabriel added, "Can you come to Rupertsberg? Tomorrow?"

Michael glanced at Hana, who raised an eyebrow in curiosity. "We'll be there," he said.

RUPERTSBERG ABBEY LOOMED ABOVE THEM, its weathered stones bathed in the silvery glow of moonlight. The greenhouse off to the side was dark now, and only a few lights shone in the small windows of the abbey. The previous sight of this medieval structure had glowed in the sun but now felt as darkly ominous as the mystery they were intent on solving. The Rhine whispered in the distance, its current steady and unfaltering. Michael and Hana stepped out of the car, the frosty air nipping at their faces as they approached the heavy oak doors. Brother Gabriel was waiting for them, cloaked in a simple black robe, a lantern in hand.

"Welcome," he said, his eyes betraying a mix of relief and tension.

Inside, Gabriel led them through winding corridors lit by flickering sconces, the air thick with the scent of beeswax and age.

Michael asked, "Where does this Order of the Green Flame reside anyway?"

Gabriel turned briefly to answer as they walked. "We live some distance from here, at the Disibodenberg Monastery, where Saint Hildegard grew up. But we have a small residence building nearby here at the Rupertsberg Abbey where a few of our members rotate keeping watch over the grounds."

They descended a spiral staircase, its stone steps polished smooth by centuries of use, until they reached a heavy iron door. Gabriel produced a key from his robe and unlocked it with deliberate care.

"Beyond this door is the heart of the Order's archive," he said. "Few outside the Order have ever set foot here."

"Yet you say there was a break-in here two months ago?" Hana pressed.

"Yes," he admitted but didn't elaborate on how they

had apparently failed to "watch over" their interests here at the time.

The door creaked open, revealing a cavernous chamber lined with shelves filled with leather-bound tomes, scrolls, and glass cases containing delicate artifacts. At the center stood a long oak table, its surface cluttered with parchment, quills, and an array of symbols etched into the wood.

"This is incredible," Hana murmured, her journalist's instinct pulling her toward the nearest shelf.

Gabriel gestured for them to sit at the table. "The Order of the Green Flame has preserved not only Hildegard's writings but also the esoteric knowledge she passed down to her closest confidants. Much of it remains untranslated or deliberately encoded to protect its secrets. It was never our mission to interpret her writings."

Michael placed the manuscript he had brought on the table. "How does this fit into her greater teachings?"

Gabriel sat across from him, his expression grave. "Hildegard believed that divine wisdom was intertwined with the natural and the metaphysical. She left behind teachings that point to a convergence— between science, faith, and humanity's relationship with creation itself. The manuscript you hold is a key to unlocking these principles."

Hana's eyes narrowed. "And Zentara? What do they want with this?"

Gabriel hesitated, his fingers brushing the edge of the table. "Zentara operates under the guise of biogenics, but their true aim lies in manipulating the building blocks of life for their own gain. Hildegard's teachings speak of a divine balance that must not be disrupted. If Zentara uncovers her full work, they could pervert it into a tool for control or destruction. I don't know how that would be done, but Hildegard's warnings and Zentara's reputation clearly indicate this could be the case."

Michael frowned, his mind sorting through the chaos. "And the infiltration? What did they find?"

"They didn't access the heart of the archive," Gabriel said. "But their methods are sophisticated. They're persistent, and it's only a matter of time before they make another attempt. We've changed our locks but realize that might be useless. That's why we need your help to decipher what we can before they break in again. I gather from Sister Amalia that you've been able to interpret Hildegard's secret language?"

Michael admitted he had grasped at least some of it.

Gabriel retrieved a scroll from a nearby shelf and unrolled it carefully. The parchment was covered in intricate diagrams and notes in Hildegard's hand. "This is part of a codex that complements the manuscript you possess. Together, they might reveal what Zentara is truly after—and how to stop them."

Michael studied the scroll, his fingers tracing the elegant curves of Hildegard's script. "This will take time," he said.

"I'll assist you," Gabriel offered.

Michael leaned back in his chair, his mind grappling with the implications. "Whatever we learn, if Zentara gets their hands on this, they could use it for any end.

This potential knowledge should benefit humanity, not a single unscrupulous company. We can't let that happen."

"Agreed," Gabriel said. "But time is not on our side. We'll begin decoding tonight. Hana, your investigative skills may be just as vital as Michael's theological expertise."

Hana smiled subtly. "Glad to know I'm not just here for moral support."

THE HOURS STRETCHED into the early morning as the trio worked tirelessly. Occasionally, one of the sisters would enter with a tray of hot tea and flattened dry oatcakes to keep them going, then bow out just as quickly and quietly. Brother Mathias would fetch extra candles or batteries or whatever was needed when Gabriel called on him. Gabriel translated passages aloud while Michael cross-referenced them with the manuscript. Hana documented their findings, her shorthand notes filling page after page of her leather-bound journal.

"Here," Gabriel said, pointing to a passage. "Hildegard writes of a 'veil of creation,' a hidden layer of reality accessible only to those who seek it with both intellect and faith. She believed this veil held the secrets to harmony within the cosmos."

"And Zentara?" Michael asked.

"They would tear through the veil to exploit its mysteries, heedless of the consequences," Gabriel replied.

As they delved deeper, a pattern began to emerge—

symbols and phrases repeated across the texts, hinting at a hidden code. Hana caught the connections, and with her input, they began to piece together a partial translation.

As dawn broke over Rupertsberg, the trio emerged from the archive, their minds buzzing with possibilities and dangers. The knowledge they had uncovered was both a gift and a burden, and the shadow of Zentara loomed ever closer.

For Michael, the revelation was clear: this was no longer just a theological or historical puzzle. It was a battle for the soul of humanity, and he had no choice but to see it through.

NINETEEN

The early morning light filtered weakly through the narrow windows of Rupertsberg Abbey's archive, leaving long shadows on the table strewn with ancient manuscripts, scrolls, and Hana Sinclair's ever-expanding collection of notes. Father Michael Dominic leaned over the table, his fingers drumming against the oak surface as he stared at the parchment codex Gabriel had provided. Beside him, Brother Gabriel meticulously turned the delicate pages of Hildegard's manuscript, while Hana sat cross-legged on the floor, flipping through a reference book she had pulled from a nearby shelf.

"It's not just a puzzle," Gabriel said, breaking the silence. "It's a series of deliberate challenges. Each riddle is layered, I'm guessing designed to test intellect, faith, and intuition simultaneously. But it is clear that Hildegard secured something valuable at the end of this quest. I can only guess that it is either another source of growing golden castors or an understanding of the recipe to create the medicinal she held secret."

Hana frowned, brushing her dark hair out of her face. "I called Élise about a potential site for them in Italy, and she said she'd check into that possibility for us through her botanical reference books. But she also confirmed that there is more to understand about how to prepare the actual medicinal. Although the chemical composition of the golden castor is essential, like the small bits of gold she found, there are likely other essential ingredients as well. So we'll need to find that full recipe. If we do, she might still be able to replicate the remedy."

Michael squinted at the manuscript, reading the passage he had just deciphered aloud.

"Seek below for the garden of life,
Look not to stone or sky for strife,
Three virtues must converge as one.
For in the heart, the journey's begun."

He sighed and leaned back. "Hildegard loved her metaphors, didn't she?"

Gabriel offered a faint smile. "She was a mystic, Father. Her writings were meant to inspire reflection and guide seekers—not hand answers over on a silver platter."

Hana closed her book with a soft thud. "Fine. Let's reflect, then. The goal seems to be the garden of life."

Michael nodded. "What she called the *Hortus Vitae*, yes."

"And 'Three virtues converging as one'—what are we talking about? Faith, hope, and charity? Something botanical? What?"

Gabriel nodded thoughtfully. "Faith, hope, and charity are possibilities, but Hildegard also emphasized virtues as harmonies within creation. She might be speaking of elements in balance—like earth, water, and air—or even something more abstract, like body, mind, and spirit."

Hana jotted down the possibilities. "Okay, let's say it's about balance. How does that fit with the rest of the verse? 'Look not to stone or sky'—so we're not looking for something physical or celestial. That leaves...?"

"Something internal," Michael said quietly. "The 'heart, where journeys are begun.' It's about introspection, or perhaps faith itself."

Gabriel leaned forward, tracing the ornate script with his finger. "Hildegard wrote extensively about the heart being the seat of both the soul and divine inspiration. It was central to her philosophy of 'viriditas'—the greening power of life. If this riddle is about preparation, then it might be pointing to a state of readiness."

Hana exhaled sharply. "So, this isn't just a scavenger hunt. It's a moral test. Typical."

Michael smiled faintly at her sarcasm. "Would you expect anything less from a saint?"

HOURS PASSED as they worked through the manuscript's riddles, piecing together Hildegard's carefully woven words. Gabriel brought out more reference texts, and Hana scoured them for connections to the manuscript's botanical and theological clues.

They arrived at the next verse:

"Where shadow and light embrace as one,
The hidden path shall be undone.
Beneath the fronds of sacred green,
The breath of life is evergreen."

Michael leaned over the manuscript. "This has to be about a specific plant. 'Sacred green'—is it one of the plants Hildegard considered vital to her philosophy?"

Gabriel nodded. "Her writings mention several plants she deemed sacred for their healing properties. She believed they were imbued with divine wisdom, created by God to mend the fractures of the body and soul."

Hana grabbed another book from the stack, flipping through it quickly. "Okay, I found a section on her herbal practices. She often wrote about fennel, yarrow, and verbena as central to her healing methods. But look at this—here's something interesting: she once described a rare fern as representing eternal life because it thrived in the darkest conditions."

"'Beneath the fronds of sacred green,'" Michael murmured. "That fits. If this fern is significant, it could point us toward the next piece of the puzzle—or the *Hortus Vitae* itself."

Gabriel's eyes lit up with recognition. "This could be referring to the *Adiantum sanctum*, a relative to today's

157

prolific maidenhair fern, and a plant she considered symbolic of resilience and divine grace. It's nearly extinct today, but Hildegard cultivated it in her original gardens."

Hana frowned. "If it's extinct, how are we supposed to find it?"

Gabriel shook his head. "Not extinct—nearly extinct. There are still preserved specimens in some monasteries and botanical collections. It's possible the *Hortus Vitae* holds a living example."

Michael nodded. "So, the riddle is pointing us toward this fern and its connection to eternal life. That reinforces the idea that the *Hortus Vitae* isn't just a garden repository of plants—it's a place of living knowledge."

Hana tapped her pen against her notebook. "But how does 'shadow and light' fit into this? It sounds like a metaphor for balance, but could it also describe a physical place?"

Gabriel considered her question. "It could be. Hildegard often described gardens as sacred spaces where the interplay of shadow and light reflected divine harmony. If the *Hortus Vitae* exists, it may be hidden in such a space."

As THEY WORKED through the remaining riddles, a picture began to emerge. The *Hortus Vitae*, as Hildegard described it, was more than a garden. It was a living testament to her belief in the divine unity of creation.

The manuscript's final verse provided a tantalizing clue:

"Within the cradle of the earth,
Where stars above mirror life's rebirth,
The sacred bloom, unseen by eyes,
Shall lead the faithful to the prize."

Michael frowned. "A cradle of the earth—could this mean a valley? A cave? Somewhere protected?"

Gabriel nodded. "Perhaps. But the phrase 'stars above mirror life's rebirth' suggests something more specific. Hildegard believed the heavens reflected the divine order of life on earth. This could point to a location aligned with celestial patterns.

"Many medieval abbeys were constructed in alignment with certain constellations in mind."

Michael closed the manuscript gently. "So, we're looking for a place that embodies divine balance—botanical, spiritual, and cosmic. If Hildegard cultivated the *Hortus Vitae*, she would have ensured this garden of life mirrored her vision of creation."

Hana stood, stretching her legs. "Then I guess the only question left is where we start looking."

Gabriel smiled. "I have an idea. There's a site near the ruins of Hildegard's original abbey—an old orchard that fits these descriptions. The fruit trees shade the ground, and ferns grow freely. The Order has long believed it held significance, but it's never been fully explored."

Michael and Hana exchanged a glance, a spark of determination passing between them.

"Then that's where we'll go," Michael said. "If Zentara is after the essence of Hildegard's life's work, then the *Hortus Vitae* will be their goal at some point, we need to find it first. And if it's as sacred as Hildegard believed, we'll do whatever it takes to protect it."

As they gathered their notes and prepared to leave, the morning light grew stronger, spilling into the room like a benediction. The path ahead was uncertain, but they were united by the conviction that Hildegard's legacy—and the balance she sought to preserve—was worth every challenge.

The *Hortus Vitae* waited, its secrets hidden within shadow and light, ready to test their faith and resolve.

TWENTY

One day earlier, Élise Gauthier sat in her lab, a study in controlled chaos. Glass beakers, meticulously labeled vials, and half-filled notebooks littered the countertops. The faint scent of ethanol and dried herbs permeated the air, a quiet testament to her tireless work. Sunlight streamed through the narrow windows of the research facility, casting streaks of gold across the white walls. Élise stood at her workstation, peering into a microscope, the delicate contours of a fern sample magnified under the lens.

It was another day of routine analysis—or so she thought.

Her focus was broken by the soft chime of her phone, a message flashing across the screen. "Lunch?" It was from Dr. Peter Gaspard, a colleague at the botanical research institute. Élise smiled faintly. She hadn't seen

Peter in weeks, and the idea of a break from her relentless work was appealing.

An hour later, she met Peter at a quaint café near the institute. The tables were small and intimate, and the low murmur of conversations created a cocoon of privacy. Peter waved her over with a grin, already nursing a cup of espresso.

"Élise, it's been too long," he said, standing to greet her with a warm hug.

"It has," she admitted, setting her bag down. "I've been buried in work, as usual."

Peter chuckled. "Still chasing your mysteries, I see. You always were the most dedicated of us."

They ordered a light lunch, and the conversation flowed easily, touching on shared colleagues, research challenges, and the latest developments in their field. But as the meal wore on, Peter's questions began to take on a curious tone.

"So, Élise," he began, twirling the stem of his wine glass between his fingers. "I hear you've been working on something fascinating—something tied to ancient botanical knowledge. Word is you've been consulting with some rather high-profile figures."

Élise raised an eyebrow, her fork pausing midair. The crisp iceberg lettuce, fresh raspberry, and walnut-laced salad had suddenly lost its flavor. "I don't know what you're talking about."

Peter smiled disarmingly. "Come now, don't be modest. You've always had a knack for uncovering the extraordinary. And there's a lot of interest in Hildegard's writings these days, isn't there?"

The mention of Hildegard sent a jolt through her. Élise had been careful—very careful—not to discuss her findings outside a trusted circle. How did Peter know?

Her expression must have betrayed her unease because Peter leaned back, raising his hands in mock surrender. "Relax, Élise. It's just academic curiosity. I heard something through the grapevine, that's all."

"From whom?" she asked, her tone more forceful than she intended.

Peter shrugged. "A mutual acquaintance. You know how researchers talk. Everyone's always trying to stay ahead of the curve."

Élise forced a smile, though her mind was racing. The conversation soon shifted to more mundane topics, but a seed of doubt had been planted. As they parted ways, Peter gave her a friendly wave, but a quiet voice in the back of Élise's mind kept insisting something was amiss.

Back at the lab, Élise replayed the conversation in her mind. Peter had always been charming and affable, but his questions had felt too pointed, too deliberate. She turned to look across the room, where Hildegard's journal and the botanical samples lay secretly locked away. Her thoughts wandered to Hana and Michael, the only two people who knew the true scope of her research.

Michael had emailed her earlier that day to say they were flying off to Germany. They could still be en route, so calling right now seemed like too dramatic an option.

Besides, doubt edged in her mind now. Could either of them have said something that got back to Peter somehow? Too much weighed on her, and she needed to sleep on what to do.

THE FOLLOWING MORNING, Élise arrived at the lab to find a small envelope waiting on her desk. Her name was written on the front in an unfamiliar hand. She glanced around the empty room before opening it, her fingers trembling slightly. Inside was a single sheet of paper bearing a short, typed message:

"Knowledge is meant to be shared, Dr. Gauthier. Don't keep it to yourself."

Élise felt her breath hitch. She checked the envelope for any identifying marks but found none. Her mind raced as she considered the implications. Someone knew about her work, her connection to Hildegard's journal—and they wanted her to know that they knew.

She locked the lab and left immediately, her heart pounding as she made her way to a nearby café. From there, she called Hana.

Hana Sinclair answered on the second ring, her voice alert despite the early hour. "Élise? What's going on?"

"I don't know," Élise admitted, her voice trembling. "Someone left me a note. It was anonymous, but they clearly know about the journal and the samples. Yesterday, Peter Gaspard asked me strange questions about Hildegard, and now this—"

"Wait," Hana interrupted. "Who's Peter?"

"A colleague," Élise said quickly. "We've worked together for years. But our conversation felt off, like he was fishing for information. One thing was certain: he knows I'm working on a project involving Hildegard."

Hana's voice hardened. "And you think he's connected to whoever left the note?"

"I don't know," Élise said, her frustration mounting. "But I can't ignore the possibility. Hana, I think Zentara might be watching me again."

There was a pause on the line before Hana spoke again, her tone measured. "Okay, listen. Don't panic. Zentara thrives on intimidation, but this note might just be a warning shot. Are the samples and the journal secure?"

"Yes," Élise said. "They're locked up, and the lab has security protocols, but…"

"But if they wanted to, they could find a way around those," Hana finished for her.

Élise nodded, though Hana couldn't see her. "Exactly."

"Where are you?"

"I'm at a café. Very public. I thought that way—"

"And you were right," Hana said. "Stay put. I'll call for the jet, and we'll be there as soon as possible. Whatever's going on, we'll figure it out."

LATER THAT AFTERNOON, after numerous cups of espresso and a generous tip to the patient staff, Élise received another message, this time via email. The sender's address was untraceable, but the subject line was chilling:

"Time to share is running out."

The email contained a single image—a blurred photograph of her lab, taken from outside the building. Élise's stomach turned. Someone was watching her, and they wanted her to know it. She had no doubt about Peter now—he would be the one to "share" with, but no way would she do that.

She clutched her bag tightly in her lap. She scanned the street outside the café window, her eyes darting to every parked car, every passing pedestrian. Was she being watched even now?

Her phone buzzed, and she nearly dropped it in her haste to answer.

"Hana," she said, relief flooding her voice.

"Élise, we just landed," Hana said. "Michael's here too. We'll meet you at your apartment. But stay somewhere public until we call to say we're closer."

Élise hung up and ordered one more espresso, this one decaf.

THAT EVENING, Élise sat in her small living room, the curtains drawn tightly shut. Hana and Michael sat across from her, listening intently as she recounted everything that had happened over the past two days.

"Peter's questions were specific," Élise said. "He asked about Hildegard's writings, and he stated I've been in contact with 'high profile' figures related to that."

Michael and Hana looked at each other with raised brows. Michael offered, "Well, certainly Hana is now high profile, considering her inheritance. But how would this man know…?" He left the question hanging.

Élise nodded. "Exactly. Even at the time, I felt uneasy about it. But now…"

"Now you think he's working with Zentara," Michael said, his tone grim.

"And that my lab has been bugged. It's the only explanation that makes sense. And the note, the email—it all fits together."

Hana leaned forward. "We need to assume your lab has been compromised. Zentara might not have raided it yet, but they're clearly watching you. Do you have a backup location for the journal and samples and whatever you need for your research?"

Élise hesitated. "I have a secure storage facility, but moving everything will take time."

"Then we'll help you," Michael said. "But we need to act quickly. I suspect Zentara doesn't leave loose ends, and if they've marked you as a target, it's only a matter of time before they escalate."

Élise swallowed hard, the burden of his words pressing down on her. "What do we do?"

Michael exchanged a glance with Hana. "We'll move the samples and the journal to a safer location, somewhere Zentara won't think to look. Then we'll figure out who's feeding them information and cut off their access."

Hana nodded. "And Élise, from now on, you're not alone in this. If Zentara thinks they can intimidate you, they're going to find out they've underestimated us."

As the three of them began planning their next steps, Élise felt a flicker of hope amid the fear. Zentara might have cast its shadow over her work, but she wasn't facing them alone. With Hana and Michael by her side, she knew they had a fighting chance to protect Hildegard's lifelong work—and themselves—from the unseen enemy closing in around them.

TWENTY-ONE

T he crisp morning air lingered over Rupertsberg Abbey as Hana, Michael, and Gabriel approached the ancient gates for the third time, with Élise joining them. Though they had grown familiar with the abbey's serene beauty and towering stone walls, this return carried new urgency. The riddles in Hildegard's manuscript had pointed them here once again, this time in search of the legendary *Hortus Vitae*.

Sister Amalia awaited them in the courtyard, her calm demeanor masking the unease that flickered in her eyes. She folded her hands as the group approached.

"Welcome back," Amalia said, her voice steady but suffused with concern. "Have you made progress?"

"We have," Gabriel replied, stepping forward. "Hildegard's writings suggest that the *Hortus Vitae*—her sacred garden—lies beneath this abbey. I'm thinking that might be the old orchard area. We believe it holds the key to her work."

Amalia's lips thinned in quiet resolve. "The *Hortus Vitae*," she said softly, as though the words themselves carried weight. "Few know of its legend, and fewer still have sought it. If it is here, it has remained hidden for centuries, unknown even to the nuns who have resided here for hundreds of years."

She glanced at Hana, her gaze thoughtful. "You are certain this is where you must look? That old orchard spans several hectares of the hillside. Where would you even begin?"

Hana nodded. "The manuscript mentions carvings and symbols that point the way. We believe they may be found within the abbey."

Amalia studied them for a moment longer before turning toward the abbey doors. "Then follow me."

She led them through the abbey's familiar corridors, the scent of incense mingling with the faint aroma of aged stone and wood. The towering stained-glass windows in the main hall cast fractured rainbows across the floor, and the faint echo of their footsteps filled the sacred space.

She stopped outside the scriptorium, her hand resting on the heavy wooden door. "The scriptorium is one of the oldest parts of the abbey. If the markings you seek exist, they may lie within these walls."

She opened the door with a groan of ancient hinges, revealing rows of towering shelves lined with leather-bound tomes. Dust motes danced in the sunlight streaming through high windows, and the air was thick with the scent of parchment and ink.

Gabriel turned to the group, his voice hushed.

"Hildegard often left her messages in places of reflection and study. We need to examine the walls and pillars carefully."

The group spread out, each member focusing on a different section of the room. Hana ran her fingers along the stone walls, searching for irregularities. Élise crouched by a pillar, shining her flashlight along its base. Michael scanned the shelves, looking for signs of concealed writings. Gabriel lingered near the back wall, his hands moving methodically over the cold stone.

It was Hana who made the first discovery. "Here," she called softly, pointing to a faint engraving on the wall. "It's almost invisible unless the light hits it just right."

Gabriel hurried to her side, kneeling to inspect the markings. The faint lines formed a delicate pattern of vines entwined with Latin text. He traced the carvings with his fingers, murmuring the words as he deciphered them.

"*Quod vita celat, lumen revelabit.*" He paused, translating aloud. "'What life conceals, light will reveal.'"

Michael leaned closer, thoughtful. "It's a clue. We might need a specific light source to reveal the full meaning."

Élise angled her flashlight over the markings, adjusting the beam until faint additional lines began to emerge—lines that formed a rudimentary diagram.

"It's a map," she murmured, her voice filled with awe. "These markings outline the abbey's foundations."

Gabriel's fingers followed the map. "These markings

outline the abbey's foundations. And these markings lead to the eastern section of the old vineyard."

Sister Amalia, who had remained silent, stepped forward. "The vineyard hasn't been cultivated in decades. It is quiet and overgrown, but its roots run deep."

Hana tilted her head, examining the map further. "Look here," she said, pointing to an intricate symbol near the center of the engraving. It resembled a compass rose, surrounded by smaller carvings of plants and stars.

Gabriel inhaled brusquely. "That's Hildegard's emblem. She used it to mark places of profound significance. This must be the entrance to the *Hortus Vitae*."

From across the river, the sound of Eibingen Abbey's bells interrupted their discovery, quickly repeated by the Rupertsberg Abbey bells above them, signaling the hour. Sister Amalia straightened, her expression resolute.

"It will be too dark soon to negotiate the protruding roots of that orchard, even with torches. We have rooms for you for the night. Hana and Élise can stay here in the abbey while Father Dominic can accompany Gabriel to the monks' housing to the east. Tomorrow you can commence your search. But tread carefully for another reason as well: if Zentara is watching, they will not hesitate to strike."

Michael nodded, his voice firm. "We'll be cautious. Hildegard's work cannot fall into their hands."

The group exited the scriptorium, their minds racing

with the implications of what they had found. The *Hortus Vitae*, hidden just down the hill from the abbey for centuries, now seemed within reach. But they knew the closer they came to uncovering it, the greater the danger they faced.

Hana glanced back at the faintly glowing map, her resolve hardening. "Now let's find that entrance," she said.

As they moved toward the eastern wing of the abbey, the ancient stones seemed to hum with an unspoken promise: that life's greatest secrets, concealed for centuries, were waiting to be revealed.

TWENTY-TWO

The sun dipped low over Rupertsberg Abbey, its fading light throwing shadows across the stone walls. Hana stood at the edge of the abbey's courtyard, watching as the nuns filed silently into the chapel for evening prayers. Their movements, precise and serene, seemed untouched by the tension that had begun to settle over the abbey.

She wasn't so sure.

"Something's off," Hana muttered, half to herself, as she turned away from the scene. Her steps carried her toward the abbey library, where Michael was likely still poring over Hildegard's writings.

The hallways of the abbey, once a source of peace, now felt unnervingly quiet. Hana's journalist instincts prickled at the edges of her mind. The mission's scope and Zentara's threat weren't the only concerns; something more pressing existed. Something closer.

Michael was exactly where she expected, seated at

one of the long wooden tables in the library before leaving for the monks' quarters. The warm light of an oil lamp illuminated the ancient texts spread before him. His brow was scrunched in concentration as he scrawled notes on a yellowed piece of parchment.

"You're still at it," Hana said as she approached, pulling out a chair across from him.

The young priest glanced up, offering a faint smile. "Hildegard wasn't one for simplicity. Her writings are layered with meaning."

"She didn't have Zentara breathing down her neck," Hana replied, settling into the chair. "Or spies in her abbey."

Michael straightened, his pen stilling. "You're still on about that?"

"Yes," Hana said firmly. "Something isn't right, Michael. Amalia told us the abbey is secure, and I know the monks are nearby to secure things, but there's been someone watching us. I can feel it."

Michael leaned back, folding his arms. "And what evidence do you have?"

Hana hesitated. She couldn't point to anything concrete—just fleeting glimpses of a figure lingering too long near the library or the sudden silences when she entered a room. But her instincts were rarely wrong.

"Call it intuition," she said finally. "But Zentara doesn't strike me as the kind of organization to leave us alone. They know we're close to finding the *Hortus Vitae*."

Michael sighed, rubbing the bridge of his nose. "Hana, this is a place of faith and sanctuary. The sisters here and the nearby monks have dedicated their lives to serving God. I find it hard to believe any of them would betray that trust."

"Maybe not willingly," Hana countered. "But Zentara has money, power, and no scruples. They could easily coerce someone—or plant one of their own here."

Michael was silent for a moment, his gaze drifting toward the vaulted ceiling of the library. When he spoke, his voice was softer. "Faith protects more than you think."

Hana opened her mouth to retort, but the sound of footsteps approaching the library door made her freeze. Both of them turned toward the entrance as a young novice stepped inside, her face flushed from exertion.

"Sister Amalia asks for you both," she said, her voice trembling slightly. "There's been... an incident."

THE INCIDENT TURNED out to be in the abbey's storage room, a tucked-away space beneath the main building where supplies were kept. When Hana and Michael arrived, Sister Amalia was already there, flanked by two other nuns. Amalia's face was a careful mask, but the tension in her posture was unmistakable.

"What happened?" Michael asked, stepping forward.

Amalia gestured to a wooden crate that had been pried open. Its contents—mostly old ledgers and documents—were scattered across the floor. A few papers bore fresh tears, as if someone had rifled through them in a hurry.

"We found this a short time ago," Amalia said. "One of the sisters came to retrieve an old inventory list and discovered the mess."

Hana crouched beside the crate, picking up one of the torn documents. It was a handwritten inventory of the abbey's archives from nearly fifty years ago—nothing particularly valuable or relevant to their search.

"Did anyone see who did it?" Hana asked, scanning the room.

Amalia shook her head. "No. The storage room is usually locked, but someone must have found a way in."

Hana stood, her jaw tightening. "This doesn't feel random. Zentara has someone in the abbey."

Amalia's face fell, drained of its earlier warmth. "That's a serious accusation."

"It's not an accusation—it's a fact," Hana said. "Zentara knows we're here, and they're not going to sit back and wait for us to find the *Hortus Vitae*. They'll do whatever it takes to get there first."

Michael stepped between them, his voice calm but firm. "Let's not jump to conclusions. This could have been a careless mistake."

Hana turned on him, her frustration bubbling to the surface. "A mistake? Michael, someone broke in here and tore through these documents. Zentara's fingerprints are all over this."

Amalia held up a hand, her tone brokering no argument. "Enough. Whether this was Zentara's doing or not, the abbey will take precautions. I will ensure the storage room is secured, and the sisters will be more vigilant."

Hana nodded reluctantly, but her unease remained. As she and Michael left the storage room, an unsettling thought clung to her that they were being watched.

THAT NIGHT, Hana sat in her small guest room, the glow of her laptop casting a faint light over the bed. She had intended to review her notes, but her mind kept circling back to the break-in. The abbey, for all its peace and sanctity, no longer felt like a refuge. It felt like a trap.

TWENTY-THREE

S ilence settled over the dining hall as three of the nuns passed out bowls of the evening's repast. Michael, Gabriel, Hana, and Élise sat at a table to themselves. The silence was common for this abbey during mealtimes, a sign of respect and gratitude for God's abundance and favor. But this particular meal held a grave sadness to its silence. The day had been spent fruitlessly searching the old orchard. The conclusion was simple: they had misunderstood the passages they had interpreted from Hildegard's manuscript. The one thing they still felt certain about was that the *Horus Vitae* existed, and that must be their next objective.

Michael spooned the last of the thick stew of venison and carrots and other wild roots into his mouth and sat back with a satisfied sigh. He looked over to the nuns who were collecting the bowls. His hands rose as if in prayer, and he nodded his thanks to them. They smiled in return.

Once the tables were cleared, the nuns felt inclined to begin small whisperings of what was happening in their abbey. Everyone knew the mission that Hana's team had brought to their grounds. They knew that the combination of their work and that of their sisters from centuries past could finally be coming to light. And yet, today had been unsuccessful to light the way for that to happen.

Michael spoke first. "This isn't the end, you know," he said. "We can go back to those passages, rethink them."

Gabriel shook his head. "No, there's more somewhere that we're just missing. I don't think the failure is in understanding those passages on their own. There's more that Hildegard would have indicated, and I'm sure it still lies within the pages of the manuscript that Hana received."

"Yes, you may be right," Michael agreed. "The codex you afforded us in your own Order's archives was invaluable in translating what she'd written. I'd only been able to go so far without it. But translating it into English is only the first step; the second understanding it." He looked down at his hands, folded on the table, as if still in prayer over their evening meal.

Hana reached over, about to touch his arm, but then hesitated. She looked at him and asked, "What is it, Michael? There's something else bothering you. Tell us what it is."

Michael's eyes scanned the room as the nuns were

leaving. "Yes, there is. Zentara knew that we would be at the Black Forest that day. They also knew that you, Hana, were involved with this mission, and they infiltrated your grandfather's estate. Some of their actions could be the result of a bug in Élise's lab, but not all of it. Plus, she's moved to another facility now. Yet, somehow, Zentara still seems to be in lockstep with us, and I don't understand how that could be. We know that they're relentless, powerful, and likely very persuasive in ways we don't want to comprehend. But how are they doing this?"

"So what are you thinking, Michael? That there is a spy here among us somehow?" Hana, too, now glanced at the last of the two sisters leaving the dining hall.

"Just that there is something we aren't aware of, some way they know what we're doing."

Gabriel spoke up, determined as ever. "Whatever we need to do, Father Dominic, it needs to be done in the utmost secrecy. For centuries we have kept Hildegard's secrets away from prying eyes. We need to do more in today's society where communications are instantaneous, and greed runs even more rampant than in times past."

The three of them nodded, unsure what to do at that moment. But all three were ready for a night of sleep and reflection on how to safeguard something so sacred and special that, in the right hands, could benefit the world.

Or cause more pain in the wrong hands.

TWENTY-FOUR

The abbey's stone corridors seemed colder than usual, their silence carrying an unnatural weight. Brother Gabriel walked briskly in the direction of the chapel, his hands clasped tightly in front of him. His mind churned with doubts, replaying the conversation he had never anticipated having.

Christophe Vaux, Zentara's enigmatic emissary, had approached Gabriel that morning. The man had appeared out of nowhere, his polished demeanor and chilling confidence a stark contrast to the sanctity of the abbey. Gabriel had listened in stunned silence as Vaux laid out his terms: betrayal in exchange for the safety of the abbey's residents and a substantial sum to "support their mission."

Gabriel's stomach twisted. The *Hortus Vitae* was more than just a repository of knowledge. It was a testament to Hildegard's vision—a delicate balance of faith and nature that Zentara would corrupt beyond recognition. And yet, Vaux's threats rang in his ears. The abbey and all its residents were at risk.

In the library, Hana sat at a long wooden table, her notebook open and a pen tapping against its pages. Michael was seated across from her, a worried expression creasing his brow.

"Gabriel is shaken," the priest said. "He didn't say much, but I can tell he's struggling with what happened this morning."

Hana didn't look up from her notes. "He's not the only one. Zentara's getting bolder, and we still haven't found the *Hortus Vitae*. If they're threatening the leader of the Order of the Green Flame and getting to Élise's colleagues, they won't stop there. They'll come for anyone connected to us."

Michael sighed, leaning back in his chair. "Gabriel's faith is his strength, but it's also a vulnerability. If Vaux offered him a way out—any way to keep people safe—he might consider it."

"He wouldn't have confided in us about that offer if he had any intention of fulfilling Zentara's demands," Hana said, finally meeting Michael's gaze. "But others may not be so strong in their ethics."

Michael studied her for a moment. "You've got that look."

"What look?"

"The one that means you're thinking of something."

Hana's lips curved into a sly smile. "I am. And it's time we figured this out."

Hana's plan was simple but effective. That evening, she gathered the group in the abbey's library—Gabriel,

Michael, and Élise. The room was heavy with tension, the toll of Zentara's growing presence pressing on everyone's shoulders.

"I know we're all feeling the pressure," Hana began, her tone measured. "Zentara's getting closer, and we don't know how they know our plans. When did it start? What was Zentara's first presence?"

"That's easy. My kidnapping," Élise answered.

"And who besides us three knew at that point what we were looking into?"

Élise gasped, her hand suddenly at her mouth, her eyes wide.

"What is it, Élise?" Hana asked.

"I… I said something to a colleague. He's been my mentor, and I trust him explicitly. There's no way—"

"Where were you when you told him?" Michael's question was pointed, firm.

She swallowed, her voice quiet now, unsure. "I… we were at a café, and it was innocent; I mean, I barely said anything about—"

"But *where*?" Michael's tone was strident now.

"Oh, at the square in Geneva, off the Boulevard du Theatre…" Her eyes widened as she realized Michael's implication.

Hana nodded. "And just two blocks from one of Zentara's main offices."

Élise's face paled as she twisted her hands in her lap.

"Okay," Michael offered, "let's keep going. They knew enough that Élise was involved with something, and after that, she was kidnapped. So, when did we encounter Zentara next?"

Hana answered, "In the Black Forest."

They all turned to Élise. "I didn't even know about that until after they kidnapped me. I only found out when Hana told me about your plans on the phone the next day."

Michael snapped his fingers. "The phone! Did you have the phone with you when they kidnapped you? Could they have had access to it while you were with them?"

"Yes, I had it, and, in fact, they had it while I was hooded. They had to give it back to me in order for me to transmit the files that I told them were what they needed. The files weren't, of course, but yes, they did have access to my phone. What are you thinking?"

Gabriel nodded at this point. "You're right, Michael. The phone is probably now bugged, and all of her conversations are being transmitted to Zentara."

Hana agreed. "They not only knew about us going to the Black Forest but likely knew the best time to have Peter ask you out for lunch and have likely since learned anything else that you've discussed on the phone."

Élise looked down at her pocket where she kept her phone as if some dangerous weapon resided there.

Hana continued, "But this is our opportunity. We can test out this theory and gain some leverage in the process."

"How do you propose we do that?" Élise asked.

Hana pulled out a folded sheet of paper and placed it on the table. "We're going to bait them. Zentara's after the *Hortus Vitae*, but they don't know where it is. What if we made them think we've found it?"

Michael's eyes narrowed. "A false lead?"

"Exactly," Hana said. Gabriel hesitated. "And what happens when Zentara acts on this false information? What if it endangers innocent lives?"

"We'll control the narrative," Hana assured him. "We'll keep Zentara chasing shadows while we move forward with the real search. No one gets hurt."

Michael spoke up, his voice calm but firm. "Gabriel, we have to protect Hildegard's legacy. If Zentara has infiltrated the abbey, they've already put lives at risk. This is our best chance to root them out."

Gabriel looked between the faces in the room, his inner conflict clear. Finally, he nodded. "Very well. But we must tread carefully. If Zentara realizes we're deceiving them, their response will be swift and ruthless."

Hana smiled, her confidence unwavering. "That's why we'll ensure they don't see it coming. Élise, I need you to make a call for us."

TWENTY-FIVE

Daniel and his three minions had waited for hours before getting the word. By that time, they had taken turns sitting and pacing at the airport in Rome, snacking on cold pizza and drinking can after can of Cedrata and Spuma. They'd had their eyes on the private sector of the airport consistently, awaiting the jet that was to bring Hana Sinclair and her fiancé, Father Dominic, back to Italy.

Earlier, Zentara had intercepted a message stating the Sinclair jet had already taken off from Germany, destined for Rome and a new location for live plants. Christophe Vaux had heard on recordings earlier that the Sinclair woman suspected another source in Italy. The orders Vaux gave Daniel ended clearly with, "*And don't burn down the damned place this time—we need every live specimen we can get to propagate those galls.*"

Daniel and his men had scrambled to get there in time, and they knew they had. Only hours later, however, they found themselves bored and frustrated when no jet landed.

"I gotta go pee," Tom announced as he stood.

"Again?" Daniel groused. "Quit drinking so much of that Cedrata, will you?"

Erik chimed in, "Yeah, it's the citrus in it. Does that to the prostate. Stick to Spuma and you won't—"

"Just go, already," Daniel snapped, and the others shut up.

They continued to update Vaux that no jet arrived. Vaux eventually sent someone to the airport in Germany and determined the jet still sat on the ground in Frankfurt, the pilot reading *Aviation News* in the cockpit.

Daniel then got the call from Vaux that something had gone wrong, and their boss's anger clearly penetrated over the phone. But he was no angrier than Daniel and his men. They had wasted time and were bored stupid in the process. And people like Daniel didn't appreciate being frustrated or wasting time. He would be sure someone paid for that.

As the men tossed their final cans of soda in a trash bin and headed out, two men in the corner of that wing of the airport nodded to each other. They looked like normal tourists, in nondescript traveling clothes, sunglasses, and dragging suitcases, awaiting the arrival of a plane. One turned to the other and said, "Time to make that call."

A moment later, Swiss Guard Karl Dengler called his cousin Hana. "You were right; they were the same guys we saw in the Black Forest. And they finally gave up.

Guess we know now how the information was passed along."

Hana thanked the two guards for checking it out for them, and after she hung up, she turned to the other three. "It looks like we found our leak. And Hildegard's secrets are still safe. At least for now. We just need to figure out what she means in her messages so we can stay ahead of Zentara."

Gabriel nodded slowly, though his doubts lingered. " Maybe we figured this out. But what else does Zentara have up their sleeves?"

CHAPTER

TWENTY-SIX

The next riddle Michael translated from the original manuscript stumped them, its poetic phrasing an enigma they couldn't unravel. Michael read the riddle aloud again, his voice calm and deliberate:

> "Where divine truth and earthly ways meet,
> A faithful heart shall guide the feet.
> Within the circle, bound by grace,
> A sacred light reveals its place."

Hana leaned back in her chair, the abbey library quiet as she thought, tapping her pen against the table. "The 'circle' could be literal—like a physical object—or symbolic. And what about the 'faithful heart'? Is that another test, like the first riddle?"

Michael didn't answer immediately. Instead, he reached for a theological text he had set aside earlier, flipping through its pages with a practiced hand. "Hildegard often used circles in her writings and artwork to represent divine harmony—the balance between heaven and earth. But the 'faithful heart' suggests something more personal, something tied to belief or intention."

His hand stilled, his eyes narrowing as he focused on a passage in the theological text. "Wait," he said, his voice suddenly keen with realization. "I've seen this phrase before—'bound by grace.' It's in one of her visions, recorded in the *Scivias*."

Hana leaned forward, her curiosity piqued. "The *Scivias*? That's her collection of visions, right?"

Michael nodded, pulling another book from the stack beside him. "Yes. In one vision, she describes a 'circle of divine grace'—a celestial map that connects earthly paths with heavenly guidance. She claimed it was a tool for seekers, meant to guide them toward enlightenment."

Hana's pen froze mid-note. "A tool? Are you saying she created a physical version of this celestial map?"

"It's possible."

Guided by Michael's interpretation, the group began combing through the abbey's archives for any mention of a physical artifact tied to Hildegard's vision. Hours passed in silence, broken only by the occasional sound of a turning page or a whispered comment.

Finally, Gabriel called out from across the room. "Here! I think I've found something."

Hana and Michael hurried to his side as Gabriel pointed to a faded entry in a dusty ledger. "It mentions a 'compass of divine grace,' crafted by Hildegard herself. According to this, it was stored in the abbey's reliquary centuries ago, but there's no record of what happened to it after that."

Hana's eyes lit up. "A compass? That makes sense. It would fit the riddle perfectly—something to guide the faithful."

Michael scanned the entry, his mind eliminating the improbable. "If it was part of the reliquary, it might still be here. Many of the abbey's relics were moved to a hidden vault during the war to protect them. We need to check."

The reliquary vault was located beneath the abbey, its entrance hidden behind a plain wooden panel in the sacristy. Gabriel led the way, his hands trembling slightly as he unlocked the heavy iron door.

The air inside was cool and dry, the faint scent of aged wood and incense lingering in the dimly lit space. Rows of shelves lined the walls, filled with ornate boxes and reliquaries bearing centuries of history.

Michael strode ahead, scanning the labels on each box. Hana followed closely, her flashlight cutting through the shadows.

"Here," Michael said, stopping in front of a small, unassuming chest. The label read simply: *Instrumentum Gratiae Divinae*—"Instrument of Divine Grace."

Gabriel stepped forward and lifted the lid carefully, revealing a finely crafted object nestled within. The device was intricate, made of brass, and inlaid with tiny, colorful gemstones that formed a pattern resembling a celestial map. At its center was a circular disc etched with Latin inscriptions and delicate markings that appeared to correspond to Hildegard's writings.

Hana let out a low whistle. "That's just… beautiful. And it definitely fits the description."

Michael held the compass-like artifact with reverence, his fingers tracing the inscriptions. "This is it," he said softly. "The circle bound by grace."

Gabriel peered over his shoulder. "How does it work?"

Michael studied the device momentarily before pointing to a small dial on the side. "Hildegard's writings describe divine guidance as a union of faith and reason. This compass likely requires both—an alignment of the celestial and the spiritual."

He adjusted the dial carefully, aligning it with the markings on the outer ring. As he held it up, the gemstones began to glow faintly reflecting the ambient light in the room, their light growing brighter as the openings in the outer ring aligned to the positions of the gems, allowing them to shimmer from the light behind them.

"It works," Michael said, his voice filled with awe.

He held it up to the window's light and the gemstone colors projected a faint pattern onto the opposite wall—like a colorful constellation.

Hana stepped back, taking in the image. "That's incredible. It's like a star chart, but it's pointing somewhere specific."

Michael nodded, his gaze fixed on the map. "I'd guess it's guiding us to the *Hortus Vitae*."

Gabriel crossed himself, his voice trembling.

"Hildegard's vision was real. She truly left this for us to find."

As they returned to the library, the group was filled with a renewed sense of purpose. The compass was more than just an artifact—it was a tangible connection to Hildegard and a key to unlocking the mysteries of the *Hortus Vitae.*

Hana glanced at Michael as they spread out a map of the abbey's property on the table. He held the compass above it as Hana lit it with her flashlight from above. They spent some time moving the compass up and down to align the colors to the map, but finally, it all fit. The gemstone colors shone onto the map on the table, indicating the location of the *Hortus Vitae.*

The three of them caught their breaths—they knew where to go now.

"Do you think Zentara knows about this?" Hana asked quietly.

Michael's expression hardened. What they had just discovered was known only to their small team. Yet, time and again, Zentara seemed to know what they were doing and where they were going. Somehow, they were tracking them, which meant they would likely do it again this time. "Well, we know not to use Élise's phone for anything important anymore. But whether they do know now or not, it's only a matter of time before they try to figure it out."

Gabriel nodded. "If the *Hortus Vitae* holds the answers we seek, Zentara won't stop until they've taken it—or destroyed it."

Hana's eyes gleamed with determination. "Then we'd better get there first."

The group worked late into the night, preparing for the journey ahead. With its glowing gemstones and celestial guidance, the compass was their beacon in the dark—a testament to Hildegard's brilliance and a symbol of the hope they carried.

The path to the *Hortus Vitae* was becoming clearer, but the dangers ahead were greater than ever. The stakes had never been higher for Michael, Hana, and Gabriel, and failure wasn't an option.

TWENTY-SEVEN

A harsh blue glow from monitors lit the darkened room. A dozen screens displayed fragmented data streams—cellular connections, audio waveforms, and location triangulations—each feeding into a labyrinth of code. At the center of it all sat Christophe Vaux, his posture rigid as he leaned forward and motioned to the technician to play the recording one more time as he listened intently.

A clipped voice echoed in the chamber:

"...Yes, that's right. Hana and Michael are on their way already. Michael discovered something in Hildegard's manuscript that pinpointed an area in Italy where the plant grows. He needs you to be at his office at the Vatican, ready to assist him when they arrive."

The recording ended shortly after that, truncated by

the sound of a disconnected line. Vaux's expression remained stoic, though his piercing gaze betrayed a flicker of anger.

He waved a hand at the technician, and the man scurried away, glad to be out from under his boss's angry mood.

Vaux's techs had exploited the cellular network by adjusting the controls on the Signaling System 7 interception terminal. Every entire conversation had been recorded since they had bugged Élise Gauthier's phone during the kidnapping. But they had been found out. How much of what they had heard had been false?

Vaux kicked at a nearby trash bin, its contents tipping out, spilling like all the leads they'd had so far, scattered with nothing useful to show for it. Without live plants, they had no galls. And without the galls, Blackthorn would have his head.

He had no choice now. He picked up the phone, and moments later, he heard Blackthorn's voice.

"What do you have for me?" he said tersely.

Vaux took a breath. "Our bug on the woman's phone must have been discovered. The jet never even took off from Frankfurt. Our operatives are returning to headquarters, but we don't know more about the—"

"Right."

Vaux frowned. Blackthorn didn't sound angry, didn't even sound interested. Sarcastic, maybe? Vaux couldn't determine his boss's response and hesitated to say more.

Blackthorn continued, "So you failed again, eh? And just what do you plan to do about that?"

Vaux swallowed, yet still the man's words didn't

ring with anger for some reason. "I have an operative entrenched in their group. It's only a matter of time before I get the intel we need. Good intel. If they have any other source of the plant, I'll know soon enough. Or if there is that formula we need, one where we can simulate that plant's properties, we'll get it, I assure you." He got no response, and Vaux hesitated to ask but couldn't help himself, "What is going on?"

"Well, let's see." Blackthorn seemed to warm to the question. "Remember those galls your team gathered before they stupidly burned out every source the world still has of them? Those galls have been proven in my labs to be a cure for cancer. Among other things."

"That's… good, right?" Tension filled him as Vaux puzzled out his boss's calm and silence. Then it hit him. "What other things?"

His boss's tone changed, a carefully measured clip to his voice that instantly put Vaux on alert. "Yes. Other things. The botanical elements in those galls, galls from the *Ricinus aureum* plant, in the same family of the *Rictus* plants from which we can derive ricin? These galls have a different—and more potent—form of ricin in them. Death from it so unrelenting, so untreatable, so agonizing that every government's military and terrorist group on earth would pay anything to get their hands on it."

Suddenly, Blackthorn's voice snapped with a malicious, evil snarl as he ended, "I don't care what you do or how you do it. You find me another source of those plants. If you don't, you'll be the first to enjoy the benefits of the ricin we extracted from those few precious Black Forest golden galls of yours." The line went dead.

TWENTY-EIGHT

The gnarled vines and forgotten trees of the gardens behind the abbey, untended for years, threw wide shadows in the afternoon light.

Hana, Michael, Gabriel, and Élise pushed through the dense foliage, the air growing cooler as they approached the back wall of the abbey. There they found a rocky slope, where nothing grew among the large boulders and sharp stones, making walking perilous. It was no wonder the nuns never tended to this area. Michael frequently referred to the map in his hand, sketched from the directions provided by the compass. He walked one way, then another, carefully negotiating the rocks.

"Here," he said, crouching beside a tangle of vines at the edge of the rocky slope. He brushed away the leaves and soil, revealing a large, flat stone embedded in the ground.

Gabriel knelt beside him, using the spade to pry at

the edges of the stone. "It's sealed, but not naturally. Someone placed this here deliberately."

Michael joined him, his hands steady as he helped lift the stone. Beneath it was a narrow shaft, its walls lined with weathered stone bricks.

Hana peered into the darkness, her flashlight cutting through the gloom. "There's a ladder. Looks like it leads to a chamber below."

Michael nodded. "This could be it. Let's go. Turn on your flashlights. Gabriel, seal the stone behind us."

THE CHAMBER beneath the abbey was small and cool, its walls carved from the bedrock. From that chamber, the underground tunnels stretched out like veins through the earth, their walls damp with condensation and streaked with centuries of wear. Michael led the group carefully, his flashlight casting a narrow beam of light that flickered across the uneven floor. Hana followed close behind, her alert eyes scanning the shadows for any sign of danger.

Gabriel brought up the rear behind Élise, his breath uneven as the group descended farther into the labyrinth. The air was cool and heavy, and each step echoed faintly as they moved deeper into the abbey's hidden network.

"You're sure this is the right way?" Hana asked, her voice low but urgent.

Michael nodded. "Hildegard's map is precise. The *Hortus Vitae* lies at the center of these tunnels, beneath the oldest part of the abbey. If we stay on this path, we'll reach it."

Élise glanced down at the map in Michael's hands, illuminated by her flashlight. "The tunnels branch ahead," she said, pointing to a spot on the map. "We'll need to take the left passage. The right leads to a dead end."

Hana frowned. "That sounds like a perfect spot for an ambush."

Michael's jaw tightened. "Stay alert."

The group moved cautiously, the silence around them amplifying every creak of the floor and drip of water. Michael's grip on the map tightened as they approached the fork in the tunnels. The left passage yawned before them, its narrow confines cloaked in darkness.

"Stay close," Michael said, stepping into the passage. He studied the map again. "It's just ahead, another hundred feet. There's a chamber marked here—it must be the entrance."

The chamber at the end of the passage was larger than they expected, its walls carved from the same ancient stone that made up the abbey's foundation. At its center stood an ornate iron door, its surface etched with Latin inscriptions and symbols reminiscent of Hildegard's writings.

Élise approached the door cautiously, her flashlight revealing an intricate locking mechanism built into its center. "This is it," she said, her voice laced with awe.

Michael joined her, his eyes scanning the inscriptions. "It's a test," he said. "Hildegard left this to ensure that only someone who understood her teachings could enter."

As Michael and Gabriel worked on deciphering the lock, Hana kept her flashlight trained on the passage behind them. The tension was excruciating.

Michael let out a triumphant breath as the iron door clicked open. "The vault is unlocked!"

Inside, the air was cold and still. The chamber was lined with stone shelves filled with ancient manuscripts, vials of preserved plants, and intricate tools. At the center of the room stood a large, glowing artifact—a crystalline orb that seemed to pulse with life from an overhead light well penetrating the ceiling.

Michael and Gabriel stared in awe, the magnitude of Hildegard's sensibilities pressing upon them. The orb's nearly mystical colorations, reflecting the light and fracturing their images in its multiple facets of glass-like surface, held their rapt attention until Élise said, "But this isn't a garden at all. This can't be the *Hortus Vitae*."

CHAPTER
TWENTY-NINE

"No," Gabriel said. "But this is."

They turned to see the monk looking behind them to the side of the metal door where they had just entered. An area had been dug out under the rocky hillside just beyond the abbey's walls. A narrow doorway opened to a vast underground garden. The air was cool and rich with the scent of earth and growing things as Michael, Hana, Élise, and Gabriel ducked through the doorway. The *Hortus Vitae*, the culmination of Hildegard von Bingen's life's work, unfolded before them in breathtaking splendor.

It was unlike anything they had imagined.

The space was naturally illuminated by beams of golden light that streamed through small holes in the rocky ceiling above. These apertures acted as skylights, their placement precise, allowing the sun's rays and rainfall to reach the chamber below, replenishing an ancient natural irrigation system carved into the floor.

The light shifted gently with the movement of the sun, casting shimmering patterns across the plants.

Hana's voice was hushed, reverent. "It's… beautiful."

Rows of lush greenery stretched out across the chamber, each plant thriving in carefully arranged plots of soil. Delicate flowers in shades of violet and gold swayed in an unseen breeze. Vines twisted up ancient wooden trellises, their leaves glinting in the soft light. At the far end of the garden, a cluster of trees reached toward the ceiling, their branches heavy with fruit.

"It's alive," Gabriel whispered, his voice trembling. "After all this time, it's still alive."

Michael stepped onward, his gaze scanning the space. Hildegard's work extended beyond preserving plants. With the right understanding of nature and faith in her mission, she had demonstrated—centuries later—that a garden of life could be everlasting. It was true proof of the power of her philosophy—a balance between nature and faith.

The group moved cautiously through the *Hortus Vitae*, marveling at its meticulous design. Paths of stone and moss wound through the garden, leading to different sections, each devoted to specific plants.

In one corner, Hana paused to examine a collection of herbs. The labels, written in Latin, described their uses: *Valeriana officinalis* for calming the nerves, *Hypericum perforatum* for lifting the spirit.

"This is more than a garden," she said. "It's a living apothecary."

Gabriel knelt beside her, his fingers brushing the

leaves of a small shrub. "Hildegard believed plants held the key to healing not just the body, but the soul. Every one of these species would have been chosen for a specific purpose."

Michael called out from a nearby section, his tone urgent. "Over here. You need to see this."

The group gathered around a central plot of land, where a plant unlike any other stood tall and proud. Its golden leaves shimmered in the sunlight, and its clusters of small, fuzzy red flowers seemed to pulse with vitality.

Hana's eyes widened. "Is that…?"

"*Ricinus aureum*," Michael confirmed, his voice hushed. "The golden castor."

The leaves were slightly more pointed than the specimens found in the forest, the plant triple the height, and the leaves more golden than green. Clearly, the perfect environmental conditions existed here for the plant to flourish, unlike the wilds of the forest, where extreme weather and marauding animals disturbed their growth. This plant exhibited the characteristics of other species of *Ricinus*, which grew to maturity as perennials rather than their lives being short-circuited into annuals.

Gabriel stared at the plant, awe etched across his face. "It's thriving here, under conditions Hildegard must have controlled perfectly. This chamber—it's more than just a repository. It's an ecosystem."

Hana nodded. "The light, the temperature, even the humidity—it's all perfectly calibrated. But not mechanically. Hildegard used natural principles to create this balance."

Michael examined the soil around the plant. "She understood how to work with creation, not against it. This isn't science or faith alone—it's both, intertwined."

Nearby, a simple wooden desk caught their attention. Its surface was cluttered with parchments and quills, as if Hildegard herself had just stepped away. The group approached cautiously, their footsteps muffled by the soft earth.

Michael picked up one of the parchments, his hands steady despite the strain of the moment. The Latin text was written in Hildegard's distinctive hand, her words as vivid and compelling as ever:

"Let no one who enters this place do so without reverence for the Creator's design. These plants are not mere objects for study or profit. They are living testimonies to the balance of life and the divine order. Beware, for greed corrupts even the most sacred of gifts."

Hana read over Michael's shoulder, her brow furrowing. "She knew this would be a temptation for people. That's why she hid it so carefully."

Gabriel's voice was somber. "And why Zentara can't be allowed to find it. If they exploit this knowledge…"

Michael set the parchment down gently. "It would be catastrophic. The very balance Hildegard sought to protect would be destroyed."

As they explored further, the group discovered a small altar at the far end of the chamber. Above it, a simple cross was carved into the stone, illuminated by a concentrated beam of sunlight. Beneath the cross lay a metal box, its surface etched with the same symbols that adorned the compass they had used to find the *Hortus Vitae*.

Michael opened the box carefully, revealing a set of vials filled with a dried golden powder, identical to the ones left to Hana in Armand's safe.

Gabriel peered closely at the vials. "It's more extract —likely from the *Ricinus aureum*. Hildegard must have been experimenting with its properties."

Michael held up one of the vials, the dried powder inside catching the light. "She described this in her writings. It's both a medicine and a warning. In the right hands, it can heal. In the wrong hands…"

"It could destroy," Hana finished, her voice heavy with understanding.

As they stood in silence, the heft of their discovery pressing upon them, a faint sound echoed through the chamber—the distant stumble of footsteps on the stones of the hillside above their heads.

Hana spun around, her instincts alert. "Zentara!" She spoke in an anxious whisper.

Gabriel looked panicked. "What do we do? We can't let them take this place."

Hana's eyes darted toward the entrance. "We've got the advantage. They don't know the entrance to the *Hortus Vitae*, but we do."

Michael nodded. They stood still, quiet, listening to the footfalls above them. A grunt and muffled curse bore witness to the difficulties of the person trying to negotiate the rocky hillside. Slowly, the sounds faded. Moments passed.

Gabriel glanced at Michael, his fear still evident. "They're gone. For now."

Michael's jaw tightened. "Then let's make sure they find nothing if they return."

As the foursome emerged into the fading light aboveground, they worked quietly to secure the stone seal, carefully spreading the vines back over it.

Together, they turned toward the abbey, knowing their journey was far from over. The *Hortus Vitae* had been unveiled, its secrets laid bare—but the fight to safeguard its treasures had only just begun.

THIRTY

The air above Rupertsberg Abbey shimmered with the autumn haze of late afternoon, golden sunlight cascading over the Rhine River. It cast a tranquil veil over the abbey's sprawling grounds, a deceptive calm in the face of mounting tension. Inside the abbey, Hana, Michael, Élise, and Brother Gabriel poured over a trove of ancient documents and botanical samples they had carried back with them from the *Hortus Vitae* chamber.

Hana straightened, brushing back a loose strand of her chestnut brown hair, her eyes narrowing as she scanned the faded Latin script. "This reference to *flos vitae*—the flower of life—it keeps appearing, but the details are maddeningly vague."

Brother Gabriel nodded solemnly. "Hildegard's writings often contained deliberate obfuscations, perhaps to deter those with ill intent. It's likely coded."

Michael leaned over, his eyes glinting with

determination. "Then we decode it. If Zentara is as close as we suspect, they'll exploit any advantage they can find. We can't afford to let this knowledge fall into their hands."

Their conversation was interrupted by the loud trill of Hana's phone. She retrieved it from the table, her brow furrowing as she read the incoming message. "Marcus, Karl, and Lukas are here."

Michael exhaled a breath of relief. "Good. Reinforcements couldn't have come at a better time."

The jet-black SUV wound up the cobblestone drive, its tinted windows reflecting the vibrant hues of the abbey's gardens. As the vehicle came to a stop, the doors opened, and Lukas stepped out first, his tall, broad-shouldered frame imposing even in the casual jacket he wore. Karl followed, his lithe figure radiating the calm efficiency of a man who had seen his share of crises.

From the rear passenger door, Marcus Russo emerged, his rugged face shadowed with a day's stubble, his leather satchel slung across his shoulder. He took a moment to take in the abbey, his archaeologist's eye sweeping over the ancient architecture. "Impressive," he murmured, his voice carrying a note of admiration. "It's like stepping into the twelfth century." He turned to Karl.

"Michael has a talent for dragging me into interesting scenarios. What's the situation?"

"Let's get inside," Karl replied, his tone firm. "Michael can brief us all."

Behind them, a truck pulled up, and Lukas stayed

behind a moment to direct it to a parking space. He then offered Sister Amalia instructions. Soon, the abbey grounds became a flurry of quiet but purposeful activity. Sister Amalia directed a group of nuns unloading crates of supplies, their habit-clad forms a curious sight against the backdrop of modern military-grade equipment being stowed for the property's protection.

The group gathered in a hastily assembled makeshift command center in the abbey's central hall. Maps of the surrounding region were pinned to the walls, alongside aerial photographs and a growing dossier of Zentara's known operatives. A laptop sat open on the central table, its screen displaying a live satellite feed.

Hana greeted the newcomers with a tight smile. "Welcome to the front line. It's not exactly the Vatican, but it has its charms."

Karl returned the smile briefly before turning serious. "We've intercepted communications suggesting Zentara's operatives are mobilizing in this area. The abbey is an obvious target. They'll want whatever's hidden here, especially after the sabotage at Élise's lab. We took it upon ourselves to order what we need for protection here."

"Intercepted?" Hana questioned, realizing what her cousin had said.

The two Swiss Guards grinned at each other. "Yeah," Karl explained. "It seems a guy named Tom had a bladder issue while at the airport and got bumped into by a would-be traveler in the men's room. Now we can pick up whatever is said when Tom is present, which isn't everything we need, but it's enough for now."

Michael grinned at these proactive allies and Marcus gave the guards a thumbs up. They had all worked together before, and Marcus was pleased his job as the Vatican's chief archaeologist had pulled him into some of Michael's endeavors at solving mysteries found in the Church's archives. He had only learned a bit from the Swiss Guards on the drive in and listened carefully to the current plans.

Standing by the map, Lukas pointed to several marked locations. "We studied the area online on our way here and identified potential ingress points based on the terrain. The abbey's defenses are minimal—low walls, dense foliage, and narrow access routes. We need to fortify these areas immediately. What about the local authorities?"

Gabriel and Michael glanced at each other. Gabriel answered, "We've discussed that, but it isn't the best idea—maybe even the worst. We both suspect the possibility that Zentara could have an operative, or at least paid helpers, on the force. Their type of financial incentives can be overpowering even for the best of men. Plus, considering the distance to the town, how few police are usually on duty, and needing a force in place for who knows how long, well, I don't think that is an option. That is one reason the Order of the Green Flame was founded centuries ago. Protecting the abbey is our one historical and immediate mission and our sole duty. I've called on my brothers, and they should be arriving shortly. I'll put them under your leadership if that works for you."

Karl gave a slight nod. "Of course."

"Good. Talk to Brother Mathias when they arrive."

Marcus leaned over the map, his expression thoughtful. "The abbey's history might work in our favor. If Zentara tries to breach it, they'll have to navigate terrain that hasn't changed much in centuries. With the right preparations, we can make it a nightmare for them."

Michael stepped forward, his calm demeanor grounding the room's charged energy. "Marcus, your expertise in medieval architecture could be crucial. If there are hidden passages or reinforced areas we can utilize, we need to know."

Marcus nodded. "I'll need to explore the abbey, but I can start right away."

Karl folded his arms, his piercing gaze sweeping over the group. "We don't have much time. Zentara's operatives could be here within the next twenty-four hours. We need to move quickly."

As dusk settled over the abbey, the preparations were in full swing. Lukas worked alongside monks of the Order of the Green Flame, who arrived quickly from the Disibodenberg Monastery. They were told the greenhouse was likely a primary target, and Brother Mathias, Gabriel's second-in-command, soon had the monks busy setting up motion sensors and portable cameras around the perimeter. Karl coordinated with Hana to establish a secure communications link with the Vatican, ensuring they could call for backup if necessary.

Marcus, guided by Sister Amalia, explored the abbey's older sections. He carried a flashlight, its beam slicing through the dim corridors as he examined the stonework and carvings. "This abbey is a masterpiece," he murmured. "The craftsmanship is exquisite—and practical. These walls are thicker than they appear, designed to withstand sieges."

Sister Amalia smiled faintly. "Hildegard von Bingen was a visionary, not only in her spiritual work but in ensuring this place would endure."

Back in the command center, Lukas approached Karl with a grim expression. "We've intercepted another transmission. Zentara's operatives are on the move, and they're heading straight for Rupertsberg."

Karl's jaw tightened. "How many?"

"At least a dozen, heavily armed," Lukas replied. "This isn't a simple reconnaissance mission. They're coming for the vault."

Michael, overhearing, joined them. "Then we need to be ready. They won't expect us to be prepared."

Karl glanced at Michael, his expression unwavering. "Let's make sure they regret underestimating us."

Night fell, cloaking the abbey in shadows as the team finalized their preparations. The once-tranquil sanctuary now bristled with silent vigilance, its defenders steeling themselves for the confrontation ahead. Michael and Hana stood side by side in the quiet of the abbey's library, their gazes fixed on the ancient documents spread before them.

"Do you think we're ready?" Hana asked softly.

Michael's expression was resolute. "We have to be. The stakes are too high."

Outside, the abbey's bells tolled the hour, their

somber tones echoing across the Rhine. The battle for Rupertsberg Abbey was about to begin.

THIRTY-ONE

T he abbey was cloaked in a quiet intensity as everyone manned a post, ready for whatever Zentara might bring. Candles flickered, their soft light tossing dancing shadows over the documents spread across the library's heavy oak table. Hana, Michael, Élise, Marcus, and Brother Gabriel worked in focused silence, deciphering another section of Hildegard's journal as they waited. The faint scent of old books and wax mingled with the acrid tang of ink as Élise meticulously sketched a diagram from the manuscript.

"This part," Hana murmured, her finger tracing an illuminated paragraph, "mentions something called *viridi arca*—the green ark."

"An ark of preserved seeds," Michael translated, leaning closer. His head jerked up, and he stared at the others.

All of them looked at him, eyes wide.

"Seeds!" Gabriel exclaimed. "Of course! Hildegard couldn't have grown the plant in the *Hortus Vitae* without seeds. And the plant we saw was blooming. Surely, she harvested seeds throughout her years nurturing the plants."

"And saved them for posterity," Hana finished. A grin started on her lips before a scowl followed. "So where are they?"

Michael bent again to the document, translating as quickly as he could, stumbling and backing up a time or two. Finally, he looked up.

"Translated, it says, '*Guarded in the chamber where life grows, within the gaze of men.*'" He looked up at Marcus. "That's not the *Hortus Vitae* that we've already discovered. It isn't within the sight of men."

"Are you sure it says 'within' and not 'outside'?" Marcus questioned.

Michael bent again, his fingers working the codex Gabriel had given him. "No, it is 'within the sight of men.' Which seems odd, don't you think? Hiding something so precious in clear sight?"

"The Purloined Letter," Élise said.

"Of course," Hana agreed. "Edgar Allan Poe's famous short story. It proved that sometimes keeping something precious in plain sight is the best way to hide it. No one thinks of looking for something out in the open that is supposed to be hidden."

Marcus, seated across from him, rubbed his stubbled jaw thoughtfully. "If Hildegard hid a cache of seeds in a chamber where life grows and in plain sight, that could mean the greenhouse I saw as we drove up or a similar space where plants could thrive."

Brother Gabriel tilted his head. "The greenhouse itself is relatively new, but it's built on the foundations of an older structure. It might still exist beneath it."

Michael nodded. "Then that's our next step. Marcus, you and I will check the greenhouse. Élise, keep working on the journal with Hana and Gabriel. If anything else comes up, let us know immediately."

Before anyone could respond, a piercing alarm shattered the calm. Everyone froze, their heads snapping toward the source of the sound. Hana's phone buzzed on the table, and she grabbed it, her face paling as she read the notification.

"The greenhouse security system," she said, her voice tense. "A tampering alert just went off. Someone's already inside."

The group moved swiftly through the abbey's darkened halls, their footsteps echoing against the stone. Outside, the night air was cool and brisk, the faint scent of damp earth rising from the gardens. Karl and Lukas met them near the greenhouse, both armed and alert.

"What's the situation?" Karl demanded, his voice low but commanding.

Hana handed him her phone. "The alert came from the east side. Motion detected inside, but no sign of forced entry."

Lukas frowned, scanning the surrounding area. "If they bypassed the locks without triggering them, they're professionals."

Marcus glanced at Michael. "Could be Zentara."

Michael's expression was grim. "We have to assume it is."

Karl signaled to Lukas, who moved toward the greenhouse's entrance, his movements fluid and silent. The rest of the group followed, their breaths visible in the cool air. The greenhouse loomed before them, its glass panes gleaming faintly in the moonlight. Inside, the shadows of plants stretched across the ground like skeletal fingers.

Lukas signaled for them to wait as he stepped inside, his flashlight cutting through the darkness. The others held their breath, their eyes straining to see through the glass. Moments later, Lukas reappeared, his face taut.

"No one's visible, but something's been disturbed," he reported. "Several trays of plants have been overturned, and a storage cabinet is open. Whoever was here may still be inside."

Karl nodded. "We move carefully. If they're here, we capture them and force the truth from them. If not, we'll have to determine what they were after."

Inside the greenhouse, the air was humid and unrelenting, the faint scent of soil and foliage mingling with a pungent, metallic tang that set everyone on edge. The group split up, their flashlights casting narrow beams over rows of plants, trellises, and workbenches.

Marcus examined the overturned trays, his fingers brushing the disturbed soil. "These plants were uprooted deliberately, not haphazardly. They were looking for something."

Hana crouched beside him, her eyes scanning the ground. "Whether they were after the *Ricinus aureum* plants or galls or seeds, they wouldn't find them here. As Gabriel explained, this greenhouse didn't exist in Hildegard's time."

Lukas's voice called out from the far end of the greenhouse. "Tracks. Someone left through the back door."

The group hurried to his side, their lights revealing faint footprints in the moist soil. One set led to a narrow door that opened onto the abbey grounds. Karl crouched, examining the prints.

"Boots, medium size, heading inside. No prints retreating," he muttered. "That means they are still inside." They all turned to look back inside, eyes fixed to detect any movement.

Karl and Lukas continued to move through the massive greenhouse like predators, their footfalls soundless on the stone floor. Behind them, Michael, Marcus, Hana, Gabriel, and Élise followed at a cautious distance, their breaths shallow as they scanned the darkened space for movement.

Karl raised a hand, signaling the group to stop. He crouched beside an overturned potting tray, his gloved fingers brushing the disturbed soil. "I think others are still in here," he murmured, his voice barely audible. He pointed to a faint smear of mud leading deeper into the greenhouse. "Split up. Lukas, take the right. Michael and Marcus, the left. Hana and Élise, stay back and cover the entrance."

Michael exchanged a glance with Marcus before nodding. "Everyone be careful."

The group fanned out, their flashlights slicing

through the darkness in narrow beams. The greenhouse, usually a haven of serene botanical study, now felt like a threatening labyrinth of shadows. Tall racks of plants created shifting silhouettes, their leaves trembling as if they, too, felt the tension.

Michael and Marcus moved along the left side, their footsteps light on the stone path. Marcus stopped suddenly, his eyes narrowing as he gestured toward a row of delicate vines. Several stems had been crushed when someone haphazardly rushed by.

A faint rustle drew their attention. Both men froze, their flashlights sweeping the area. Marcus pointed toward a shadow that shifted unnaturally near a cluster of ferns. Michael signaled for silence as they crept closer.

On the opposite side of the greenhouse, Karl and Lukas closed in on their own quarry. Lukas, his eyes scanning the rows of potted herbs, caught sight of a flicker of movement. He motioned to Karl, who nodded and circled wide to flank the target.

A sudden clatter broke the stillness as a metal watering can toppled from a shelf. The noise drew a sharp curse from the shadows, and a figure darted out, their form silhouetted briefly against the moonlit glass. Lukas lunged, his speed and precision honed by years of training. He tackled the intruder to the ground, pinning them with practiced ease.

"Got one!" Lukas called, his voice low but urgent.

Karl turned to assist, but another figure emerged from the darkness, wielding a metal pole like a weapon. Karl dodged the swing and countered with a swift strike to the attacker's wrist, disarming them. He twisted their arm behind their back and forced them to their knees.

"Two down," Karl growled. "But I doubt they're alone."

Hana and Élise waited near the entrance, their nerves stretched taut. Hana gripped her phone, ready to alert the others if anything went wrong. Élise clutched a flashlight in one hand and a small spray bottle of ethanol in the other—a makeshift defense, but it was better than nothing.

A sudden crash from deeper inside the greenhouse made them both jump. Hana's heart raced as she strained to see through the rows of plants. "Stay close," she whispered to Élise, who nodded, her face pale but determined.

Their tension mounted as footsteps approached. Hana tightened her grip on her phone, ready to call for help, but the figure that emerged from the shadows was Marcus. His expression was urgent.

"We think there are more," Marcus said quietly. "Stay here and stay alert."

He disappeared back into the greenhouse before Hana could respond.

The confrontation reached its peak near the greenhouse's center. Michael and Marcus caught sight of two more intruders, their dark clothing blending with the shadows. One carried a canvas bag likely filled with stolen samples, while the other was crouched near a rack of vials, examining labels with a flashlight.

Michael gestured for Marcus to circle around as he approached from the opposite side. Timing their movements perfectly, they pounced. Michael tackled the figure with the bag, knocking them off balance, while Marcus grabbed the other by the wrist, forcing them to drop their flashlight.

A struggle ensued, the quiet greenhouse erupting into grunts and the sound of shuffling feet. One of the intruders lashed out, shoving a shelf of plants to the ground in an effort to escape. Trays crashed to the floor, soil and fragile leaves scattering across the stone.

"Watch out!" Marcus shouted as a heavy pot teetered on the edge of a nearby table. Michael barely managed to dodge as it shattered centimeters from where he had been standing.

Karl and Lukas arrived moments later, securing the remaining intruders with zip ties. The team stood over the subdued operatives, their breaths heavy, as they surveyed the damage.

The aftermath was sobering. Broken pots, crushed plants, and spilled soil littered the greenhouse floor. Élise knelt beside a particularly delicate vine, her fingers trembling as she examined its snapped stem.

"This is a disaster," she whispered. "Some of these plants are irreplaceable."

Marcus crouched beside her, his expression sympathetic. "We'll salvage what we can. Zentara didn't get away with anything, and we've secured their operatives. That's a win."

"It doesn't feel like one," Élise murmured, her eyes shining with unshed tears.

Lukas spoke up, "They aren't the best trained, but

they do have military-grade equipment. Zentara doesn't do things halfway."

Marcus swore under his breath. "Which means they'll send more operatives. It's just a matter of time."

Michael gathered the team near the greenhouse entrance. "This was a close call, but Marcus is right—it won't be the last. Zentara knows we're here, and they're not going to stop."

Karl folded his arms, his expression grim. "Then we dig in. Fortify the abbey, double the patrols, and stay vigilant. We can't afford any more losses."

Hana looked at the wreckage in the greenhouse, her jaw tightening. "And we find Hildegard's *viridi arca*—the green ark. Whatever's in there could be the key to ending this."

Michael nodded, determination hardening his gaze. "Then we work fast. Zentara won't give us another chance."

Outside, the first light of dawn began to creep over the horizon, casting the abbey in hues of gold and crimson. The battle for Rupertsberg was far from over.

THE INTRUDERS WOULDN'T TALK, which was no surprise, and the team wasn't inclined to call the local authorities until later that morning. While Karl and Lukas took their prisoners to a heavily fortified locked room inside the abbey, with a couple of the monks guarding it, the rest of the team returned to the greenhouse, the air inside heavy with tension. Hana flipped through Hildegard's journal, her movements laced with frustration. "Whoever they were, they're getting closer. We're running out of time."

Marcus placed a steadying hand on her shoulder. "We'll find it. Let's focus."

Michael leaned over the table, his eyes scanning the manuscript. "The key hidden in plain sight… It has to be in the greenhouse, connected to the remains of the original greenhouse Hildegard used."

Élise, her voice soft but firm, spoke up. "What if the key isn't physical? Hildegard often used symbolism—light, shadow, patterns in nature. What if we're looking for something conceptual?"

The room fell silent as her words sank in. Then Marcus straightened, his face alight with realization. "The vines."

Hana blinked. "What?"

"The vines etched into the stone near the greenhouse," Marcus explained. "I noticed them when Sister Amalia showed me the abbey. I'm thinking they're not just decorative. They're a map—or a clue. Hildegard was known for weaving messages into her surroundings."

Michael grabbed a flashlight. "Then we need to examine them. Now."

Outside, the abbey's bells tolled early morning, their solemn chimes echoing across the Rhine. The group hurried to the greenhouse's outer wall, where Marcus directed his flashlight over the intricate carvings. The vines twisted and coiled, their patterns mesmerizing.

"There," he said, pointing to a cluster of symbols nestled among the leaves. "It's another constellation."

Hana's breath hitched. "And constellations were often used as markers—guides to something hidden."

Michael traced the symbols with his fingers. "If we align these with the layout of the abbey…"

Hana opened up a copy of the abbey layout she had been carrying throughout their searches and held it up, turning it so its major features fit the constellation made by the symbols in the vine etchings. Once aligned, the remaining symbols on the stone wall pointed to one location… but they realized it was simply the very location where they stood.

"Oh, fine! We'd just pinpointed where we already stand," Hana spat in frustration, jabbing her finger to that spot on the wall, but jumped back when the stone gave way at her touch. A section of the wall shifted, revealing a narrow passage leading to a wooden door. The group exchanged tense glances before Michael stepped forward, his expression resolute.

"Okay. We've found the opening to the *viridi arca* chamber," he said. "Now behind this door we need to see what Hildegard was hiding."

THIRTY-TWO

The early morning light filtered through the intricate stained-glass windows of Rupertsberg Abbey, casting vibrant colors across the stone walls of the hallway leading to the greenhouse. The abbey hummed with a serenity that seemed almost at odds with the team's current mission. Michael, Hana, Marcus, and Élise, now equipped with more flashlights, notebooks, and tools, gathered again at the opening in the stone wall that housed a small wooden door Marcus had identified near the greenhouse.

"This is it," Marcus said, his voice low but resolute as he knelt to examine the ancient wood. The carvings on the door—an intricate pattern of vines and flowers intertwined with Latin script—seemed to echo Hildegard's teachings on the unity of faith and nature.

Michael knelt beside him, his hand brushing over the worn surface. "It's more than decorative. Look at the way these symbols align. They're forming a coded prayer."

Hana leaned closer, notebook in hand. "A prayer? Or a set of instructions?" She pointed to a faint indentation beneath one of the vines. "Could this be a keyhole?"

Marcus nodded, already pulling a small brass key from his satchel. Sister Amalia had entrusted it to them, explaining it was found among Hildegard's relics. With a gentle turn, the key clicked into place, and the door creaked open, releasing a faint, earthy scent that had been sealed away for centuries beyond the stone steps that faced them.

"Here we go," Michael said, stepping back to let the others enter.

The steps were narrow but extended deep into the stone foundation of the current greenhouse and opened to a small chamber. Dust motes danced in the beams of their flashlights, illuminating shelves carved into the rock, each lined with clay jars and small wooden boxes. The air was heavy with the aroma of dried herbs and old parchment.

"Seeds!" Élise whispered, her voice reflecting awe. She reached for one of the clay jars, carefully wiping away the grime to reveal an inscription. "This one… *Ricinus aureum*."

Michael's breath caught as he read the name over her shoulder. "Hildegard's golden castor plant."

Hana's fingers flew over her notebook, documenting every detail. "This could change everything. If these seeds are viable…"

Élise opened the jar. Inside, dozens of small, golden

brown seeds lay nestled like treasures. "It's impossible to know their condition until we test them, but the fact that they've been stored here, sealed away... it's remarkable."

Marcus, meanwhile, was inspecting the walls and floor of the chamber. His flashlight revealed faint carvings near the back. "Over here," he called, his voice echoing slightly. "I think I've found something."

The others joined him, their lights converging on a small plaque embedded in the stone. The Latin inscription read:

In manus Dei vitae redivivae. Solum purum, caelum serenum, et fides immutata requiruntur.

Michael translated aloud. "Into the hands of God, life renewed. Pure soil, clear skies, and unwavering faith are required."

Hana scribbled the phrase into her notebook. "It's almost like a formula," she murmured.

Michael nodded, his eyes scanning the plaque. "This isn't just about growing a plant; it's about creating the conditions for it to thrive."

"Which means," Marcus added, "we need to find more than just the seeds. We need the exact conditions she described. Soil composition, temperature, even the timing could be critical."

Élise frowned. "That soil might not exist anymore. And if it does, we'll need to analyze it meticulously to replicate it."

"Oh, but it does," Hana said. "Remember the full-grown specimen in the *Hortus Vitae*? Surely, the soil it grows in will tell us what we need to know."

Before they could respond, Hana's phone buzzed. She glanced at the screen, and unease flickered across her face. "It's Karl. He says there's movement near the abbey. Zentara might be closer than we thought."

Michael's jaw tightened. "We need to secure these findings now. If Zentara gets their hands on this, they'll try to weaponize it somehow."

"Agreed," Marcus said, stepping back from the plaque. "Hana, Élise, you handle documenting everything here. Michael and I will check the greenhouse for vulnerabilities. We'll need to make sure there's no way Zentara can access this chamber."

Élise nodded, already pulling out her portable analysis kit. "I can take preliminary samples for testing. The more we know about these seeds, the better we can protect them."

"I'll help with the notes," Hana said, positioning herself near the shelves. "Let's make this airtight."

Michael and Marcus exited the chamber, their footsteps fading as they ascended the stairs. The tension in the air was palpable as Hana and Élise worked in focused silence. Every seed, jar, and inscription was carefully documented and photographed. Hana's fingers flew over her keyboard, while Élise's precise movements ensured no detail was overlooked.

After nearly an hour, Marcus's voice crackled over the walkie-talkie. "Michael and I have secured the greenhouse. Karl's spotted movement outside the abbey. We're locking it down."

Hana grabbed the speaker. "Understood. We're finishing up here. Be ready to move if Zentara gets too close."

"Copy that," Marcus replied.

As the chamber fell silent again, Hana glanced at Élise. "We're out of time. Let's conceal what we can here and move the most critical items to a safer location."

Élise nodded, carefully resealing the jars and replacing them on the shelves. Hana photographed the remaining documents, then tucked them into a secure bag. Together, they worked quickly, their movements deliberate but unhurried.

As they finished, Hana's gaze lingered on the ancient plaque. The cryptic phrases, the delicate balance of science and faith—it all felt like pieces of a puzzle still waiting to be solved. She suspected this discovery was only the beginning.

"Hana," Élise said, breaking her reverie. "We need to go."

Hana nodded, securing her bag and stepping toward the door. As they ascended the stairs, the consequence of their discovery pressed heavily on her mind. The seeds, the soil, the ritual—it all pointed to a deeper truth about Hildegard's work and its place in the modern world.

The abbey above was quiet, but the tension was unmistakable. Karl and Lukas stood guard near the greenhouse, their sharp eyes scanning the surrounding woods. Michael and Marcus emerged from the far side of the courtyard, their expressions grim.

"We're secure for now," Michael said, his voice

steady, as Marcus hurried over to move the stone wall back in place to hide the wooden door. "But Zentara won't give up easily. We need to stay vigilant."

Hana glanced back toward the greenhouse and then to the team. "We have something worth protecting," she said firmly. "And we'll do whatever it takes to keep it safe."

The others nodded, their resolve evident in their faces.

THIRTY-THREE

The makeshift lab, nestled in a quiet corner of Rupertsberg Abbey's expansive grounds, was a blend of ancient reverence and modern practicality. Wooden beams arched overhead, a testament to centuries of craftsmanship, while a computer and some lab equipment lined the countertops, humming softly in the background. The air carried the faint aroma of herbs and chemicals, a fitting backdrop for the groundbreaking work being done within.

Élise Gauthier stood at the center of it all, her focus razor-sharp as she adjusted the settings on a high-powered microscope. A delicate glass slide rested beneath the lens, holding a minute sample of golden granules extracted from one of the *Ricinus aureum* seeds. She worked with the precision of an artisan, her gloved hands moving fluidly between instruments as she recorded her findings.

Hana and Michael watched from a nearby table, their expressions a mix of anticipation and anxiety. Marcus leaned against the wall, his arms crossed as he studied Élise's every move. The tension in the room was palpable; they all understood the stakes.

"Anything?" Hana finally asked, her voice breaking the silence.

Élise didn't look up, her eyes fixed on the monitor displaying a magnified view of the sample. "There's definitely something here," she murmured. "The structure of these compounds… it's unlike anything I've seen in modern botany. It's incredibly complex, almost engineered."

Michael stepped closer, his curiosity piqued. "Engineered? Are you suggesting Hildegard manipulated these seeds somehow?"

Élise shook her head. "Not intentionally. But the way these compounds are arranged… it's as if nature itself refined them for a very specific purpose. This plant was more than just a medicinal herb. It was something extraordinary."

Hana leaned forward, her notebook open and pen poised. "But are the seeds viable? Can they grow?"

At this, Élise's expression darkened. She picked up a handheld scanner, running it over one of the seeds.

"The seeds appear biologically intact," she said, her tone cautious. "But dormant for now. There is no way of knowing if they're just waiting for the right conditions, as all seeds do through a winter or dry period. Or if they're beyond germination…"

Marcus pushed off the wall. "Due to age?"

Élise sat back, setting the scanner down. "That's what I would have thought at first. But their chemical integrity is far too well-preserved for something this old. Maybe it is wishful thinking, but it's almost as if they're waiting for a very specific condition to activate."

Michael's eyes narrowed. "And you think Hildegard knew what that condition was."

"She must have," Élise replied, turning to the open pages of Hildegard's journal spread out on the lab table. Her finger traced the elegant Latin script. "Here are the clues: *matris novae lucis*; Mother's new light. And *terra vitae*; Life-giving soil. She's explicit about it. The seeds require a particular type of soil to grow, one that's enriched in ways we don't fully understand yet."

"This section here corroborates that," Marcus said, his voice low but urgent, pointing to a line of Latin scrawled in Hildegard von Bingen's distinctive hand. "It mentions something about altering the environment to mimic the plant's natural growth conditions. It's encoded, but the phrasing suggests she had a way to speed up *Ricinus aureum*'s development."

Using a magnifying glass, Michael leaned closer to the parchment. The intricate illustrations of vines and feathery red flowers seemed almost alive under the golden light. His finger traced a set of symbols at the edge of the page. "These patterns—they're not just decorative. They correspond to the phases of the moon. It's a timing mechanism."

Marcus frowned, scribbling notes in a battered journal. "A lunar calendar? That's not just science; that's a spiritual practice. The lunar phases, in fact, are the method by which the Church determines each year's date for Easter."

"Exactly," Michael replied. "Hildegard blended the two seamlessly. If we follow these phases and her instructions, we could cultivate *Ricinus aureum* quickly and ensure it remains viable."

Élise said, "Here." She grabbed a book from a nearby shelf, thumbed through it quickly, and then looked up. "Remember the clue of 'Mother's new light' in her journal? I've been thinking about that. Planting by the moon has been traditional since long before Hildegard's time. I'm guessing that phrase means planting at the time of the new moon. Which"—she pointed at the opened page in the almanac—"is the day after tomorrow at eight in the evening."

Hana scribbled furiously in her notebook. "What do we know about this soil, though? Does she describe its composition?"

Élise shook her head. "Not directly. She uses poetic language—'soil kissed by divine breath,' 'purified by fire and water,' things like that. But we can infer some elements. It's not just about nutrients; it's about balance. The soil has to be pure and harmonious, as if it's a living entity itself."

Michael rubbed his chin thoughtfully. "So, we're looking for a soil that's rare, possibly unique, and somehow tied to her spiritual beliefs. And we need to find it in two days. That's a tall order."

Marcus grinned. "We have some of that soil."

Élise turned to him. "Where… oh, but of course! The live plant in the *Hortus Vitae*!" Then she paused. "Only we would need enough of it and, honestly, from what little I saw of that plant and its plot of soil, I wouldn't want to jeopardize taking much at all from it. The very fact that it has lived this long means it thrives on a very delicate balance, one we don't dare disturb."

"Can't we take enough just for you to analyze?"

"Yes, but that won't be enough to get us far in trying to grow the seeds. We really need a supply of it, and I fear it's an organic mix that must be cultivated and matured over time, not just chemicals mixed together. Remember, Hildegard called it 'kissed by divine breath.'"

Hana suddenly froze, her pen hovering over her notebook. "Kissed by divine breath?" Her mind raced back to Geneva, to the greenhouse her grandfather had maintained with such care. The soil there had always struck her as unusual, rich and almost luminous under certain lights. And when she had asked him why it was so special and he told her it was kissed by divine breath. She had laughed at the time, had dismissed it as part of the greenhouse's meticulous upkeep, and her grandfather's poetic nature. But now…

"Wait," she said, her voice urgent. "The greenhouse at my grandfather's estate. The soil there… it's different. I always thought it was just well-maintained, and he used that very term for it. Could he have known the soil formula? Or could it have been handed down for generations? What if it's *terra vitae*?"

Élise's head snapped up. "In your grandfather's greenhouse?"

Hana nodded. "It was his sanctuary, almost like a shrine. He had plants there I've never seen anywhere else. And the soil… it always seemed almost alive."

Michael's eyes lit up with realization. "If your grandfather knew about Hildegard's work, he might have been cultivating the right conditions all along."

Marcus crossed his arms, his gaze becoming more acute. "Do you think he left any records? Notes about the soil's composition or its origins?"

"Maybe," Hana said. "I didn't find anything obvious when I first explored the estate papers, but I wasn't looking for anything related to soil composition. If it's there, I'll find it."

Élise grabbed a nearby bag, already preparing to pack the seeds and tools for transport. "If there's even a chance your grandfather's soil matches Hildegard's description, we need to test it. I can run a full analysis once we get there."

Michael stepped forward, his expression resolute. "We can't waste time. Zentara's already shown they're willing to go to any lengths to obtain the plants. By now, they know Italy was a ploy. And they've already attempted a break-in of the abbey's greenhouse."

Hana's jaw tightened. "Then let's get going."

As THE TEAM gathered their materials, a quiet determination settled over them. The pieces of

Hildegard's secrets were slowly falling into place, but the path ahead was fraught with challenges. The prospect of *terra vitae* offered hope, but it also raised new questions about how deeply her knowledge had been preserved and passed down.

Minutes later, they stepped out of the lab into the abbey's tranquil courtyard. The sun was beginning to dip below the horizon, casting a warm golden glow over the ancient stone walls. Karl and Lukas were stationed near the entrance, their watchful eyes scanning the perimeter, as a few monks appeared in prayer at various benches, their robes hiding their weapons.

"We're heading to Geneva," Michael informed them. "The next piece of the puzzle might be there."

Karl nodded, his expression grim. "I'll let Gabriel know. We'll hold things down here. Zentara's been quiet for now, but that could change any moment."

"Stay vigilant," Marcus said. "If anything happens, you know how to reach us."

As Hana and the others made their way to the waiting vehicle, she felt a renewed sense of purpose. The memory of her grandfather's greenhouse loomed large in her mind, a place she had always associated with quiet reflection but now saw as a potential key to unlocking Hildegard's greatest secret.

She glanced at Michael, who met her gaze with a small, reassuring smile. "We're close," he said softly.

Hana nodded, clutching her notebook tightly. "Let's hope we're not too late."

The car pulled away from the abbey, its headlights

cutting through the encroaching darkness. Behind them, Rupertsberg stood as a silent sentinel, guarding the secrets of a bygone era. Ahead, the team faced the unknown, driven by the belief that Hildegard's legacy was worth every risk they took to protect it.

THIRTY-FOUR

T he gentle hum of the jet engines filled the cabin as Hana's private aircraft cut through the clouds over Frankfurt, heading toward Geneva. Hana had called the estate's security chief from the jet and explained the situation, telling him to increase their detail to monitor the estate's perimeter. Despite the luxurious leather seats and the serene view of a sunset stretching across the horizon, the atmosphere inside was anything but relaxed. Michael, Marcus, and Hana were deep in discussion over Hildegard's writings, while Élise reviewed her notes on the *Ricinus aureum* seeds and the enigmatic "*terra vitae.*"

"If this soil matches Hildegard's description, it could explain how your grandfather managed to cultivate such rare plants," Michael said, leaning forward. "But why would he keep it a secret?"

Hana frowned, staring out the window for a moment before turning back to the group. "My grandfather was a meticulous man. He loved mysteries and took pride in preserving the family's legacy. If he knew about Hildegard's work, he might have seen it as something too valuable to share, or too dangerous."

Marcus tapped the table with his pen thoughtfully. "The Saint-Clairs have a long history of safeguarding artifacts and knowledge. It wouldn't be surprising if he felt this was part of that responsibility."

Élise looked up from her tablet, her expression determined. "Whatever his reasons, we need to focus on analyzing that soil. If it's truly *terra vitae*, it could be the key to reviving those seeds." She had taken a small soil sample from the massive plant in the *Hortus Vitae* and planned to compare it to Hana's grandfather's "potting soil" as soon as they arrived.

As the jet descended into Geneva's private airstrip, Hana couldn't shake the unease settling in her chest. Her grandfather's home had always been a place of comfort, a refuge from the chaos of the world. But now, it felt like a puzzle she was only beginning to understand.

THE SAINT-CLAIR ESTATE loomed ahead as the team's car wound through the tree-lined driveway. The grand manor, with its ivy-covered walls and intricate wrought iron gates, exuded an air of timeless elegance. Hana's memories of playing in the sprawling gardens as a child came flooding back, but the gravity of their mission tempered her nostalgia.

"This place is incredible," Marcus said as they got out of the car. "It's like stepping into another century."

"It's always felt like its own world," Hana replied, leading them toward the greenhouse nestled in the eastern corner of the estate. The glass structure shimmered in the late afternoon light, its panes catching the golden hues of the setting sun.

Inside, the air was warm and fragrant, filled with the scent of blooming orchids, citrus trees, and exotic plants. Hana paused, her gaze sweeping over the rows of meticulously arranged flora. "He spent more time here than anywhere else. It was his sanctuary."

Élise's eyes lit up as she surveyed the space. "This is remarkable. Some of these species are incredibly rare."

Michael moved toward the central planter, where a patch of soil stood out amidst the surrounding greenery. It was darker, richer, with a faint shimmer that seemed almost unnatural. "This must be it," he said, kneeling to inspect it.

"Let's find out," Élise said, pulling out her portable analysis kit. She knelt beside Michael, scooping a small sample of soil into a vial. Her hands moved with practiced efficiency as she prepared the sample for testing, adding reagents and placing it under a handheld microscope. She did the same for the sample she had taken from the *Hortus Vitae*.

The rest of the team watched in silence as Élise worked. Minutes stretched into what felt like hours until she finally leaned back, a look of astonishment on her face.

"It's a match," she said, her voice flushed with awe.

"The composition is almost identical to what that plant is thriving on in the *Hortus Vitae*. The balance of minerals, organic matter, even trace elements of volcanic ash—it's all here. This is *terra vitae*."

Hana let out a breath she hadn't realized she was holding. "He knew. He must have."

Michael's gaze softened as he placed a hand on her shoulder. "Your grandfather understood the importance of preserving this. It's thanks to him that we're even this close to unlocking Hildegard's work."

Marcus's eyes narrowed as he examined the surrounding plants. "But why stop here? If he had the soil, why didn't he attempt to grow more?"

"Maybe he didn't have the seeds," Michael suggested. "Or maybe he didn't understand their significance."

"Remember, however," Élise cautioned, "the soil alone isn't enough. We need to control the temperature, humidity, and probably other variables we haven't identified yet."

Hana nodded, a tangle of thoughts coiling tightly in her mind. "We'll do whatever it takes. This greenhouse has all the equipment we'll need. We can make it work."

Michael's face darkened slightly. "We also need to be cautious. Zentara's not going to stop looking for us. If they find out what we've discovered here…"

"Then we make sure they don't," Hana said firmly. "They don't even know we've discovered the seeds, let alone the right soil. This estate is private and secure. My grandfather's security systems are still active. We'll double-check everything and keep this under wraps."

Marcus exchanged a glance with Michael. "We'll need to work quickly. The longer we're here, the greater the risk."

Élise began packing up her tools, her expression resolute. "I'll start designing the growth conditions based on Hildegard's notes and what we know about the soil. But we'll need to test it step by step. There's no room for error."

As the team prepared to secure the greenhouse and set up their test planting for the next night, the sun dipped lower, leaving long shadows across the grounds. The air was charged with a mix of urgency and determination, each member driven by the significance of their discovery.

But as they worked, a faint unease lingered. Somewhere in the distance, unseen forces were undoubtedly moving against them, and the secrets of the Saint-Clair estate had drawn a dangerous spotlight.

"So, they still have that plant, eh? And seeds now as well?" Christophe Vaux's eyes glistened with the promise of success. It was about time his mole paid off with something substantial.

He wanted to tell Blackthorn, but not yet. Not until he had what that man wanted in his hand. He just needed a bit more time first.

He picked up the phone again and started the calls to mobilize two teams this time. He knew now where that live plant had been hidden, in something called the *Hortus Vitae*, and the team sent there had strict instructions to preserve the plant at all costs, bringing back a living sample of what Blackthorn so desperately wanted. Whatever galls they could inflict on it with insects or other irritants would be immediately useful for Zentara's experiments.

His spy didn't know the reason Sinclair's team had flown to her estate in Geneva, but he knew they had taken the seeds. That was all Vaux needed to know.

The second team he sent also had orders, and once they confiscated the seeds, he made it clear that nothing should be left behind.

No pristine estate on the hill.

No living witnesses.

THIRTY-FIVE

The Saint-Clair home was bathed in the soft glow of the Geneva twilight, its manicured lawns and towering trees throwing long shadows under the fading light. Hana had called the compound's security chief from her jet and explained the situation, telling him to increase their detail to monitor the estate's perimeter. Now safely inside the greenhouse, extra security already in place, Hana, Michael, Marcus, and Élise worked in tense but focused silence, their attention concentrated on Hildegard's seeds.

Hana's phone vibrated on the nearby workstation, jolting her from her thoughts. The message was from one of her estate's security staff: "**Unusual activity detected near the south perimeter**."

"It's starting," she murmured, her voice tight with concern.

Michael glanced up from his notes. "Zentara?"

"Most likely," Hana replied, tucking her phone into her pocket. "They've been circling ever since we got here. The security team is investigating."

Marcus set down his magnifying glass and moved closer. "If they're already at the estate's perimeter, it's only a matter of time before they try something more direct."

Élise nodded, her expression grim. "We need to secure the soil and seeds. Zentara won't stop until they've taken everything."

Michael placed a hand on Hana's shoulder, his steady presence grounding her. "We'll protect what we've found. But you need to stay vigilant. As Armand's, and therefore Hildegard's, only living familial heir, you still pose a legal threat to them as well. Zentara isn't just after Hildegard's work; they're trying to break you, too."

Hana's jaw tightened, her resolve hardening. "Let them try. They'll find I'm not so easily broken."

AT GERMANY'S RUPERTSBERG ABBEY, the atmosphere was no less tense. Karl and Lukas, stationed at the abbey's eastern gate, surveyed the wooded area surrounding the grounds. A few hours earlier, one of the Green Flame monks had reported seeing unfamiliar figures near the outer fence, and both men had been on high alert ever since. Monks covered various positions over the abbey's acreage, but the property was large, and access points were too many.

Karl adjusted the strap of his rifle, scanning the

shadows for movement. Lukas saw his partner's action and said, his tone low, "We're ready for them, Karl. They won't breach these walls."

The Zentara radio, taken from one of the prisoners and now clipped to Karl's vest, crackled to life. "Heading to the slope left off the north chapel entrance," a voice reported.

Karl and Lukas exchanged a look, their expressions grim. Without a word, they moved quickly and quietly toward the north chapel, their footsteps muffled against the stone path. As they approached, Karl signaled for Lukas to take the left flank while he advanced from the right.

The chapel's silhouette loomed in the darkness, its stained-glass windows glinting faintly under the moonlight. Karl's eyes swept over the area, his pulse steady as he tightened his grip on his weapon. The sound of gravel crunching, then rocks slipping underfoot, came from just beyond the north entrance.

Lukas moved silently, positioning himself to cut off any potential breach. Karl raised a hand, signaling for Lukas to hold position, then stepped forward. "Come out slowly," he called, his voice firm but controlled. "You're surrounded."

For a moment, there was only silence. Then, a figure emerged from the shadows, their hands raised. The intruder was clad in black tactical gear, their face partially obscured by a mask. Karl's eyes narrowed as he recognized the emblem stitched onto their shoulder —Zentara.

"Identify yourself," Karl demanded, keeping his weapon trained on the operative.

The intruder remained silent, their posture rigid.

Lukas moved in from the side, securing the operative's hands with zip ties. "You've got a lot to answer for," he muttered, patting the operative down for weapons or equipment.

As they escorted the operative toward the abbey's secure area, Karl's mind raced. They had apprehended the man at the rocky slope that led to the entrance to the *Hortus Vitae*. This was no coincidence and no frontal team assault but reconnaissance by one person, for now. Zentara knew too much, but how? Only one thing was certain. Whatever they were planning, it was escalating.

Back at the estate in Geneva, the tension reached a boiling point. Hana, Michael, Marcus, and Élise gathered in the central office, poring over security footage of the perimeter. The monitors displayed grainy images of figures lurking in the shadows just beyond the gates.

"They're testing us," Michael said, his voice tight. "Looking for weaknesses."

"They won't find any," Hana replied, her fingers flying across the keyboard as she enhanced the footage. "The estate's defenses are top-of-the-line, and I've reinforced everything since we arrived."

Élise leaned closer to the screen. "This isn't just about reconnaissance. Look at their equipment. They're prepared for extraction. They mean to take something."

A flicker of menace settled over Marcus's features. "We need to act fast. If they breach the perimeter, they could do more damage than just stealing the seeds. They'll destroy everything we've worked for."

As Hana prepared to alert the estate's security team, her phone buzzed. She glanced at the screen, her breath catching as she read the message:

"You have something that belongs to us. Surrender the seeds, or the world will learn every secret your family has worked so hard to hide."

The message was unsigned, but the implication was clear. Zentara's CEO had made their move.

"Hana?" Michael asked, noticing the color drain from her face.

She held up the phone, the screen glowing with the damning text. "They know about the seeds. And they're threatening to expose my family's secrets." She stared at him in both bewilderment and fear.

Michael took the phone, reading the message carefully before handing it to Marcus. "Do you know what they're talking about?"

Hana hesitated, her mind swirling over the nine decades of her grandfather's life: his undercover actions in the war, his rise to financial power, his connections worldwide. What secrets did he have? What bargains were struck or compromises made to become a leader of nations and a financial powerhouse? Suddenly, all the years of his tender hand on her head and then on her shoulder and then backing her every career move… all tainted by this evil man's threats of exposing truths she likely couldn't bear.

"Hana?" Michael pressed.

She looked up, aware she had held silent too long. "No! No, I know of nothing, but…" Her hand shook as she held the phone away from her as if to insulate herself from some unforgivable truth.

"Hana, listen to me," Michael took her hand, removed the phone, and stepped up to hold her. "They're bluffing. Zentara's power lies in its own secrecy. If they go public, they risk exposing themselves, too."

Hana's hands clenched into fists. "But what if they're not bluffing? What if they've already uncovered something they can use against us?"

Élise stepped forward, her voice steady and calm. "Then we fight back with the truth. Zentara thrives on fear and manipulation. If we show the world who they really are, their threats will lose their power."

Hana nodded, her resolve hardening. She thought of the hard-edged young man her grandfather had been, defying Nazi aggression at every turn. "Then that's what we'll do. They want a fight? We'll give them one."

Michael placed a reassuring hand on her shoulder. "Zentara won't win."

As the team prepared for what was certain to be a battle on multiple fronts, the shadows outside the estate seemed to grow darker. Zentara's presence loomed large, but within the walls of the Saint-Clair estate and the abbey at Rupertsberg, a light of determination burned bright. They would protect Hildegard's mission —and their own—no matter the cost.

THIRTY-SIX

E ight o'clock at night and the Saint-Clair greenhouse was silent but for the faint hum of grow lights and the occasional rustle of leaves. The air was heavy with anticipation as Hana and Michael stood before the central workstation, its surface meticulously arranged with Hildegard's journal, a basin of water, and an assortment of tools. In the heart of the greenhouse, a patch of *terra vitae* soil cradled in a planter awaited the culmination of their efforts.

"We've prepared everything exactly as Hildegard described," Michael said, his voice low. "But this isn't just about following instructions. There's a spiritual element to her process, a connection we need to honor."

Hana nodded, glancing at the open journal. The Latin text glowed softly under the lights, its elegant script a blend of scientific precision and poetic devotion. "She believed the act of renewal was as much about faith as it was about science," she said. "Let's hope we can live up to her expectations."

Michael stepped close, holding the journal in one hand and a small vial of purified water in the other. "The ritual begins with purification. Hildegard emphasized the importance of sanctifying both the environment and ourselves before attempting to awaken the seeds."

He dipped his fingers into the water and made the sign of the cross over himself, then over Hana. She mirrored his actions, her movements steady despite the significance of the moment. Together, they approached the soil patch, where Michael sprinkled the remaining water over its surface.

"*In mater novo veritatis lumine, vita crescit,*" Michael intoned, reading from the journal. "In the mother's new light of truth, life grows."

Hana repeated the phrase, her voice firm. She reached for a small container of ash, another element described in Hildegard's text. "She said the ash represents the trials the seeds have endured. It's a reminder of the strength required to bring new life."

Carefully, Hana scattered the ash across the soil, watching as it blended seamlessly into the dark, fertile earth. Michael followed with a mixture of crushed herbs and minerals, each chosen and detailed in the journal for its symbolic significance—resilience, harmony, and vitality.

The final step was the seed itself. Hana retrieved one of the precious *Ricinus aureum* seeds from its protective container, cradling it in her palm as if it were the most delicate of treasures. The seed's golden-brown surface shimmered faintly, almost as if it held a light of its own.

"This is it," she said, her voice barely above a whisper.

Michael nodded, his expression solemn. "Place it in the soil. Slowly, deliberately. Hildegard believed the act of planting was a form of prayer."

Hana bent to the soil, her hands trembling slightly as she pressed the seed into the earth. She covered it gently, her fingers lingering for a moment before pulling away.

"Now we wait," Michael said, stepping back. He looked up through the greenhouse's glass wall at the darkening sky. The others followed his gaze. A faint crescent of the new moon rose over the horizon, signaling a new cycle of time and, hopefully, a new cycle of life. "And we trust."

Élise nodded. "If these conditions are correct, we should see early signs of growth within a few days," she said.

As they locked the greenhouse for the night, the faint glow of the grow lights illuminated the soil, a silent promise of the life it might one day bring forth. But in the shadows beyond the estate's gates, a storm was already brewing.

THE HOURS that followed were a study in patience and hope. Marcus joined them in the greenhouse, having documented every detail of the process for the Vatican archives. He photographed the soil, the seed, and the steps outlined in Hildegard's journal, his notes meticulous and exhaustive.

"This could be the ticket," Marcus said as he adjusted the focus on his camera for yet another photo. "If this works, it'll be the first successful cultivated germination of a *Ricinus aureum* seed by humans in centuries."

"If it works," Hana echoed, her eyes fixed on the soil. "We're putting a lot of faith in an ancient text and a handful of clues."

"Hildegard's work has proven reliable so far," Michael said. "She understood the balance between the natural and the divine better than anyone. If anyone could guide us, it's her."

As the evening wore on, the team's vigilance never wavered. They took turns monitoring the greenhouse, each member driven by a shared sense of purpose. Hana and Michael revisited Hildegard's journal, searching for any additional insights, while Marcus double-checked the environmental controls.

Finally, as the first rays of dawn filtered through the greenhouse's glass panes, something shifted. Hana, who had been resting in a chair nearby, noticed it first.

"Michael," she called, her voice urgent. "Come look."

He hurried to her side, his gaze following her pointing finger. At the center of the soil patch, a tiny green shoot had emerged, its delicate leaves still curled about its stem as if stretching up for its first breath of life before unfurling.

"It's growing," Michael said, his voice permeated with awe.

Élise, who had just entered the greenhouse, stopped in her tracks, her eyes wide. "This is incredible. The soil, the ritual—it all worked."

Marcus snapped photo after photo, his excitement barely contained. "This is history in the making. We need to document every stage of its growth."

Hana knelt beside the seedling, her heart swelling with a mixture of pride and gratitude. "This isn't just about us. It's about honoring Hildegard's hard work and everything she stood for. This is her work brought back to life."

Michael placed a hand on her shoulder, his expression serene. "And it's a reminder of what's possible when we trust in something greater than ourselves."

But as the team celebrated their success, a darker shadow loomed in Geneva. Across the city, Zentara's operatives were moving with precision and purpose, their target clear: Élise's new lab.

In the secret laboratory of a nondescript building, security cameras captured the figures as they breached the perimeter. Dressed in unmarked tactical gear, they moved with practiced efficiency, disabling alarms and bypassing locks with ease. Within minutes, they were inside, combing through the lab's meticulously organized files and equipment.

"We're in," one of the operatives said, his voice low

and clipped. "Start extracting data. Priority is on anything related to Hildegard von Bingen."

Laptops were powered on, external drives plugged in, and file cabinets rifled through. The team worked quickly, copying research notes, chemical analyses, and digital records. They ignored everything else, laser-focused on their objective.

One of the operatives paused as he came across a locked drawer. Pulling a small device from his pocket, he pressed it against the lock, which clicked open seconds later. Inside was a sealed envelope, its contents labeled in Élise's neat handwriting: *Ricinus aureum - Preliminary Findings.*

"Got it," the operative said, holding up the envelope. "This is what we came for."

As they gathered their spoils and prepared to leave, the leader of the team issued a final directive. "Wipe the drives and destroy the backups. Leave no trace."

By the time the lab's security system rebooted, Zentara's operatives were gone, leaving behind a trail of destruction and a void where critical research once existed.

At the Saint-Clair estate, the greenhouse was filled with cautious optimism as the team marveled at the seedling's progress. But the celebration was short-lived. Hana's phone buzzed on the workstation, and when she answered, her lips pressed into a firm, unforgiving line.

"It's my security team," she said, her voice tight. "Élise's secret lab was hit. Zentara took everything."

Élise's face went pale. "My research… they have it all."

Michael's jaw clenched, his nerves buzzing with restless energy. "They're getting bolder, escalating."

"And they won't stop there," Marcus added. "We need to secure this greenhouse and the seedling immediately. Zentara knows too much now."

Hana squared her shoulders, her resolve hardening. "Then we fight back. They might have taken Élise's research, but they don't have Hildegard's journal. And they definitely don't have the seeds or this seedling."

Michael nodded. "We'll protect it however we can. Everything depends on it."

"How do we do that? Protect it?"

Michael smiled. "I have an idea."

As the team prepared for the next stage of their battle against Zentara, the tiny seedling stood as a beacon of hope—a fragile yet powerful symbol of renewal in the face of overwhelming adversity.

ANOTHER MONK PASSED Karl at his post, and they nodded to each other. Vigilance was still the keyword, and the Green Flame monks had switched out with fresh ones arriving from the Disibodenberg Monastery earlier that day.

The operatives they had apprehended trying to find the entrance to the *Hortus Vitae* had been questioned but to no avail. Whatever threats Zentara held over the heads of their agents were greater than any fear Karl or Lukas could instill. And the threat of imprisonment only brought smirks. Karl figured the men knew Zentara would spring them in short order. An organization like theirs had both the kind of money and people in their pockets to open jail cells.

Karl's phone beeped; he answered quickly.

"South side, breach in progress," Lukas called out, the signal going simultaneously to all the monks' devices.

Karl rushed to the south, his weapon drawn. Several monks, their hoods flying back, joined him en route. "There!" He saw a line of black-clad assailants rushing through the tree line. The battle had begun.

An hour later, Karl and Lukas watched as the authorities hauled away the last of the intruders. Lukas had radioed the police in Bingen right after his call to Karl and the monks, and the uniforms had arrived before much blood was shed, coming in from behind the assailants. Cornered, the men finally gave in, and after the men had been arrested and statements taken by the police, Karl started to make the call to Michael to fill him in. "Karl?" He heard Lukas's voice, a puzzle in the question.

Karl turned and looked back at his partner. Behind him, Sisters Amalia and Clara were running toward them from the abbey.

"We saw them leaving, we couldn't stop them!" Sister Amalia shouted out.

Karl and Lukas looked at each other and then back at

the sisters. "What do you mean? The police took them—"

"No!" Sister Clara pointed behind at the abbey. "There was a truck. On the north side. We didn't hear it or see it, we were watching you here when—"

But Karl and Lukas were already at a run and didn't hear the rest as they raced to the north side of the abbey, to the stone entrance of the *Hortus Vitae.*

They came to a sudden stop.

The large stone cover lay upside-down, discarded on the rocky ground, the entrance to the *Hortus Vitae* wide open.

A faint trail of glistening soil, like the lifeblood of the one remaining live golden castor, stained the rocky ground from that opening across the slope and ended at truck tracks that led to the forest.

HANA SAT with her head in her hands, Élise stood with tears in her eyes, and the men sat is shocked disbelief after Michael closed out the call from Karl. The image of that golden-leafed miracle plant that had grown in the garden of life filled all of their minds.

Gabriel was the first to speak. "That whole team of assailants was no more than a distraction, fodder that Zentara found expendable to just buy their second team time."

Michael nodded. "And it did. They have the mother plant now. But at least we have seeds. And the right soil. And we've assumed Zentara doesn't know that. Except…"

Michael and Marcus looked at Gabriel.

"What?" Hana asked, seeing their glances.

Michael answered, "Zentara knew a live plant existed, knew exactly where to access the *Hortus Vitae*. None of that was ever discussed over Élise's phone. So, we can only assume we have another leak. Meaning, we have no idea how much Zentara knows."

Gabriel swallowed; his face suddenly reddened. "I know what you're thinking. There is no way any of my men could have informed Zentara."

Marcus squinted at him. "How many monks do you have? What do they all think of your life of poverty and self-sacrifice? How many men in history have succumbed to bribery and riches, the promise of more than what they have, of fulfilling their desires?"

"No! I can't… I won't believe that."

Michael stepped toward the monk. "But what of threats? Even you were approached by Zentara and with threats that had you questioning yourself, right?"

Gabriel's complexion drained, and his shoulders sagged. "Okay, okay. I know you could both be right." He took in a full breath and addressed them all. "I'll find out who did this. No matter who it is or how it happened, I won't let the impact of this one person's dereliction destroy everything my Order has stood for. Somehow, we will make this right."

CHAPTER
THIRTY-SEVEN

The Saint-Clair estate buzzed with quiet urgency as the team prepared for their next moves. After Zentara's brazen thefts of both Élise's research and the golden castor plant, it was clear they were running out of time. The *Ricinus aureum* seedling stood as a tender, uncertain promise of hope—and a vulnerable and valuable target of interest.

Hana stood in the estate's central office, her arms crossed as she studied a map of Geneva on the digital display. Beside her, Élise typed furiously on her laptop, drafting press releases and coordinating with trusted media contacts.

"We need to control the narrative," Hana said, her tone firm. "If Zentara gets ahead of us, they'll twist the truth into something unrecognizable. The public needs to know what they're really after."

Élise nodded without looking up. "I'm contacting every scientific journalist I trust. We'll frame this as a fight for ethical research and historical preservation. If Zentara tries to discredit us, they'll face a wall of public scrutiny."

Michael entered the room, his expression serious. "Hana, Marcus and I are leaving for Zurich in an hour. We've arranged a meeting with Father Benedetto, a Vatican colleague there. He's discreet and well-connected. If anyone can help us secure additional resources to protect what we have, it's him."

Hana turned to face him, her brow furrowing. "Be careful. Zentara isn't going to sit back and let us strengthen our position. They'll be watching every move we make."

Michael placed a reassuring hand on her shoulder. "We'll be fine. Focus on the media strategy and securing the estate. We'll bring back what we need to keep the seedling safe."

Marcus appeared in the doorway, a duffel bag slung over his shoulder. "The plane's ready. Zurich isn't far. We should be there in less than an hour."

With a quick nod of agreement, Michael and Marcus departed, leaving Hana, Élise, and Gabriel to their work. The estate's atmosphere grew heavier as the hours passed, each person acutely aware of the precarious balance they were trying to maintain.

THE CITY of Zurich's sleek skyline shimmered under a pale autumn sun. Michael and Marcus navigated the bustling streets in a rented black sedan, their eyes constantly scanning for signs of surveillance.

"Benedetto's expecting us at the Jesuit retreat center," Michael said, glancing at his phone for directions. "He's arranged for a private meeting in the library. It should be secure."

Marcus adjusted his seatbelt, his gaze fixed on the rearview mirror. "Let's hope he has more than words to offer. We need actionable intelligence and resources."

The retreat center was a modest stone building tucked away in a quiet neighborhood. Its unassuming exterior belied the wealth of knowledge and influence housed within. Michael and Marcus entered through a side door, following a narrow hallway to the library where Father Benedetto waited.

The elderly priest greeted them warmly, his eyes twinkling with a mix of curiosity and concern. "Michael, Marcus, it's good to see you both. Though I wish it were under less dire circumstances."

"Thank you for meeting with us, Father," Michael said, shaking his hand. "We need your help. A pernicious enemy is escalating their efforts against us in an important matter, and we're running out of time."

Benedetto gestured for them to sit, his expression growing serious. "Tell me everything."

Michael and Marcus outlined the situation, from Hildegard's writings to the seedling's fragile growth and Zentara's relentless pursuit. Benedetto listened intently, occasionally interjecting with questions that demonstrated his deep understanding of both theology and science.

When they finished, he leaned back in his chair, his hands steepled. "This is indeed a grave matter. I can provide funds and secure transport for the seedling if relocation becomes necessary. Additionally, I'll reach out to my contacts in the Swiss Guard. They're discreet and loyal; their involvement could bolster your defenses."

Marcus nodded appreciatively. "That would be invaluable. Do you have any insight into Zentara's operations in the region? Their network is wider and more aggressive than we anticipated."

A shadow passed over Benedetto's face. "Zentara has allies in high places, both within governments and private sectors. But they've grown overconfident, leaving traces of their activities. I'll share what I know with your team."

Michael clasped the priest's shoulder. "Thank you, Father. Your support means more than we can express."

MEANWHILE, in Geneva, Hana and Élise were finalizing their media strategy in the estate's command center. The room's large monitors displayed a flurry of headlines and social media feeds, each one a potential tool or threat in their battle against Zentara.

"The press is biting," Élise said, scrolling through an email thread. "Several outlets are interested in running stories about Hildegard's work and the ethical implications of Zentara's actions. If we position this correctly, it could turn public opinion against them."

Hana nodded, her fingers flying over her keyboard. "Good. But we need more than just sympathy. We need outrage. Zentara's funding sources and hidden alliances need to be exposed."

Élise hesitated. "That's a dangerous line to walk. If we reveal too much, we risk putting ourselves in danger."

"We're already in danger," Hana replied, her tone steely. "This is the only way to fight back."

As they worked, a notification pinged on Hana's phone. She glanced at the screen and froze. The message was from an anonymous number: "**We know where the seedling is. Consider this your only warning**."

Hana's heart pounded as she showed the message to Élise. "They know about the seedling," she said, her voice low.

Élise's eyes widened. "How? We've been so careful!"

"It doesn't matter," Hana said, rising from her chair. "We need to act now."

AT THE SAME TIME, in Zurich, a Zentara operative sat in a dimly lit cafe, his laptop open to an encrypted messaging platform. His fingers flew across the keyboard as he sent a detailed report to the organization's CEO.

"Saint-Clair estate confirmed as location of *Ricinus aureum* seedling. Awaiting further instructions."

The message was sent, and the operative leaned back, a faint grin playing across his lips.

THIRTY-EIGHT

The tranquility of the Saint-Clair estate was shattered by the wail of an alarm cutting through the crisp evening air. Hana, working late in the greenhouse, froze as the sound sent a jolt of adrenaline through her veins. She instinctively grabbed the radio on the nearby workstation.

"Security breach!" a guard's voice crackled over the line. "Perimeter compromised. Zentara agents are inside."

Hana's heart sank. She had feared this moment, knowing Zentara would stop at nothing to claim the *Ricinus aureum* seedling. But the reality was more terrifying than she had imagined.

She glanced at the tiny green shoot in the central planter of her workstation, its two delicate primary leaves just starting to open, illuminated under the grow lights.

"Hana, stay put," Gabriel's voice broke through the static, calm but firm. "The security team is engaging the intruders. I'm on my way."

"Understood," Hana replied, her voice steadier than she felt. She scanned the greenhouse, her mind working at a feverish pace. They had prepared for this possibility. Emergency protocols were in place, but Zentara's aggression had escalated faster than anyone had expected.

OUTSIDE, the estate's security guards moved with precision, their training evident in their coordinated efforts. Security cameras had captured the intruders scaling the fence and disabling motion sensors. Now, shadows darted between the trees, their movements swift and calculated.

"Three agents moving toward the greenhouse," one guard reported over the radio. "Another pair near the main house. Team Beta, cover the flank."

The guards split into teams, their weapons drawn as they advanced through the darkened grounds. A rustling sound to the left caught one guard's attention. He pivoted, raising his weapon just as a masked figure lunged from the shadows. The agent swung a baton, but the guard sidestepped, delivering a precise blow to the attacker's ribs. The intruder stumbled but quickly recovered, retreating into the darkness.

"They're testing us," the guard muttered, his grip tightening on his weapon. "Stay alert."

. . .

INSIDE THE GREENHOUSE, Hana had already taken the measures they had rehearsed earlier, including having locked the doors and activated the reinforced shutters. The structure, though designed for research, had been fortified after Zentara's first attack attempt. She felt a small measure of relief as the steel barriers slid into place, but it was short-lived.

A loud bang reverberated through the building as Zentara agents attempted to breach the entrance. The sound of metal grinding against metal filled the air, and Hana realized the shutters wouldn't hold for long.

The banging grew louder, more insistent. Hana's breath quickened. She reached for her radio.

"They're almost in," she said.

"We're coming," the lead guard replied. "Hold your position."

THE GREENHOUSE DOORS gave way with a deafening crash, and Zentara agents poured inside. They moved with methodical efficiency, fanning out as they began their search. Hana ducked behind a row of tall plants, her heart pounding as she watched them sweep the room.

"Spread out," one agent said, his voice muffled by his mask. "Find it."

Hana gripped the radio tightly, a knot of tension tightening in her mind. If they found the seedling, it was over. She needed to buy time.

Drawing a deep breath, she grabbed a nearby rack of gardening tools and tipped it over, sending shovels and rakes clattering to the ground. The noise drew the agents' attention, and they moved toward the disturbance.

From her hiding spot, Hana slipped to the opposite side of the greenhouse, her movements silent and deliberate.

OUTSIDE, the security team coordinated their counterattack. One guard had already neutralized an intruder near the main house, but the remaining agents were proving more difficult to pin down. One guard moved swiftly, flanking the agents near the greenhouse. With a sharp whistle, he drew their gaze, then fired a warning shot into the air. The intruders hesitated, momentarily distracted, before splitting their forces to pursue him.

INSIDE, Hana reached the back of the greenhouse, watching as one of the intruders called out, "Got it!" from her earlier workstation.

Suddenly, one of the agents rounded the corner where she hid, his flashlight cutting through the shadows. Hana froze.

"Don't move," the agent barked, raising a weapon.

Before he could advance, a deafening crack echoed through the greenhouse. The agent stumbled, clutching his arm as the lead guard emerged from the shadows, his rifle still raised.

"On your knees," the guard ordered, his voice cold. "Now."

The agent hesitated, then lowered himself to his knees. The guard zip-tied him for later arrest. He turned to Hana, his expression tense but relieved.

"Are you hurt?" he asked.

Hana shook her head. "No. But I heard them say they have the seedling. They broke into the workstation before I could stop them."

The guard's jaw clenched.

By the time the intruders withdrew, the estate was in disarray. Broken glass and scattered equipment littered the greenhouse, a stark reminder of the night's events. Zentara had succeeded in stealing the seedling she had left at her workstation.

Hana, the security team, and Élise regrouped in the estate's command center, their faces etched with determination.

"We've taken a hit," Gabriel admitted, his tone grave. "They were more brazen and aggressive than we'd figured. But we're not out of the fight. They think they've won, but they don't know what they have."

Hana unlocked and opened a compartment under her workstation and pulled out a container. She set it on the table, revealing the shiny, minuscule leaves of the golden castor seedling, its leaves looking remarkably like the yellowed sunflower seedling they just sprouted in nitrogen-poor soil. "That sunflower seedling they stole has bought us some time," she said. "Maybe we can still finish what we started. But we need to act fast. Zentara won't be fooled for long."

As the team strategized their next steps, the heft of their mission pressed heavily on their shoulders. The battle was far from over, but their ploy gave them a glimmer of hope in the face of overwhelming odds.

CHAPTER

THIRTY-NINE

Z urich's bustling streets gleamed under the midday sun, the city's efficiency and order an almost surreal contrast to the chaos unfolding behind the scenes. Marcus and Michael sat in a quiet corner of a small café, their laptops open and documents spread across the table. The team's efforts to track Zentara had finally borne fruit, but the picture emerging was far from reassuring.

"Southern Germany," Marcus said, tapping a highlighted region on the digital map displayed on his screen. "Zentara's activities converge here. Logistics hubs, secure shipments, and personnel transfers—it's their epicenter."

Michael leaned forward, studying the map. "That lines up with the intel Benedetto provided. If they're producing a formula based on any galls they obtained from the *Ricinus aureum* in the Black Forest, it's happening there."

Marcus nodded, his jaw tightening. "And if they've started trials, the results could be catastrophic."

Michael's phone hummed. Seeing it was Hana calling, Michael put her on speaker. "Zentara hit us again. Two of their agents have been taken into custody by Geneva police, but our security team here confirmed the other agents have retreated," she said. "They left with the sunflower seedling. Our little golden miracle seedling is still safe."

Michael looked at Marcus and they both grinned. "Well, that buys us a bit of time. Meanwhile, we think we're close to knowing the laboratory they're using. I'll let you know when we have more."

HANA HAD SPENT hours researching the employees suspected of working for Zentara. Élise helped, contacting various colleagues in the field, confidently using a new burner phone, her old device long since destroyed. In the end, they had a list of high-level scientists, those capable of providing great botanical and chemical expertise to a firm like Zentara—men and women both highly intelligent yet potentially vulnerable to Zentara's persuasion. Then they narrowed it down to those currently residing in southern Germany, on sabbatical in unknown locations, or who had recently dropped off the radar. The tension was unrelenting, but they refused to let it show. The stakes were too high.

Hana's phone lit up with Michael's name on the screen. "I just got off the phone with a colleague here,

Father Benedetto," he said. "He's confirmed our intel. Zentara's facility is located near Lake Constance in Baden-Württemberg, Germany. It's heavily guarded, but there are weak points in their supply chain we can exploit. They seem to be setting up for full-scale testing."

"Do we have a timeline?" Hana asked.

"Two days, maybe three. After that, Zentara's operations will be fully operational. If we're going to act, it has to be soon. We're on our way back to you now. We'll need to gather as much intelligence as possible before moving in. If we're going to stop Zentara, we can't afford to miss anything.

"Too, it looks like we may have caught a break. Father Benedetto knows a prominent scientist in Zentara's R&D division who's upset with many of the company's unethical practices, and could be just on the verge of whistleblowing. His name is Dr. Fabian Keller, so find a way to make his acquaintance while you're there."

"Outstanding news! I think we've got information that will help with that," Hana said, her voice steady. She glanced at Élise. "We will certainly find him once we're on the inside."

THE HOURS STRETCHED into the evening, the team working with a singular focus. Michael and Hana finalized plans for a reconnaissance mission to the facility in southern Germany.

"We'll need eyes on the ground before we move in,"

Michael said, laying out a map of the area. "Drones can give us a preliminary view, but we'll need someone inside to confirm the intel."

As the team rallied around their mission, the impact of Zentara's threat loomed large. But their determination only grew stronger in the face of fear and intimidation. The chase was on, and they had no intention of letting Zentara win.

FORTY

The Zentara research facility loomed ahead, its stark, modern architecture a chilling monument to secrecy. The glass-and-steel façade shimmered faintly under the overcast German sky, concealing the true purpose of the company's work. Hana and Élise, wigs and makeup in place, exchanged a brief glance as their rented sedan rolled to a stop in the visitors' parking lot.

"Ready?" Hana asked, her tone cool but tinged with an undercurrent of tension.

Élise adjusted her wire-rimmed glasses and smoothed the lapel of her lab coat. "As ready as I'll ever be. We can't afford mistakes."

Hana nodded, gripping the sleek briefcase that held their forged credentials and infiltration tools. As they approached the facility entrance, the imposing figure of a security checkpoint came into view. Two guards in navy-blue uniforms stood at attention, their sharp eyes scrutinizing every movement.

"Names and purpose of visit?" one of the guards asked briskly.

"Hélène Fournier," Hana replied, her French accent crisp as she handed over her forged ID. "This is my colleague, Dr. Élodie Chastain. We're here representing l'Institut Français de Biotechnologie Appliquée to consult on Zentara's R&D initiatives."

The guard scanned their IDs, checking a tablet on his desk. After a pause, he nodded. "You're cleared. Welcome to Zentara."

The guards waved them through, and Hana allowed herself a small exhale of relief. They had passed the first hurdle.

The lobby was a vision of sleek modernity, all polished surfaces and minimalist décor. A woman in a tailored black suit approached them with the precision of a machine, her expression unreadable.

"Dr. Fournier, Dr. Chastain," she said, her German accent clipped and professional. "I'm Greta Adler, head of project coordination. Welcome."

"Thank you," Hana said with a polite smile, shaking Adler's hand. "We're eager to collaborate."

Adler offered a curt nod. "Follow me. The facility has restricted access, so you'll be accompanied at all times. The projects we're working on require the utmost confidentiality."

As Adler led them through a maze of gleaming hallways, Élise discreetly noted the extensive security infrastructure—cameras in every corner, biometric scanners at every door. Zentara had clearly spared no expense in safeguarding their secrets. Hana, walking beside Adler, noted the lab names etched on glass doors: Genomic Suppression, Therapeutic Viability Monitoring, Proprietary Oncology Research.

The air grew colder as they entered the main research lab, where scientists in white coats worked in focused silence. Adler gestured toward a sealed chamber at the rear. "This is our controlled cultivation lab," she explained.

Inside, rows of Petri dishes sat on a long counter, each accompanied by a sheet of what would be the data for that culture. Hana's eyes scanned the room, her gaze landing on the environmental control gauges on the wall.

Adler stepped aside as a tall, pale man approached, his demeanor tense.

"This is Dr. Fabian Keller," she said. "He'll provide you with everything you need."

It was all Hana could do to contain her shock at this unexpected opportunity. She briefly glanced at Élise.

Keller shook their hands stiffly, his eyes darting nervously to the door. "Follow me," he said, his voice low.

"Dr. Keller, I should mention that Father Benedetto sends his regards. We're close colleagues…" She gave the man a knowing look, one he seemed to understand immediately.

In the chamber, Keller closed the door and gestured toward the console on the side wall. "This contains all the data on the properties, modifications, and potential applications of the galls obtained in the Black Forest."

Élise stepped forward, her hands steady as she accessed the files. She scrolled through pages of genetic sequences and cultivation protocols, her expression darkening. "These modifications... they're designed to *suppress* therapeutic efficacy."

Keller's shoulders stiffened, and he cast a wary glance at the door. "Zentara's directive is to ensure that no viable treatment for cancer reaches the market," he said, his voice barely above a whisper. "They've spent years acquiring patents and burying breakthroughs."

Hana's reaction was one of surprise. "Why suppress treatments? There's huge profit in curing diseases."

Keller's bitter laugh was devoid of humor. "Not when you can profit indefinitely from ongoing treatment. Zentara ensures the monopoly remains untouched, even if it means sabotaging potential cures."

Élise froze, her hand hovering over the console. "This data—it's not just research. It's sabotage."

Keller nodded grimly. "They're using the knowledge obtained from those galls to cultivate chemicals to suppress plants with therapeutic properties. They're actively ensuring that natural treatments never see the light of day."

Hana spoke quietly, even though she knew the environmentally controlled room was likely soundproof. "You're doing the right thing in helping us, Dr. Keller... " She saw the man's eyes shift, his expression tight. "What? Are you afraid?"

"No. It's just that... there's more."

"What do you mean?

He reached over to the console, clicking into another file, entering his password and stepping back.

Élise leaned over the data, her fingers scrolling, her eyes widening. "The galls. Of course, it makes sense. Their purpose is twofold: to protect a plant from an exterior invasion, by insects or disease, by providing a potent cure, which is what we've been concentrating on. But the other purpose is to destroy whatever is infiltrating it." She looked at Hana.

"You mean, like a poison?"

"Not just any poison…" Keller swallowed hard before explaining. "Another *Rictus* species is used to produce ricin. The galls from the golden castor produce a similar substance likely to be more devastating as well as incurable. Death from it would be unbearable. And they're about to start the trials."

Hana exchanged a look with Élise, her jaw tightening. "We need to corrupt this data."

They looked at Keller, who nodded and looked away. Élise inserted a flash drive into the console. While the files transferred, Keller glanced back at the door again, his tension palpable.

"Once you're finished, leave," Keller said. "Quickly."

The falsification took minutes, but it felt like hours. As Élise completed the upload, Keller guided them out of the chamber, his face a mask of neutrality. Back in the main lab, Hana and Élise maintained their façade, asking Adler benign questions about Zentara's broader operations.

After the tour concluded, Adler saw them back to

the lobby. "We'll be in touch to coordinate further collaboration."

"It's been a pleasure," Hana replied, though the words felt bitter in her mouth.

As they exited the building, Élise released a shaky breath as they climbed into their car. "Well, we've stopped them for the moment. Plus, we got what we came for. Now let's analyze it."

In the safety of their rented apartment, Hana and Élise removed their disguises, preparing to open the files they had copied from the Zentara server.

"This is monstrous," Élise said, her voice trembling. "I'd thought they wanted to corner the market on a cancer cure. Instead, they plan to keep people sick. And purposely kill others."

Hana's gaze hardened. "We've set them back for now with what you inserted into their files, but this is only a small piece of the puzzle. The idea of a ricin-like agent coming out of this research as well is the very reason Hildegard took such pains to secure her work, hiding facts in clues and secreting what was needed in hidden chambers. Somehow, she knew the dangers."

Her phone buzzed with an unknown number. Frowning, she opened the message:

"Look to other sources, other places. — K"

Hana stared at the note, her pulse quickening. Élise, seeing Hana's expression, leaned over.

"What is it?"

Hana handed her the note.

The two women went to work, scouring the stolen Zentara files. Moments later, they sat back, stunned.

The data confirmed Zentara's chilling motives, but not just related to the golden castor. Their suppression efforts spanned decades, targeting promising therapies derived from plants, fungi, and other natural sources. Entire species had been eradicated from their habitats to prevent independent research.

Hana read the file, her face paling. "This isn't just about cancer treatment. This is global control." She grabbed her phone and typed a message to Michael. What Zentara was doing was far more sinister than they had imagined. And they were running out of time to stop it.

FORTY-ONE

Zentara's headquarters in Geneva stood like a monument to power and secrecy, its sleek, glass exterior gleaming in the sunlight. Inside, however, the company's carefully crafted façade was beginning to crack. The media fallout from the leaked trials had sent shockwaves through its ranks, exposing the ruthless strategies that had brought the corporation to prominence.

From the Saint-Clair estate, Michael, Hana, and Marcus watched the tension unfold through their hacked surveillance feed of Zentara's boardroom. The team had taken up temporary residence at the estate to monitor and counter Zentara's activities, their makeshift command center brimming with laptops, monitors, and hastily gathered files.

"They're unraveling," Marcus observed, pointing at the live feed provided by Keller. "Blackthorn's grip on the board is slipping."

Michael stood behind him, arms crossed, his face a mask of focus. "Not fast enough. If Alton Blackthorn manages to reassert control, we'll lose the chance to fracture Zentara from within."

Hana adjusted her headset, her eyes scanning a separate screen displaying recent activity logs. "We still have cards to play. That leaked trial data was only the tip of the iceberg. The real damage will come from tying Blackthorn directly to Zentara's suppression tactics, decades in the making."

Marcus smiled faintly. "Lucky for us, he's not exactly subtle. The South America operation where he'd killed off a species that could cure diabetes alone would be enough to bury him."

"Then let's make sure it does," Michael said.

Inside Zentara's boardroom, the tension was palpable. Alton Blackthorn, the CEO, sat at the head of the table, his posture commanding even as dissent rippled through the room. Around him, the board members were locked in heated discussion, their voices rising in anger and frustration.

"This exposure is catastrophic!" snapped Leonie Strauss, one of the senior members, waving a printout of the leaked documents. "The world knows we've conducted unethical trials, and now they're digging deeper."

Blackthorn's expression was cool, his gray eyes narrowing as he leaned back in his chair. "This is a temporary storm. It will pass, like all the others."

"It won't pass if we keep making enemies," Farhad Khan interjected. "This isn't just bad press, Alton. Governments are starting to look at us."

"And regulators," Willem Koenig added. "If they uncover the full extent of what we've done—"

"What you've done," Leonie interrupted, her tone accusatory. "This was your operation, Alton. You signed off on it."

Blackthorn's calm façade cracked slightly, his voice gaining an edge. "Let's not pretend you're innocent in this. Every one of you has benefited from our actions."

"Benefited, yes," Farhad said, his voice growing quieter but more forceful. "But there's a difference between profit and recklessness. You've gone too far."

The argument escalated, the room descending into chaos as voices overlapped in anger and accusations. Blackthorn's jaw tightened, his knuckles whitening as he gripped the armrests of his chair. Finally, he stood, his voice slicing through the cacophony.

"You're weak," he said coldly. "All of you. I built this company, and I'll ensure it survives. But if you're not with me, you're against me."

The board members fell silent, their anger replaced by unease as Blackthorn swept out of the room, his expression thunderous.

BACK AT THE ESTATE, Hana exhaled slowly as she watched Blackthorn leave the boardroom. "He's losing control, but he's not out yet. That kind of arrogance doesn't disappear overnight."

Marcus leaned back in his chair, crossing his arms. "He'll retaliate. The question is how."

FORTY-TWO

In her grandfather's library, Hana sat with her laptop open, headphones perched on her head. Her investigative instincts were in full swing as she navigated encrypted networks and sent messages to her most trusted contacts. The screen displayed a flurry of activity: correspondence with journalists, digital archives, and whistleblowers eager to bring Zentara's corruption to light.

"This piece of data," Hana muttered, pulling up an internal Zentara report, "shows how they've suppressed research globally for over a decade. Entire regions were targeted—scientists silenced, patents buried."

She paused, composing an email to an investigative journalist at *Le Monde*. Her words were precise, the tone professional but urgent: ***"The world deserves to know how Zentara has blocked lifesaving cancer treatments. Here's the proof—share it widely."***

Élise entered the library, carrying a tray with two steaming cups of coffee. "You look like you haven't moved in hours," she said, setting the tray down beside Hana.

"I haven't," Hana replied, pulling off her headphones and rubbing her temples. "The deeper I dig, the worse it gets. Zentara hasn't just blocked progress; they've orchestrated a global campaign to maintain control of treatment markets. Every story we leak, every piece of evidence we expose—it's a step closer to dismantling their monopoly."

Élise nodded, her expression darkening. "And they'll stop at nothing to keep that monopoly."

"That's why we need to get ahead of them," Hana said, taking a sip of coffee. "We've done about all we can here. Now it's up to Karl and Lukas at the abbey to keep everything else of Hildegard's safe."

By EVENING, the team reconvened in the study, the atmosphere charged with discovery and tension. Marcus was on a video call with Karl and Lukas at Rupertsberg Abbey, their faces appearing on the laptop screen. Behind them, the abbey's stone walls and flickering candlelight were visible.

"There's been movement near the greenhouse," Karl reported, his tone clipped. "Strangers posing as pilgrims, asking too many questions about Hildegard's manuscripts and the abbey's history."

Lukas chimed in. "They haven't done anything overt yet, but their presence is unsettling. We've increased patrols, but if Zentara's planning something, we're going to need more than vigilance."

Marcus frowned. "Do you have any evidence they're connected to Zentara?"

"Not yet," Karl admitted, "but the timing is suspicious. The moment Zentara was exposed and its actions related to the abbey, these so-called pilgrims showed up. Supposedly, they're here out of respect for St. Hildegard, and like the aftermath of any accident scene, some people like to see where 'the action' has been. But any of them could also be one of Zentara's people."

Michael leaned into the frame. "Keep a close watch. If anything happens, alert us immediately. We'll figure out how to counter them."

Karl nodded. "Understood."

As the call ended, Hana's laptop pinged with a notification. She opened it, her eyes narrowing as she scanned the encrypted file. "This just came through from one of my sources," she said, her voice tense.

"What is it?" Michael asked, moving to her side.

Hana's fingers flew over the keyboard, decrypting the message. A Zentara directive appeared on the screen, stark and chilling in its clarity: ***"Initiate Operation Sanctum. Target: Rupertsberg Abbey greenhouse. Priority: Eliminate all assets tied to Ricinus aureum."***

"They're going after the abbey," Hana said, her voice tight. "And they're not just looking—they're planning to destroy everything."

Michael's expression hardened. "We need to act now.

If they succeed, Hildegard's legacy could be lost forever."

Marcus grabbed his phone, his voice resolute. "Then we prepare. Rupertsberg is not falling on our watch."

FORTY-THREE

T he autumn morning at Rupertsberg Abbey was serene, the soft light illuminating the abbey's weathered stone walls. Inside, the quiet hum of daily life blended with the distant toll of bells. Pilgrims meandered through the gardens, their voices hushed in reverence for the sacred grounds. Beneath the tranquil exterior, however, tension simmered among those sworn to protect Hildegard's mission in life.

Karl stood by the greenhouse, scanning the grounds. He wore a simple jacket to blend in with the abbey's pilgrims, but his posture betrayed his readiness. Lukas approached, his footsteps barely audible on the gravel path.

"They're here," Lukas murmured, nodding toward a group of five visitors clustered near the abbey's chapel. "They've been asking questions about the greenhouse and Hildegard's manuscripts. They're careful, but their interest is too specific."

Karl's jaw tightened. "They're waiting for the right moment."

Lukas nodded grimly. "We should alert the sisters to prepare. If Zentara's sending operatives, they'll act soon."

Inside the abbey's main hall, Sister Amalia moved with calm authority, directing the other nuns in their daily tasks. When Karl and Lukas entered, she paused, her serene expression giving way to concern as she listened to their report.

"We believe Zentara operatives have infiltrated the abbey," Karl said quietly. "They're posing as pilgrims, but their behavior suggests they're here for the greenhouse."

Sister Amalia's face hardened. "Hildegard's accomplishments cannot fall into their hands. What do you need from us?"

"Discretion," Lukas replied. "If they suspect we're onto them, they may act unpredictably. We'll coordinate with you and the other sisters to secure the greenhouse."

Sister Amalia nodded. "Consider it done."

From the Saint-Clair estate in Geneva, Marcus bent over a map of the abbey, his phone propped up on the desk for a video call with Karl and Lukas. The map, a detailed layout of Rupertsberg's grounds, was marked with annotations from Marcus's earlier explorations.

"The greenhouse has two main access points," Marcus said, his voice steady. "The east entrance is the most vulnerable. If they plan to attack, they'll likely use it to avoid detection."

Karl studied the map on his screen, nodding. "And the west side?"

"It's better fortified," Marcus replied. "But don't rule it out. Zentara's operatives are thorough. They might stage another diversion. This time on the east side while targeting the west."

"What about the sisters?" Lukas asked.

Marcus paused. "Station a few in the garden as lookouts. Their presence will seem natural, but they'll be able to spot any unusual activity."

Hana, seated at her laptop in the same room, monitored Zentara's digital communications. Using a secure backdoor into their network, acquired through the download they had obtained at the Zentara laboratory, she tracked encrypted messages and movement logs. Her eyes focused as a new directive flashed on her screen.

"They're moving tonight," she announced, her voice cutting through the quiet. "The message doesn't specify the exact plan, but it confirms their operatives will target the greenhouse under cover of darkness."

Marcus relayed the update to Karl and Lukas. "Stay alert. If they're acting tonight, we need to be ready."

As night fell over the abbey, the serene grounds took on an ominous stillness. The sisters moved about their tasks as usual, but a sense of anticipation hung heavy in the air. Karl and Lukas patrolled the perimeter along with several of the Green Flame monks, their keen eyes scanning for signs of movement.

Near the greenhouse, Sister Amalia and two other nuns worked among the plants, their presence a subtle but deliberate deterrent. Inside, the precious manuscripts and botanical samples tied to Hildegard's legacy were secured behind locked cabinets.

Just after midnight, Karl spotted a shadow moving along the eastern wall. He signaled to Lukas, who moved silently to flank the figure. As they approached, two more shadows emerged from the woods, their movements purposeful. The first shadow approached them and paused, a hand reaching out to pass something to the others. Then the first person returned to the abbey, and as he slipped around a corner, Karl recognized he wore a monk's garb.

"We've got our mole, entering the abbey from the east," Karl whispered into his comm link, his voice barely audible. "Now we have three at the east entrance. No sign of activity on the west yet."

Marcus's voice came through the earpiece. "Stay with the group at the east. If they breach the entrance, the manuscripts could be at risk."

The operatives moved quickly, their tools gleaming faintly in the moonlight as they worked to disable the greenhouse's electronic lock. Lukas crept closer, his footsteps soundless on the damp grass. When the lock clicked open, the lead operative gestured for the others to enter.

Karl waited until all three were inside before signaling to the sisters in the garden. With practiced coordination, the sisters quietly moved to block the operatives' escape routes with rakes inserted through handles and wheelbarrows in front of side doors, while Karl and Lukas entered the greenhouse.

Inside, the air was oppressive with humidity and the scent of soil. The operatives moved with precision, heading straight for the secured cabinets. One produced a crowbar, while another set a small device against the cabinet door, likely a makeshift explosive.

Karl's voice rang out, low but commanding. "Step away. Now."

The operatives froze, each head turning toward the source of the voice. One of them lunged for the device, but Lukas was faster. He tackled the operative to the ground, disarming him with a swift motion. Karl moved to cover the other two, his imposing presence stopping them in their tracks. Then he snatched up the would-be explosive, ensuring it couldn't do any harm.

As the confrontation unfolded, Hana intercepted another Zentara communication on her screen. Her heart sank as she read the message.

"They've got someone inside the abbey," she said, her voice tight. "A sleeper agent."

Marcus turned abruptly to face her. "Who?"

Hana shook her head. "The message doesn't say. It only refers to the agent by their role: a close associate of the sisters."

Marcus's mind raced. "Someone trusted enough to have access to sensitive information. It could be anyone."

BACK AT THE ABBEY, the captured operatives remained silent as Karl and Lukas secured them. The greenhouse was safe, but the air was heavy with unease.

Sister Amalia arrived, her face pale but resolute. "Do you think there are more of them?" she asked.

Karl exchanged a glance with Lukas. "We don't know. But until we do, we can't assume the threat is neutralized."

As they spoke, a figure emerged from the shadows, their presence both unexpected and unsettling. It was Brother Mathias, one of the abbey's longest-serving monks and a trusted confidant of the sisters.

"I heard the commotion," Mathias said, his tone calm. "What's happened?"

Karl's eyes narrowed. "We've intercepted Zentara operatives. What are you doing out here?"

Mathias hesitated, his gaze flickering to the subdued intruders. "I thought I could help."

But something in his voice was off—too measured, too rehearsed. Lukas stepped closer, his instincts flaring. "Where were you before this?"

Before Mathias could answer, Karl noticed something glinting in his hand—a small device, similar to the one the operatives had been carrying. Recognition dawned, and his voice hardened.

"Stop right there, Mathias," Karl said slowly, "you have some explaining to do."

The monk's face darkened, and without warning, he bolted into the shadows. Karl and Lukas gave chase, their shouts echoing across the abbey grounds. Behind them, the sisters and remaining monks secured the greenhouse, their resolve unshaken even as the betrayal cut deep.

CHAPTER

FORTY-FOUR

The late afternoon sun streamed through the tall windows of the Saint-Clair residence, casting golden light across the cluttered study. Hana sat at her laptop, her gaze fixed on the screen. She scrolled through a set of encrypted emails, smuggled to her by Fabian Keller, Zentara's whistleblower, each bearing his company's distinctive digital signature. Since his quiet defection, Keller had been feeding Hana critical intelligence, risking his life to undermine the corporation from within.

Another message arrived, flagged as urgent. Hana opened it, her stomach twisting as she read the contents.

"Keller's intel is invaluable," Hana murmured, leaning back in her chair. "Zentara isn't just suppressing cancer cures—they're coordinating with major pharmaceutical giants to maintain control over treatment markets, so that even the cures that are currently available take more time and require more treatments than would be necessary."

Élise, seated nearby and analyzing financial documents, looked up suddenly. "That explains their reach. If Zentara is the enforcer, the pharmaceutical conglomerates are the puppet masters."

Hana nodded, pulling up a spreadsheet Keller had sent. "These transactions link Zentara to at least five of the world's largest pharmaceutical companies. They're funding Zentara's suppression campaigns while ensuring any viable natural treatments are buried."

Élise's face paled. "It's a cartel. They're not just blocking cures—they're profiting from prolonged suffering."

"Then we have to get this out."

LATER THAT EVENING, the team gathered in the study. Élise had finished setting up the climate chamber, the faint hum of its controls blending with the rustle of papers and the tap of keys. Hana stood at the head of the desk, her laptop open to the files Keller had sent.

"This is what Keller uncovered," she began, her tone measured but urgent. "Zentara's suppression strategies are tied to a network of major pharmaceutical corporations. They've been silencing independent researchers, burying patents, and sabotaging natural therapies."

She turned the screen to show a series of financial trails. "These companies funnel money to Zentara, ensuring they have the resources to eliminate the competition. It's a symbiotic relationship—Zentara does the dirty work, and the corporations reap the benefits."

Marcus leaned forward. "So Zentara isn't acting alone. This is bigger than we thought."

Michael crossed his arms, his expression grim. "And Keller's intel is the key to exposing it. How much have you leaked so far?"

"Enough to start a fire," Hana replied. "I've sent the first wave to *Le Monde* and other outlets. The preliminary stories are already sparking investigations."

"And the rest?" Élise asked.

Hana smiled a bit smugly. "We hold onto it until the moment it'll do the most damage."

As the group strategized, Hana's laptop pinged with an alert. She opened it, her face tightening as she read the decrypted message from Keller.

"What is it?" Michael asked, stepping closer.

Hana's voice was tense. "Keller says Zentara recognized the corruption Élise inserted into their database, remedied it, and started live human trials." She looked up, her eyes blinking at the realization. "They don't care if it has cancer-curing properties; they want to demonstrate the ricin-like substance from the galls. The details are vague, but…" She trailed off, scanning further. "Keller managed to extract data from their test logs. The results are catastrophic."

Michael frowned. "How catastrophic?"

Hana turned the screen toward him, revealing clinical reports Keller had smuggled out. The logs detailed horrifying side effects: organ failure, neurological collapse, and in all cases, death within hours of administration.

"They're killing people," Hana said, her voice trembling with anger. "These aren't trials—they're executions."

Marcus's hands clenched into fists. "Do we know where the trials are happening?"

Hana shook her head. "Keller's still working on that. He says the facility is isolated, but he's close to pinpointing the location."

Michael's gaze hardened. "If we find it, we can stop them."

"And if we don't," Hana said, her voice steely, "we expose it for the world to see."

The room fell silent as the lingering consequences of their discovery settled over them. Across the room, Élise adjusted the climate chamber, her face set with determination. "Saving lives is what matters. Both by protecting and nurturing these seeds into gall-productive plants and stopping the misuse of nature for such heinous purposes."

Michael nodded, crossing himself in a silent prayer for guidance on just how to do that. As if in answer, his gaze fell on Hildegard's journal when he opened his eyes. They had come so far, he thought. They had discovered the galls and their location in the Black Forest; solved riddles that led them to Hildegard's *Hortus Vitae* and the living plant; uncovered the seed bank chamber where the precious seeds were stored; even determined the exact soil and process to grow the seeds. All for naught? The seeds they had now would take months to produce fruit and maybe years to develop galls on their mature leaves. Zentara had the only fully grown plant, already fruiting and potentially with galls now forming from their botanists' efforts. Surely, there was something still missing that Hildegard could tell them, something hidden yet in her cryptic words. He picked up the journal, moved off to the side from the others, and began, again, reading deeper into its pages.

Marcus researched locations near the Zentara lab that might be isolated enough for their human trials.

Élise spoke softly to the seeds hidden under the magic soil as if to coax them to life. Hana glanced at her laptop, a message from Keller still open on the screen. Despite the darkness surrounding them, his quiet rebellion offered a glimmer of hope.

As the night deepened, the team pressed on, each set to their own task, knowing that every moment brought them closer to a confrontation with Zentara—and the truth that could dismantle its empire.

A WRAITHLIKE FIGURE moved quietly in the shadows of the estate's precisely sculpted bushes of the massive acreage. Security cameras had been pinpointed, and each movement avoided their piercing eyes as this figure slipped silently from one undetectable area to another.

The residents had finally retired for the night, leaving only dim security lights still filtering on the pathways through Armand's greenhouse. Slowly, the figure reached the greenhouse door, used a handheld device to open the electronic lock, and slipped inside unnoticed. He scowled, determined and stealthy.

There would be no mistaking plants this time. No sunflower seedlings nor a false seed stash, if they had even thought of that this time. No, he knew exactly what he was looking for. Every action mattered now. He had failed once. He wouldn't this time. He reached to the pack on his back and pulled out the accelerant and other items he needed to destroy, for good, what would remain of this place after his theft. First, it was a matter of finding what he needed to take with him back to Zentara. Then, just a bit of the right powder sprinkled here and there, one lit match and he would be on his way. The rewards were staggering. The promises given to him by Christophe Vaux glittered like jewels in his mind. He had suffered enough in silence and poverty. It was his time to excel and live a full and pleasurable life.

Besides, the alternative he had been given, as one of the subjects of their latest testing, left no question about his mission result: Succeed or die.

Moments later, he found the climate-controlled chamber and flats of glistening soil that promised to be the plantings of the golden castor. Off to the side, he found a locked box, the same one that had been found in the seed chamber at the abbey.

Using a pick from his pocket, he unlocked the ancient clasp, opened the box, and there, nestled carefully, were the golden seeds that seemed to shimmer in the dimmed light beam from his flashlight. He closed the box and shoved it into his jacket's oversized pocket.

Then, with a mighty shove, he tipped the table over that held the trays where the other seeds had been planted and quickly looked about the other tables for the single seedling he had been told had already sprouted.

There… in the corner where a light mist periodically sprayed life-giving water on it, a tiny seedling seemed to sway in the dull security lighting. The man approached it and carefully examined it. Yes, there was no mistaking this one. He grabbed the spindly stem, crushed it between his fingers, ripped it out, and threw it atop the spilled soil of the planting trays now on the floor.

Quickly, he sprinkled the ground with the powder from a canister in his breast pocket and stood back, satisfied. He pulled out a lighter and flicked a flame to life, tossing it onto the powder with a grin.

Whoosh!

The powder caught, flames jumped up and raced quickly across the remaining powder, spreading a film of deadly fire atop the entire floor. He jumped, surprised at the immediacy of the reaction, and turned to run out when suddenly alarms blared and a deluge of water crashed on his head, pushing him to his knees. He scrambled to get up, but the slippery mud under his feet sent him sprawling. Water cascaded over him like a waterfall, holding him down.

The alarm continually sounded, shouts now adding to the cacophony. He forced himself up, gained footing against the still flowing water, grabbed the door handle and pulled—nothing!

More shouts, this time right outside the door, and he

turned, trying desperately to find another exit, but the low light and pouring water obscured any escape.

Suddenly, the door crashed open behind him, and rough hands grabbed him, pulling him out of the greenhouse as others rushed inside.

AN HOUR LATER, Brother Mathias sat, still soaking wet, but now handcuffed on the steps of the estate. A police car's flashing lights swirled against the dark of night across the estate's walls.

He had been questioned and sat silent and sullen throughout. The penetrating cold on his wet skin now set him shivering, and when Father Dominic came to stand before him, he felt like the weight of the Church and the law now condemned him.

"Why, Brother?" Michael asked. The question came quietly, not like the demands of the law enforcement officers earlier. And for some unknown reason, Mathias felt all reasons for remaining quiet had been washed away. He would die. It was a certainty. Zentara had its reach inside the prisons, into the courts, into, well, everything. He would likely be found dead in his cell. Or maybe they *would* get him out, but then, he shivered, thinking death in a prison cell the better of the two.

"I had to, Father." It felt like the truth on his lips.

"No, Mathias, you didn't," came the reply that told the real truth. Michael crossed himself, asking God for forgiveness for the greed, avarice, and betrayal this man had foisted on the abbey and the Church. Then Michael turned and left him alone with his thoughts as two policemen hauled Mathias up by the shoulders to lead him to a police cruiser.

"What's the assessment?" Michael asked later as the team gathered in the estate's library hours later.

The entire team had worked with staff and security through the rest of the night on the remains of the greenhouse. The damage came not from the fire, which was quickly extinguished, but by the flood of water. Hana's grandfather had taken many measures to ensure the safety of his precious and rare plants, including a more-than-adequate fire suppression sprinkler system. His reasoning had been that plants can survive a sudden deluge of water—as they can in nature—but they cannot survive arson or fire, which was true to a degree. Some, however, were too tender to handle the weight of the water. For others, there would be much tending to them in the coming days.

But no amount of tending could heal the crushed golden castor seedling they had nurtured to life.

Marcus was the first to answer Michael's question. "Well, the seedling is gone, of course. Thankfully, the box in Mathias' pocket hadn't been swamped with water, so all those seeds are still dormant, and we can plant them as needed. And, thanks to these two women and their delicate touches, the seeds we'd planted were all retrieved."

Hana and Élise both looked at their hands, their fingernails still caked from digging through the muddy, spilled soil. Then they looked at each other and grinned. Hana said, "I think a manicure is in order, don't you, Élise?" Then she turned to the others. "And, thanks to these delicate fingers, we discovered that several of the seeds had already started to open. I think every one of them will survive this early transplant."

Élise interjected, "Well, we hope so, anyway. The chemical Mathias used could be harmful, but we won't know right away. I found one sprouting seed a bit damaged and am using it for a test. In the morning…" She paused as a yawn overtook her, the early light of sunrise already peeking through the curtains.

"For now," Michael suggested, "we all get some sleep. We can reconvene about noon?"

Élise said she would be along soon, but she wanted to test one more thing first. The others nodded and headed for their bedrooms, satisfied that the day—and night—had ended.

At noon the next day, Michael, Marcus, and Hana were sipping coffee on the estate's veranda, with a tray piled with buttery croissants next to a plate with an array of French and Swiss cheeses. As they munched, the news streamed in on their devices.

Hana received a text from Keller and shared it with the others. "Fabian says the whole Zentara complex is in an uproar. First, there are arrest warrants out for Alton Blackthorn and Christophe Vaux, apparently the henchman carrying out Blackthorn's bidding. Other scientists, like Keller, are now openly willing to divulge the Zentara agenda. But listen to this: the plant they stole from the abbey's *Hortus Vitae*? It's dead!"

"Which I'd expect," Élise broke in as she walked up

to the bench seat and sat beside Hana. "That plant only survived because of the carefully balanced nature created by the wisdom and foresight of Hildegard. We knew better than to touch anything in there and knew not to disturb more than even the tiniest sample of soil. But from what I heard, Karl saw a trail of that soil leading to the truck that carried it off. Well, with the loss of so much of that unique soil, let alone with the changed environment"—she shook her head—"I understand why the plant didn't survive for long." She reached for a croissant and bit off a piece, but the others realized she'd had a big grin even before the flavors hit her mouth.

"You look awfully happy about that," Hana puzzled.

"Well, I haven't slept yet—but, besides being dog-tired, I have news."

"Which is?" Hana prompted.

Élise took one more satisfying bite and then explained. "The accelerant powder? It includes a certain potassium compound. Thankfully, the other ingredients in it didn't affect the seeds. But that one chemical did. It acted as an irritant to the seed. But rather than killing the sprouting seed I'd tested, the seed responded." She grinned and looked like she was about to reach for yet another croissant.

Hana stilled her friend's reach."So? Explain, Élise."

"Oh, right. Remember how the mature plants form the galls to protect them from insects or damage? And the result is a powerful curative within the gall that we know can be used for cancer cures? Well, the seed responded in the same way. What I'm saying is that we don't need to wait for the plants to mature and form galls for the cure we're looking for. We just need to grow enough seeds and subject them to just the right pinch of that potassium compound as they sprout, and the same curative will be in the sprouts. Plus, because the sprout isn't fending off an insect, it doesn't respond with the ricin-like chemical at all. It can't be used for any destructive purpose—only to heal."

Marcus lifted the croissant tray and passed it to Élise. "Have another," he said, and they all laughed.

FORTY-FIVE

The next morning, the sun rose above the skyline of Geneva as the team buzzed with frenetic energy. Hana sat at the center of it all, surrounded by a tangle of cables, screens, and open files. Her fingers danced across the keyboard, finalizing the last details of the exposé that would bring Zentara to its knees.

"We've verified every source," Hana said, glancing at Élise, who stood nearby with a stack of corroborating documents. "This isn't just a story—it's an indictment."

Michael leaned against the doorway, arms crossed. "The world needs to see this, but Zentara won't go quietly. Are you ready for their response?"

Hana gave a tight nod. "Let them come. We've got the truth on our side."

Moments later, on the morning news, Hana's exposé went live. The headline blazed across the homepages of major news outlets: **"Zentara's Deadly Secrets: The**

Cartel Behind Cancer Suppression and Human Suffering."

The article laid bare Zentara's calculated suppression of cancer cures, the unethical trials of a ricin-like substance that left countless victims dead or dying in the southern German facility authorities raided, and the shadowy network of pharmaceutical giants funding their operations. It included testimonies from whistleblowers like Dr. Fabian Keller and others, leaked internal documents, and damning financial records.

Within minutes, the story ignited a firestorm.

Social media platforms erupted with outrage, hashtags condemning Zentara trending globally. Protests sprang up outside Zentara facilities in New York, London, Berlin, and Tokyo. Videos of demonstrators calling for justice flooded the internet, their voices amplified by influencers and activists.

Governments responded swiftly. Regulatory agencies launched emergency investigations, freezing Zentara's assets and halting operations at key facilities. In Geneva, where Zentara's headquarters loomed like a fortress, the building was surrounded by law enforcement officials executing search warrants.

INSIDE ZENTARA'S HEADQUARTERS, Alton Blackthorn stood in his corner office, his steely gaze fixed on the chaos unfolding below. Protestors filled the streets, their chants echoing up to the glass walls. Police vehicles lined the perimeter, their lights flashing ominously.

Behind him, a small group of loyalists gathered, their

expressions a mixture of fear and determination. One of them, a lanky man with distinct features, stepped forward. "Mr. Blackthorn, the authorities are closing in. We need to leave now."

Blackthorn turned, his face calm despite the storm raging around him. "We leave nothing behind," he said coldly. "Erase the servers, destroy the records. If they want proof, they'll find ashes."

"But the assets—" the man began, only to be cut off by Blackthorn's sharp glare.

"Money can be recovered," Blackthorn said. "Control is what matters."

Moments later, Blackthorn and his loyalists slipped out of Zentara headquarters through a series of private passages, evading the authorities swarming the building. As he stepped into an unmarked car waiting in an underground garage, the CEO allowed himself a faint smile.

"Let them celebrate their victory," he murmured. "They'll soon learn it was hollow."

The car sped away, disappearing into the night as Zentara's empire burned behind him.

AT THE SAINT-CLAIR ESTATE, Hana, Michael, and Marcus monitored the fallout. Screens displayed live footage of Zentara facilities being raided, their employees escorted out under armed guard. News anchors dissected the exposé, calling it one of the largest corporate scandals in modern history.

"This is it," Marcus said, leaning back in his chair. "The empire is crumbling."

Hana watched the footage, her face a mask of grim satisfaction. "It's not just Zentara. The pharmaceutical companies backing them are being dragged into the spotlight, too. This is bigger than we could have imagined."

Michael nodded but remained tense. "Blackthorn won't go down with the ship. He's too dangerous to be left unchecked."

As if on cue, Hana's phone buzzed with an encrypted message. She opened it, her eyes narrowing as she read the text.

"It's from Blackthorn," she said, her voice edged with unease. She read the message aloud:

"Truth is a weapon, but it's not the only one. You've won this battle, but you've only scratched the surface. There's more at stake than you realize. The Kronos Protocol will change everything."

Marcus frowned. "Kronos Protocol? What the hell is that?"

Hana shook her head, her mind racing. "Whatever it is, it's his next move."

Michael's expression darkened. "He's warning us. And if Blackthorn is planning something, it won't be small."

The team sat in the quiet aftermath of their triumph,

the power of Blackthorn's message hanging heavily over them. Hana broke the silence first.

"We've exposed Zentara, but Blackthorn's not done. Whatever the Kronos Protocol is, we need to stop it before it starts."

Michael nodded, his gaze resolute. "We will. But for now, we've dealt a blow they won't recover from easily."

As the team reflected on their hard-won victory, the night deepened, and the faint glimmers of a new battle began to take shape on the horizon.

A MONTH LATER, a few days after the next new moon, the morning sun bathed Rupertsberg Abbey in warm golden light, illuminating the ancient stone walls and casting a serene glow over the greenhouse. Sister Amalia moved with quiet purpose among the rows of *Ricinus aureum* seedlings, carefully tending to each plant. The greenhouse had once again become a peaceful sanctuary, its reinforced structure and fortified security reflecting the abbey's commitment to protecting Hildegard von Bingen's legacy.

Karl and Lukas stood at the greenhouse entrance, their alert eyes scanning the grounds. The tranquil setting belied the tension that had infiltrated this sanctuary for weeks as they thwarted Zentara's efforts. Father Benedetto had spoken to the Swiss Guard administration and, as a result, the two Swiss Guards had been on loan to the abbey for the last month now and would stay until after the annual ceremony celebrating the saint's special contributions to the Church. And with the help of Brother Gabriel, the two guards knew the pieces were now in place for the Order of the Green Flame to successfully go forward to fulfill their centuries-old duty of protection.

"These plants represent more than just Hildegard's work," Sister Amalia said as she knelt by a seedling, her voice steady but filled with reverence. "They're a symbol of resilience—of faith prevailing over greed and corruption."

Karl nodded. "And a reminder that vigilance is the price of preservation. Zentara may be down, but we can't assume they're out. Not with Blackthorn still on the loose."

Lukas glanced toward the abbey courtyard, where guests were beginning to arrive for the day's ceremony. "Let's make sure they don't get another chance."

In Geneva, Michael, Hana, Élise, and Marcus monitored the abbey's progress from a large screen in the study. A live feed from the greenhouse displayed Sister Amalia's careful work, her movements deliberate as she nurtured the fragile seedlings.

"They're thriving," Marcus said, leaning closer to the screen. "The conditions are ideal, and the growth rate is exactly what Hildegard's notes predicted."

Michael stood by the window, his arms crossed. "It's reassuring to see her vision coming to life. After everything Zentara has done to suppress this knowledge, it's a victory worth celebrating."

Seated at the desk with her laptop open, Hana glanced at the feed. "It's more than that. Hildegard's work is safe for now, but if Zentara or their allies find another way to target it, we'll need to be ready."

Élise nodded, her tone resolute. "Which is why I'm documenting everything. From Hildegard's original manuscripts to our modern interpretations, the world will finally know the full extent of her genius. Zentara's suppression tactics won't work this time."

Marcus leaned back in his chair, his expression thoughtful. "It's strange, isn't it? A medieval saint's work becoming the key to challenging one of the most powerful organizations in modern history."

Michael turned from the window, his voice steady. "It's a reminder that truth and knowledge transcend time. Hildegard understood that, and so do we."

RUPERTSBERG ABBEY'S annual ceremony began in the courtyard, where guests and pilgrims gathered to honor Hildegard's legacy. Sister Amalia stood before the crowd, her calm voice carrying across the space as she spoke.

"Today, we honor not only Hildegard von Bingen's vision but also the resilience of those who have fought to preserve her work," she said. "These plants represent hope, healing, and the triumph of truth over greed."

The greenhouse stood behind her, its glass walls shimmering in the sunlight. Inside, the *Ricinus aureum* seedlings were arranged in neat rows, a living tribute to Hildegard's wisdom and the dedication of those who had protected it.

The ceremony concluded with a hymn composed by Hildegard herself, sung by the abbey's sisters, its haunting melody a fitting tribute to the saint whose legacy continued to inspire.

FORTY-SIX

The Saint-Clair estate basked in the soft glow of the morning sun, its sprawling gardens and elegant architecture emanating a sense of quiet serenity. Inside the estate's library, the air was heavy with contemplation. Michael stood by the window, gazing out at the manicured grounds. His reflection in the glass showed a man whose faith had been tested but not broken, whose pursuit of truth had deepened his understanding of what it meant to believe.

On the table behind him, Hildegard von Bingen's manuscripts lay open, their intricate diagrams and annotations illuminated by a shaft of sunlight. Michael turned from the window, his gaze falling on the pages.

"Hildegard understood something we often forget," he murmured. "Faith and knowledge aren't enemies. They're two sides of the same coin, both essential to understanding the world and our place in it."

Élise, seated nearby and carefully cataloging notes, looked up. "She bridged the gap between science and spirituality centuries ago. In many ways, she was ahead of her time—and ours."

Michael nodded. "She believed that knowledge, when guided by moral responsibility, could be a force for good. That's the lesson we need to carry forward."

In another corner of the estate, Hana sat at a desk strewn with papers, her laptop open in front of her. A blank document stared back at her, its cursor blinking expectantly. She took a deep breath and began to type:

"In a world where power often eclipses morality, truth becomes both a weapon and a responsibility. This is the story of how a medieval saint's work challenged one of the most powerful corporations of our time—and the people who fought to protect it."

She paused, rereading the opening lines. Her mind drifted back to the journey they had taken—the betrayals, the victories, the lives lost and saved. Zentara's greed had nearly destroyed what Hildegard had left behind, but their resilience had ensured her memory and purpose would endure.

LATER THAT DAY, the Vatican released an official statement, its contents broadcast worldwide. Michael, Hana, Élise, and Marcus, gathered in the estate's study to watch the announcement, their expressions a mix of anticipation and relief.

On the screen, a cardinal stood before the press,

flanked by Vatican officials. His voice was steady as he read from the prepared text.

"The Vatican is pleased to announce the establishment of the Hildegard von Bingen Botanical Research Center, a secure facility dedicated to preserving and studying her groundbreaking work. This center will serve as a beacon of ethical science, ensuring that her legacy continues to inspire and heal for generations to come."

The room fell silent as the magnitude of the announcement settled over the group. Michael was the first to speak, his voice quiet but resolute. "Hildegard's work is safe now. And it's being used for the purpose she intended."

Marcus leaned back in his chair, a faint smile on his face. "It's a rare thing, seeing something good come out of all this chaos."

Élise nodded. "She'd be proud. And the world will finally understand how much she contributed—not just to her time, but to ours. And with a cache of the remaining seeds safely hidden away, we can rest easy as the seedlings become plants, producing seeds of their own, and the process of creating a cure for cancer can begin."

Hana crossed her arms, her gaze fixed on the screen. "Zentara may have tried to bury her, but her spirit lives stronger than ever. That's what matters."

As the sun dipped lower in the sky, casting warm

golden hues across the estate, the group gathered for a quiet dinner. The atmosphere was reflective, each of them aware that this chapter of their journey was coming to an end.

Michael raised his glass, his voice steady as he addressed the group. "To Hildegard, whose wisdom guided us. And to all of you—for your courage, your resilience, and your belief in what's right."

The clink of glasses echoed in the room, followed by quiet conversation. They spoke of the challenges they had faced and the friendships they had forged, and their plans for the future began to emerge. Élise spoke passionately about her intention to compile a definitive record of Hildegard's work, ensuring it would be accessible to scholars and the public alike. Marcus, ever the archaeologist, mused about returning to his fieldwork, albeit with a renewed focus on uncovering lost knowledge that could benefit humanity.

Hana leaned back in her chair, a thoughtful expression on her face. "For me, it's about accountability. Zentara may have fallen, but there are other forces out there—other truths waiting to be uncovered. That's where I belong."

Michael smiled, his gaze warm. "And I'll return to the Archives. There's still so much to uncover—so much worth protecting."

As the clock chimed midnight, signaling the end of another day, the team exchanged quiet goodnights. The estate grew still, its halls filled with the echoes of their shared journey.

The next morning would bring new paths for each of

them, but the bonds they had forged—and the lessons they had learned—would remain.

For now, the Saint-Clair estate rested under the light of the moon, a beacon of what could be achieved when faith, reason, and courage came together.

FORTY-SEVEN

Father Michael Dominic stood in the quiet sanctuary of the small chapel within the Vatican Gardens, the flickering candlelight casting warm, dancing shadows on the ancient stone walls. For weeks, he had wrestled with the decision before him, a choice that could forever alter the course of his life. Tonight, he felt the pressure of that choice weighing on him more than ever.

Through the good graces of Michael's father, Pope Ignatius, the Church had changed its stance, allowing priests to marry. This extraordinary shift meant that he didn't have to choose between his love for Hana and his vows of faith. But if he tried to walk both paths simultaneously, of husband and priest, would he shortchange both?

Or… he could choose to walk away from the priesthood. But the question that consumed him was this: if he left the priesthood to focus solely on a life with

Hana, he would lose the position that had defined him for years—prefect of the Vatican Secret Archives. That role was more than a job; it was a calling, a stewardship of the Church's most sacred mysteries. Could he truly walk away from it?

The door to the chapel creaked open softly, and Michael turned to see Hana stepping inside. She wore a simple dress, her hair loose around her shoulders, her expression warm but pensive. She had given him space to reflect, understanding the enormity of the choice he faced. Yet tonight, she had come not to push for an answer but simply to be present.

"I thought I might find you here," she said, her voice quiet.

He hesitated, his hands tightening at his sides. "I've been praying, thinking… agonizing. And I think I've finally reached a decision. But saying it out loud… it makes it real. It makes it permanent."

Hana stepped closer, her eyes searching his. "Whatever you choose, Michael, I'm with you. That's the only thing that's permanent."

Her words, so simple yet profound, steadied him. He drew in a deep breath and let it out slowly. "I've spent my life serving the Church, dedicating myself to something greater than myself. The Archives… they're not just a collection of documents. They're a living testament to faith, history, and truth. To walk away from that feels like walking away from a part of who I am."

"But?" she prompted gently, sensing there was more.

"But loving you has changed me," he admitted. "It's shown me that faith isn't confined to an office or a title.

It's in the choices we make, the people we love, and the lives we touch. I know I want to marry you, Hana. And if I remain a priest, my duties will keep me most often in the Archives, away from you. Plus, now that you have the demands of your grandfather's empire to handle, if anything, you need a full-time husband to support you in Geneva for your efforts as well..." He trailed off, his voice heavy with emotion. "I couldn't, wouldn't, ask you to live here with me, and I couldn't be with you as often as I would want."

Hana reached for his hands, her touch grounding him. "Michael, you don't have to choose between us and your calling. If staying in the priesthood means you can continue serving as prefect of the Archives, then we'll find a way to make it work. I'm not asking you to leave something you love just to prove your love for me. And I hope you know my love for you transcends any distance." She paused and smiled. "Scheduling, logistics, timing, will all be challenging, of course. But it doesn't matter—we can work it out. Together. As partners."

Her words struck a chord deep within him.

"I've learned much from Hildegard von Bingen, Hana. She balanced faith and nature, spirituality and purpose. Remember, I read one of her visions when we were leaving the Black Forest?" She nodded. "It was about a man who couldn't reach both his faith and a woman's hand at the same time. I misunderstood it for some time."

Hana asked, "What do you mean?"

Michael smiled. "I thought it meant he had to choose

only one. Only lately I recalled the end of that story. The man didn't choose one or the other. Instead, he reached out to do what he needed to do: in that case, to protect a plant, and it thrived. He could do what he needed to do, with both choices still standing behind him. Still in his life. I've seen by her example that if a person does each task set before him, it can be done with both Church and marriage behind him and guiding him. I just needed to be sure you, too, saw the work involved to bring our lives into that balance for what lies ahead for each of us."

Tears glistened in Hana's eyes as she listened, her grip on his hands tightening. "I do," she said, her voice trembling with emotion.

Michael looked at her, his heart swelling with love and certainty. "Those are exactly the words I want us both to say. We'll build a life together, one that honors both our love and our calling as we succeed with each task before us."

They embraced, the strain of weeks of uncertainty finally lifting. In her arms, Michael felt a profound sense of peace, a reassurance that his decision was the right one. The road ahead wouldn't be without its challenges, but for the first time, he felt ready to meet them head-on.

After a long moment, they pulled back, and Hana's smile turned playful. "So, does this mean I still get to call you Father Dominic? Or is there a more husbandly title I should use?"

Michael chuckled, a deep, genuine sound that echoed in the quiet chapel. "Let's keep it simple.

'Michael' works just fine when it's just us. But in public, I think Father Dominic might still be safest."

"Fair enough," she said, grinning. "But don't be surprised if I slip up and call you 'husband' when we're around others."

"I'll take it as a badge of honor," he replied, his smile widening. He felt an overwhelming sense of gratitude. For her love, for her unwavering support, and for the chance to continue living his faith while building a future with her.

As they strolled through the gardens, the bells in St. Peter's Basilica tolled softly in the distance, marking the hour. To Michael, it felt like a blessing, a gentle affirmation of the choice he had made. The path forward might be uncharted, filled with unknowns and challenges, but he knew one thing with certainty: he was exactly where he was meant to be.

Together, he and Hana stepped into the night, their love and faith intertwined, ready to embrace whatever the future might hold.

EPILOGUE

The morning dawned cool and clear over Geneva, the sky a gentle blue streaked with wisps of golden light. The gardens of the Saint-Clair estate were unusually quiet, their usual bustle subdued in reverence. Rows of chairs had been arranged beneath a canopy of ancient oaks, their branches arching protectively over the solemn gathering. At the center of it all stood a simple mahogany casket, draped in the French tricolor flag.

Baron Armand de Saint-Clair, Hana's grandfather and a hero of the French Resistance, was finally being laid to rest.

Hana stood to one side, dressed in black. Her eyes were dry, but her expression was etched with a quiet grief. She had organized this ceremony, ensuring that every detail honored the man who had been a pillar of courage and integrity in her life. Around her, friends, family, and dignitaries gathered, a testament to the profound impact Armand had left on so many.

Michael stood nearby, his gaze fixed on Hana. He could see the weight she carried—the mixture of sorrow and pride in her stance. She was mourning not just the loss of her grandfather, but the end of a connection to a history that had shaped her identity.

The ceremony began with a soft hymn, the notes carrying across the estate. Michael stepped forward to offer a prayer. His voice, calm and resonant, spoke of remembrance and gratitude.

"Today, we honor not only a life but a life well lived," he said, his gaze sweeping over the crowd. "Armand de Saint-Clair stood against tyranny, not with weapons alone, but with courage, wisdom, and an unyielding belief in what is right. May his memory inspire us to live with the same conviction."

Hana's mouth set into a firm line as she listened, her thoughts drifting to the stories her grandfather had shared with her as a child. Tales of evading Nazi patrols, smuggling messages through treacherous terrain, and risking everything to protect others. His courage had seemed mythical then, larger than life. Now, she understood it for what it truly was: a quiet, steady resolve to stand for what mattered, even when the odds were against him.

As the prayer ended, Hana stepped forward next. The crowd seemed to hold its breath as she approached the podium, her posture straight but her expression reflecting vulnerability. She glanced down at the small stack of notes in her hand but set them aside after a moment.

"My grandfather didn't care much for speeches," she began, her voice steady but soft. "He believed in actions, not words. But today, I feel compelled to speak—not just for him, but for the lessons he left behind."

She looked out over the crowd, her eyes briefly meeting Michael's. "Armand de Saint-Clair was a man who fought in the shadows. He never sought recognition or reward. His work with the Resistance wasn't about glory—it was about people. About ensuring that the world we inherit is one worth living in."

Her voice faltered slightly, but she pressed on. "When I think of him now, I think of the quiet moments. The times he'd tell me stories of the Resistance—not to boast, but to teach me the importance of standing for something greater than yourself. Those lessons shaped me. They're why I became a journalist. They're why I've fought so hard to uncover the truth wherever it might be found, no matter how dangerous it might be."

She paused, glancing at the casket. "In many ways, our recent fight against Zentara felt like a continuation of his mission. We stood against forces that sought to erase truth, to suppress knowledge for their own gain. And through it all, I often found myself asking: What would Grand-père do?"

The audience listened in rapt silence, Hana's words carrying the force of their shared journey. "His answer, I think, would be simple: You do what's right, no matter the cost. And you ensure that the truth—the real truth—is never buried."

She paused, her gaze falling briefly to the casket. "Grand-père, I hope I've made you proud."

The crowd sat in solemn silence as Hana stepped back, her words hanging in the air like a benediction. Michael met her as she returned to her seat, his hand briefly squeezing hers. She didn't look at him, but her fingers tightened slightly in return.

As the ceremony drew to a close, a small honor guard approached the casket. They folded the tricolor flag with precision and presented it to Hana, who accepted it with trembling hands. The moment was almost too much for her, but she drew strength from the presence of those around her.

The crowd began to disperse slowly, conversations muted out of respect. The team lingered near the casket, each member reflecting on the journey that had brought them together and the man whose legacy had been a guiding force.

Michael broke the silence first. "His heroism extended beyond his generation. He's a hero for all time."

Marcus nodded. "And a reminder that the fight for truth and justice never really ends."

Hana, holding the folded flag close, gave them a faint but genuine smile. "He would've liked all of you," she said. "He believed in people who stood for what mattered."

Karl and Lukas exchanged quiet smiles. Élise,

standing nearby, adjusted her glasses. "Then let's honor him by continuing to stand for what matters. Always."

THE AFTERNOON FADED INTO EVENING, the estate bathed in the soft hues of twilight. The team gathered in the library for one final toast. Glasses were raised, not in celebration, but in tribute—to a man whose courage had inspired them all.

"To Armand," Michael said simply. "And to the truth he fought for."

As the glasses clinked, the mood was somber yet hopeful. The team had accomplished what they had set out to do, but the lessons they had learned would guide them in the paths they now prepared to take.

The room fell quiet, each person lost in their own thoughts. For Hana, the day was a closure of sorts, but it was also a beginning. Her grandfather's life wasn't just a memory—it was a call to action. And she was ready to answer it.

The evening ended with the casket lowered into the family crypt, its resting place marked with a simple inscription: *Armand de Saint-Clair: Hero of the Resistance. A Light in the Darkness*.

As the team walked back toward the house, the night sky stretched above them, clear and infinite. They didn't speak, but the silence was companionable, filled with the unspoken bond of shared purpose.

For now, the journey was over. But the lessons they carried would ensure that the fight for truth—like Armand's memory—would endure.

FICTION, FACT, OR FUSION

Many readers have asked me to distinguish fact from fiction in my books. Generally, I like to take factual events and historical figures and build on them in creative ways, but much of what I write is historically accurate. In this book, I'll review some of the chapters where questions may arise, hoping it may help those wondering where reality meets creative writing.

FIRST, A WORD ABOUT MY INSPIRATION:

As I close the pages of this book, I want to take a moment to honor a historical figure who has profoundly inspired me during its creation: Hildegard von Bingen.

As I mentioned in the Prologue, Hildegard, born in 1098, was a Benedictine abbess, writer, composer, philosopher, mystic, and visionary. Her extraordinary contributions spanned the realms of theology, medicine, music, and natural science—fields often inaccessible to women of her time. She fearlessly navigated a patriarchal society, asserting her voice and intellect to become one of the most influential figures of the medieval era. Her writings, particularly those on natural medicine and holistic healing, remain relevant even in today's world.

What has captivated me most about Hildegard isn't just the breadth of her achievements but the spirit of her work. She embodied the belief that faith and knowledge aren't opposing forces but complementary paths to understanding the world. Her insistence on ethical responsibility in the pursuit of knowledge and her commitment to using her gifts for the betterment of humanity resonate deeply with the themes explored in this story.

As I researched Hildegard's life and works, I was struck by her courage and conviction. She spoke truth to power, often challenging ecclesiastical authorities and societal norms when she believed justice was at stake. She reminds us that the fight for truth and integrity isn't bound by time and that the preservation of knowledge is a sacred duty.

While writing this book, I frequently listened to her hymnal music, letting her ethereal melodies fill my workspace. Her compositions—soaring and transcendent—transported me to a place of quiet contemplation, as if her spirit were present, guiding the words on the page. It was in these moments of inspiration that I felt a deeper connection to her, as though her timeless wisdom and creativity were woven into the story itself. Even today, her music can be found on most streaming services.

Through this book, I hope to shine a light on the enduring relevance of her teachings and to honor her legacy. Hildegard von Bingen was more than a product of her time—she was a visionary whose influence transcends centuries, reminding us of the power of wisdom, resilience, and faith, and whose light continues to guide, inspire, and challenge us to be better stewards of truth and knowledge.

PROLOGUE:

While the names of Hildegard's parents are correct historically, they were **not connected to the Saint-Clair family** at all, which I've used here for creative purposes in the story. Hildegard did originate from a noble lineage, yet the surname of her family seldom appears or is acknowledged in historical records. During the medieval period, particularly throughout the eleventh and twelfth centuries, the concept of surnames as understood in contemporary times was neither prevalent nor formalized, especially among noble circles. People were typically distinguished by their geographical origins, titles, or familial connections rather than by surnames. So in Hildegard's case, "Hildegard von Bingen" literally means Hildegard "of Bingen" (from the small town of Bingen, Germany).

The **humoral theory of medicine**, which was the dominant medical paradigm in Europe until the late seventeenth century, believed that diseases were caused by imbalances among the four "humors": *blood, phlegm, yellow bile*, and *black bile*. Cancer was often attributed to an overproduction or malfunction of black bile.

According to this theory, each humor was associated with specific qualities (hot, cold, moist, and dry) and parts of the body, influencing both physical and psychological characteristics.

Hildegard's **Lingua Ignota** ("Unknown Language") is a constructed language she created, consisting of approximately 1,000 unique words. It's paired with an invented script and was likely intended for spiritual expression or as a mystical, symbolic code. The vocabulary draws heavily on Latin and German roots, featuring terms for celestial beings, flora, fauna, and human roles. While its exact purpose remains debated, scholars believe it reflected Hildegard's vision of a divine, universal tongue that transcended earthly languages, underscoring her creativity and deep theological insights.

Lastly, to avoid confusion with botanical realities, I contrived the plant name *Ricinus aureum* ("golden castor"), which doesn't exist. Too bad, isn't it…?

CHAPTER 6:

Rupertsberg Monastery (which I have redesignated as an "Abbey" in the book), was originally founded by Hildegard von Bingen in the twelfth century, but it's no longer functional as a monastery and exists only in ruins. The monastery was located at the confluence of the Nahe and Rhine rivers near Bingen am Rhein, Germany.

Hildegard established the monastery around 1150 after leaving the **Disibodenberg Monastery**, which included a Frauenklause, a female hermitage associated with the monastery. Rupertsberg became a center for her theological work, music composition, and herbal medicine. The monastery was destroyed during the Thirty Years' War (1618–1648), and its ruins were further dismantled over time. Only fragments of the original structure remain today. Some archaeological efforts have preserved these remnants, but the site isn't a functioning religious institution.

After founding her first monastery at Rupertsberg, Hildegard sought to expand her work. When a nearby Benedictine monastery in Eibingen fell into neglect, Hildegard acquired the property in 1165 and reestablished it as a vibrant religious community. The **Eibingen Abbey** became a place for women devoted to the spiritual practices and teachings inspired by Hildegard's visionary theology, music, and holistic approach to healing. Today, it's known as *Abtei St. Hildegard*, and continues to honor her legacy as an active Benedictine community.

CHAPTER 11:

Plant galls are fascinating natural formations that occur when plants respond to the presence of foreign organisms, such as insects, mites, fungi, bacteria, or even other plants. These abnormal growths can appear on leaves, stems, roots, or flowers and often serve as protective homes or nutrient sources for the organisms that induce them. Despite their often unusual appearance, galls showcase the remarkable adaptability and complexity of plant biology.

Throughout history, plant galls have held a place of

wonder and utility in various cultures. Ancient herbalists and healers recognized their medicinal potential, using galls for a wide range of treatments. Oak galls, for instance, were highly valued for their high tannin content, which made them effective astringents. They were used to treat wounds, reduce inflammation, and combat infections.

Beyond medicine, plant galls have played a significant role in other industries. The tannins extracted from oak galls were essential in the production of iron gall ink, a key writing material used from the Middle Ages through the nineteenth century. This durable, dark ink was used to pen some of the most important documents in history, from illuminated manuscripts to early scientific treatises.

Galls have also been utilized as natural dyes, producing rich hues of brown and yellow, and as components in traditional cosmetics and beauty treatments. Their unique chemical compositions continue to intrigue scientists, who study them for potential applications in pharmaceuticals and sustainable materials.

These unassuming botanical marvels remind us of nature's ingenuity, providing not only shelter and sustenance to their inhabitants but also a wealth of resources for humanity across the ages. Plant galls, in their quiet complexity, reveal the profound interconnectedness of life.

AUTHOR'S NOTE

Dealing with issues of theology, religious beliefs, and the fictional treatment of historical biblical events can be a daunting affair.

I would ask all readers to view this story for what it is—a work of pure fiction, adapted from the seeds of many oral traditions and the historical record, at least as we know it today.

Apart from telling an engaging story, I have no agenda here, and respect those of all beliefs, from Agnosticism to Zoroastrianism and everything in between.

Thank you for reading *The Hildegard Seeds*. I hope you enjoyed it and, if you haven't already, I suggest you pick up the stories in the earlier books of the three series: The

Magdalene Chronicles, the Vatican Secret Archive Thrillers, and the newest Vatican Archaeology series.

When you have a moment, may I ask that you leave a review on Amazon, Goodreads, Facebook, and perhaps elsewhere you find convenient? Reviews are crucial to a book's success, and I hope for all my *Thrillers* series to have long and entertaining lives.

You can easily leave your review by going to my Amazon book review page; or just search for *The Hildegard Seeds*. And thank you!

If you would like to reach out for any reason, you can email me at gary@garymcavoy.com. If you would like to learn more about me and my other books, visit my website at garymcavoy.com, where you can also sign up for my private mailing list.

With kind regards,

Gary McAvoy

ACKNOWLEDGMENTS

I have had the grateful assistance of a few friends, without whose help this would have been a more challenging project.

I am deeply grateful to my dear friend, California botanist and biologist Robin Kobaly of The Power of Plants, whose extraordinary knowledge and passion for the natural world inspired a pivotal element in this story. Robin's introduction to the fascinating world of plant galls opened my eyes to their unique biology and symbolism, providing the perfect medium to weave into the narrative. Her insights, boundless curiosity, and enthusiasm for the intricate connections within nature have enriched my understanding and profoundly influenced this book. Thank you, Robin, for sharing your wisdom and for being such a wonderful source of inspiration.

I also want to extend my heartfelt gratitude to Greg McDonald and Yale Lewis, who graciously served as ongoing readers of chapters as they grew along the way. Your thoughtful feedback, encouragement, and keen insights were invaluable in shaping this story. Knowing I could rely on your perspectives gave me both confidence and inspiration during the writing process.

Thank you for being part of this project and for your relentless support.

My editor, Sandra Herner, has been with me for fourteen books now, bringing an exceptional level of precision, insight, and dedication to every one of them. Her keen eye for detail, deep understanding of narrative structure, and steady commitment to enhancing every scene have been invaluable. Thank you, Sandra, as always.

And to the most remarkably gifted pair of copyediting eyes I've yet to encounter, those of Donna Marie West, whose meticulous attention to detail, intuitive grasp of rhythm and voice, and unwavering commitment to excellence elevated every sentence she touched. Her thoughtful suggestions and sharp eye caught what others missed, helping shape the final manuscript into its finest form.

Gary McAvoy

Made in United States
Orlando, FL
21 April 2025

60690520R00208